OVER the MOON

Angela Knight
MaryJanice Davidson
Virginia Kantra
Sunny

B
BERKLEY SENSATION, NEW YORK

THE BERKLEY PUBLISHING GROUP
Published by the Penguin Group
Penguin Group (USA) Inc.
375 Hudson Street, New York, New York 10014, USA
Penguin Group (Canada), 90 Eglinton Avenue East, Suite 700, Toronto, Ontario M4P 2Y3, Canada
(a division of Pearson Penguin Canada Inc.)
Penguin Books Ltd., 80 Strand, London WC2R 0RL, England
Penguin Group Ireland, 25 St. Stephen's Green, Dublin 2, Ireland (a division of Penguin Books Ltd.)
Penguin Group (Australia), 250 Camberwell Road, Camberwell, Victoria 3124, Australia
(a division of Pearson Australia Group Pty. Ltd.)
Penguin Books India Pvt. Ltd., 11 Community Centre, Panchsheel Park, New Delhi—110 017, India
Penguin Group (NZ), Cnr. Airborne and Rosedale Roads, Albany, Auckland 1310, New Zealand
(a division of Pearson New Zealand Ltd.)
Penguin Books (South Africa) (Pty.) Ltd., 24 Sturdee Avenue, Rosebank, Johannesburg 2196,
South Africa

Penguin Books Ltd., Registered Offices: 80 Strand, London WC2R 0RL, England

This is a work of fiction. Names, characters, places, and incidents either are the product of the authors' imagination or are used fictitiously, and any resemblance to actual persons, living or dead, business establishments, events, or locales is entirely coincidental. The publisher does not have control over and does not assume any responsibility for author or third-party websites or their content.

OVER THE MOON

A Berkley Sensation Book / published by arrangement with the authors

PRINTING HISTORY
Berkley Sensation mass-market edition / January 2007

ISBN: 978-0-425-21343-8

BERKLEY SENSATION®
Berkley Sensation Books are published by The Berkley Publishing Group,
a division of Penguin Group (USA) Inc.,
375 Hudson Street, New York, New York 10014.
BERKLEY SENSATION is a registered trademark of Penguin Group (USA) Inc.
The "B" design is a trademark belonging to Penguin Group (USA) Inc.

PRINTED IN THE UNITED STATES OF AMERICA

10 9 8 7 6 5 4 3 2 1

CONTENTS

Moon Dance

Angela Knight

1

*Between the Mountain
and the Moon*

Virginia Kantra

95

Driftwood

MaryJanice Davidson

187

Mona Lisa Three

Sunny

249

MOON DANCE

Angela Knight

♂

*This story is dedicated to
my wonderful critique partner, Diane Whiteside,
who went above and beyond the call of duty to help me
turn it into something readable.
Thanks, babe.*

♂

PROLOGUE

Rain dripped from Sergeant Lucas Rollings's uniform hat and rolled down his neck in a constant, cold stream. His feet were slowly going numb inside his uniform shoes, which squelched unpleasantly with every step across the sodden leaves. Even his bulletproof vest was wet, and the gun felt slippery in his hand. He ignored the discomfort.

Any chance they'd find the little girl was worth it.

"The dogs have lost the scent in this rain." Beside him, Ray Johnston grimly watched his two big German shepherds work a spiraling pattern through the trees. Though pushing sixty and barely five-foot-seven, Ray was wiry and tough. His angular face looked years younger than it actually was under his thatch of thick, black hair, and his eyes were a piercing Paul Newman blue. "Wish it could have held off." He shot Lucas a look. "You know, you don't have to chase this hunch with me. Everybody seems pretty sure Myer has the girl."

Somebody had called in a tip to 911, saying they thought

their pedophile next door neighbor had dragged a four-year-old who matched Jennifer Rosemond's description into his house. The SWAT team went to investigate, and he'd fired on them. Now damn near every cop in Harrisville was parked outside his house while a hostage negotiator tried to talk Jerry Myer into giving up.

"Yeah, but what if he doesn't really have the kid? What if the neighbor called in a false tip because he just wanted to get rid of the bastard?" Lucas, for some reason, had the nagging feeling that was just what happened. And his nagging feelings had an ugly habit of being right. "If you stumble on the kidnapper by yourself, he'll blow your ass away. And the kid would be toast."

Frustration flashed across Ray's face. "I'm tougher than you think."

Lucas eyed him. *Why the hell does he want me gone?* It was a troubling idea. Ray was a damn good police K-9 trainer, but he was also a civilian, which is why Lucas had been assigned to ride herd on him. Was he dreaming of a little vigilante justice?

Not that Lucas wouldn't mind beating the shit out of their target himself.

Three hours ago, four-year-old Jennifer had been out playing in the back yard while her mother read on the screened-in porch. Apparently, the dark screen had kept the kidnapper from realizing Tammy Rosemond was there. He'd emerged from the woods behind the house and snatched the little girl right off her swing set.

Tammy screamed and charged out to rescue her daughter. The man had drawn a gun and fired at her. Luckily he'd missed, but as the woman ducked for cover, he'd carried the child into the woods.

Tammy had run to the phone and called 911. Soon afterward, every cop in Harrisville County roared onto the scene, sirens screaming. Lucas, though a city cop and technically out of his jurisdiction, had been one of them. In a case like this, everybody pitched in.

They'd just gone into the second hour of the search when their helpful tipster had called. Now it was getting dark, and everybody but Lucas and Ray was off on what might be a wild-goose chase.

And if it was, the bastard would get away. Unless Ray and Lucas found him.

"Bothers me that this guy snatched the kid in the middle of the afternoon with all those neighbors around," Lucas murmured to the handler as they walked along behind the dogs, scanning the trees for any sign of the kidnapper. "He's not just a pedophile, he's nuts." Thinking about what he might be doing to the child even now made Lucas's belly twist into a sick knot.

"Yeah, I—"

Lucas threw up a hand for silence as a pile of brush suddenly drew his attention. Something about the way the limbs lay around the fallen tree trunk struck him as subtly unnatural. It looked like somebody had stacked them . . .

The wind shifted. Both dogs began to bark as if they'd suddenly caught a scent as they charged toward the brush pile.

"Ray, shut those dogs up," Lucas snapped. The last thing they needed was to spook an armed man into killing his hostage.

Ray whistled sharply. The dogs instantly went quiet, except for soft whines of excitement. They really were well-trained.

Pointing his nine-millimeter Glock at the pile, Lucas moved toward it. "Come out with your hands—"

A gun barrel thrust through the branches. In the split second that followed, Lucas realized he didn't dare fire into the brush—he'd hit the kid. He dove for the ground to the thunder-ous boom of a .45, then scrambled aside as the shooter fired again. One of the dogs yelped in agony, and the other howled.

Brush flew as the kidnapper leaped to his feet, jamming the muzzle of his gun under the jaw of the little girl he held in front of him. The child hung limp, head lolling. "Get the hell back, or I'll shoot!"

Lucas leveled his gun, rage boiling through him. "Looks like she's already dead, you son of a bitch!"

"She's just out!" He hauled the child higher until her shoulders blocked the head shot Lucas was contemplating. "Just gave her a little chloroform, that's all. Don't mean to kill her."

"Yeah, right, asshole." Lucas lowered his gun and pointed it at the guy's crotch, just below Jennifer's dangling sneak-ers. "Maybe I ought to make sure the world's little girls have nothing to worry about."

"And there'll be one less little girl in the world, because I'll—"

Ray's remaining dog suddenly began to bark in a furious salvo, advancing on the thug with stiff-legged menace. The kidnapper backed away, hastily jamming the gun tighter against Jennifer's jaw. "Call off that dog! Now!"

Oh, shit. A movement behind the thug caught Lucas's eye. Ray was circling around behind the kidnapper, using the dis-traction provided by his dog. His gaze was intent, murderous.

Lucas fought to keep the reaction off his face, though his gut clenched. Ray was three inches shorter than the guy, and he wasn't armed. Somebody was about to get killed—and it was way too likely to be Jennifer.

Lucas jerked his gun skyward and lifted his free hand—something every bit of training he had told him not to do. But he was wearing a bulletproof vest, and if the fucker shot at him, at least the gun wouldn't be pointed at the kid. *It'll give Ray his chance—as long as he doesn't shoot me in the head . . .* "Hey, hey—calm down! You win . . ."

In an eyeblink Ray had disappeared, replaced in an instant by something huge and dark. The kidnapper jerked his gun from Jennifer's jaw and fired at Lucas just as the thing grabbed him.

A bullet slammed into Lucas's hip like a baseball bat. He hit the ground on his back, fighting a scream of pain. Despite the agony, he rolled over, sought to aim his gun at the kidnapper . . .

And blinked in astonishment. A towering black creature had snatched Jennifer from the kidnapper. The man screamed and pointed his gun at it.

The monster hit him with a casual swat, slamming him into the tree behind him with a crunch. When he hit the ground, his head was twisted at an unnatural angle. His eyes went fixed and dead.

Well, Lucas thought with grim satisfaction, *that fucker won't hurt anybody again.*

"Aw, man . . ." The creature moved toward Lucas with an odd, swift grace, carrying the unconscious little girl cradled in his arms. He crouched at Lucas's side, long wolf muzzle tilting to examine him. "You're bleeding like a son of a bitch. I think he hit an artery."

The monster's eyes were Paul Newman blue.

"Ray?" Lucas husked, fighting to focus. He must be hallucinating. Ray Johnston couldn't have turned into a seven-foot werewolf . . .

"Yeah, it's me." The werewolf put Jennifer down in the leaves. "You can see why I didn't want you to come along. I could smell the bastard out here, but I wasn't sure where he was."

"The kid . . . okay?"

"Just out. Smells like chloroform. Asshole must have been telling the truth." There was compassion in those blue eyes, so human in that alien lupine face. "She'll be fine. But you . . ."

Oddly, Lucas felt no fear. Everything seemed floating, dreamlike. It no longer even hurt. "Dying . . ."

"Yeah." The werewolf searched his gaze. "I can save you, Lucas. If I bite you, the magic'll keep you alive until you can change."

He blinked and began to shiver. Cold was spreading up his torso. "Magic?"

"Yeah. That stuff about werewolves being cursed killers is all bullshit. Merlin created us to help people, not kill them. And I think you could do a lot of good as one of us." Blue eyes searched his. "The ambulance isn't going to get here in time to save you, buddy. You'll be dead in ten minutes without the bite. I'm the only shot you have. It's your choice, Lucas."

Blearily, he decided that Ray was right—maybe he could do some good as a werewolf. Besides, he wasn't ready to die yet. "Do it."

When Ray sank his fangs almost tenderly into Lucas's forearm, the pain felt as distant and dreamlike as everything else.

CHAPTER 1

Five years later . . .

"Lucas Rollings is the best chance you've got, Elena." Candice caught her wrist. In her urgency, pink-painted fingernails lengthened into claws. "He's the best chance any of us have."

"Maybe he is." Elena Livingston pulled away and rose from the sitting room couch to move restlessly to the French doors. A decorative wrought-iron grill covered the glass with lacy, fanciful shapes—leaves, unicorns, wolves, stags. Almost pretty enough to disguise the grill's real purpose: bars on Elena's gilded cage. "But this isn't his fight. Do I have the right to involve him?"

Candice made a frustrated sound and raked both ringed hands through her fine hair. She'd dyed it cotton-candy pink to go with her leather pants and cropped top. It was the kind of thing a rebellious teenager would wear. Candice James was twenty-nine, but like a teenager, she was trying to make a declaration of independence. Unfortunately, pink leather was the best she could do. "Don't be so damned noble. Do you *like* living like this? Locked up for a month every year like a horny French poodle so the neighbor's mutt can't get to you?"

"No, I don't like it." Elena ground her teeth, barely suppressing the urge to throw herself against the iron grill and rip it right off the door. She could do it. She had the strength. Unfortunately, it would set off every alarm in the house. "I'm twenty-seven years old, dammit. I should have a career. I could be married to a man who loves me, raising babies. Instead I'm a chess piece in Daddy's ongoing game with the Chosen." Letting her forehead rest against the door, she stared blindly through the grill at the forest behind the house. "And I've run out of time."

Candice rose from her chair, concern on her pretty, narrow face. "You think your father's really going to give you to Stephen Bradford?"

She shrugged. "Judith said they've been in negotiations for the past week." The maid might not go so far as to help Elena escape, but she was usually a reliable source of information.

"Stephen. Jesus. Of all the Chosen, why'd your dad have to pick him? He's the nastiest in the bunch."

Elena shot her a dry look. "Which pretty well makes him perfect, as far as my father's concerned. Stephen's arrogant and obsessed with power, and Daddy knows he'll protect the Chosen's traditions."

"Which is exactly why you need Lucas." Candice spread her ringed hands in a pleading gesture. "Look, if you won't do it for yourself, do it for the rest of us. I don't know about you, but I'm sick of living in the Middle Ages. If you can claim your father's seat, you could persuade the rest of the council to dismantle the Traditions."

"*If* I can claim the seat, and *if* I can convince them.

That's an awful lot of 'ifs.' But I *know* that if I ask this cop of yours for help, Stephen is going to challenge him, and Stephen has never lost a fight. Is the freedom of a bunch of spoiled rich girls worth a man's life?"

Candice's eyes narrowed under their dramatic eyeshadow. "Maybe not. But my daughter's freedom is."

Elena winced. "Cheap shot."

"*I don't care.* I want to know that when she gets married, her husband won't consider it his right as a Chosen Alpha to beat her if she crosses him." Candice dropped her voice to a mocking baritone. " 'She'll heal. She must learn discipline.' " Making a lewd gesture at her imaginary daughter's imaginary husband, she snarled, "Fold it into a pointy package and shove it up your hairy Alpha ass!"

"Look, I'm not going to roll over for Stephen. I'm more than capable of fighting my own battles. I just don't like the idea of using anybody else as cannon fodder."

Candice sighed. "You are not up to taking on Stephen Bradford in a fight. Lucas is." She reached into a pocket of her jeans and pulled out a folded envelope. Opening it, she produced a newspaper article and displayed it with a flourish. In a grainy color photo that took up most of the page, a tall, dark-haired man crouched, gazing intently at something on the ground. "Look at this guy. Six-foot-five, and that's when he's not furry. What's more, he's got the muscle to match. He could definitely take Stephen."

Elena took the clipping from her friend's hand and studied it. Candice was right—Lucas looked formidable, but what interested her most was the focused intensity in his gaze. It was pure Alpha male. Pure warrior. Deep inside her, something clenched and heated in response—the Burning Moon reminding her of its presence. She cleared her throat. "He does look like he could give Stephen a run for his money."

"And he's a cop in Harrisville." Harrisville was one of the larger towns in upstate South Carolina, just a three-hour drive from the Livingstons' Charleston mansion. Elena had driven through the area during her frequent trips to Charlotte, North Carolina. "What's more, he hasn't been Direkind long enough to be willing to look the other way for the Chosen. I don't know of anybody else in three states I can say that about."

Elena studied her, interested. "How did you meet this guy?"

"I ran into him a few months ago at a Direkind clan gathering. Fell instantly in lust."

Candice fell instantly in lust on a regular basis. "I'm surprised you didn't snatch him for your very own."

"I did give it some thought. Then I decided you needed him more than I did. I . . ."

"Shh!" Footsteps on the stairs—ones grown all too familiar. "Oh, hell, that's Stephen. You'd better go, Candice."

"Shit!" Her friend hastily stuffed the clipping back in the envelope and handed it over. "Oh, listen—I also printed out the directions to the Harrisville PD, where Lucas works. I put those in the envelope, too. I want you to think about this, Elena. And fast. You're running out of time."

"I'll think about it." Elena folded the envelope and slid it into the pocket of her jeans, then hurried to escort Candice to the door.

When she opened it, she found Stephen towering on the other side, tall, blond, and icily handsome. He watched Candice slip past, his eyes narrow with disapproval. "What's she doing here?"

"She's a friend, Stephen. My father still allows me to have friends."

The sarcasm, not surprisingly, flew right over his head. "Well, I don't want her here again." Stephen glowered, his gaze deliberately challenging. He was broad shouldered and long-legged in a way that should have made Elena's Burning Moon hormones hum. Yet he left her literally cold. There was just something *off* about him. Even his handsome face reflected a subtle wrongness. Despite the precisely chiseled features that were the hallmark of the Chosen, his eyes were just a fraction too close together, and his lips were just a little too thin.

Centuries of inbreeding at work, Elena thought. *Yet another argument for Lucas Rollings. . . .*

"You know, you really do smell delicious." Stephen shouldered his way into the room and closed the door behind him.

"Stephen, what the hell are you doing?" The sinister excitement in his cold blue eyes made the hair rise on the back of her neck.

This was bad. Very bad.

He inhaled deeply. "Ahh, that Burning Moon. Pheromones and sex, my favorite combination." His smile turned chilling. "Especially with a little fear thrown into the mix."

Definitely not good. She took a wary step back. "My father told me he doesn't want me alone with any male for the next month." Never mind that those instructions had pissed her off at the time. Right now, she was grateful.

Stephen's narrow mouth curled into a smile. "That order doesn't apply to me. We just put the finishing touches on the betrothal agreement. You and I are to be married."

She'd known it was coming. Why did this latest betrayal have such power to wound? Elena squared her shoulders and met his hot gaze with her best Ice-Bitch glare. "And I'll tell you what I told him—*I will not marry you.*"

"He's your Alpha. You'll do as you're told. And if that's not enough, he's dying." Nasty anticipation lit those cold eyes. "Surely you wouldn't refuse a dying father's last wish?"

The thought of Richard's death shot a little sliver of pain into Elena's heart. It saddened her that her grief was less for the man himself than for the relationship they'd never had. To Richard Livingston, she was nothing but the means to carry on Wulfgar's line.

But he had also taught her that being the descendent of the Direkind's greatest hero was a responsibility as well as an honor. Her few happy childhood memories involved sitting in Richard's lap, listening to the legends of her ancestor's heroism.

Remembering those stories, Elena knew what she had to do. "I know my duty, Stephen." She also knew what he was capable of, but she curled her lip and met his eyes anyway. "And my duty is to make sure that the blood of a self-serving bully does not run in my son's veins."

Stephen's head rocked back as if from a physical blow. "You little bitch."

She'd just declared war on the Direkind's most dangerous man. It was oddly freeing. "And you have no business leading the Chosen."

He smiled coldly. "Not just a bitch, but a *stupid* bitch. Richard warned me you'd take this attitude. That's why we're not going to wait." Slowly, Stephen began to stalk her, his big hands curling into fists.

Her pounding heart turned to ice. "What are you talking about?"

"No point in waiting until after the wedding when you won't be fertile again for another year." He bared his teeth. "So Richard told me to get you pregnant now. He wants you nice and round before he kicks off."

If she'd needed proof of how little she meant to her father, this was it. "So you're just going to rape me?"

"You're in your Burning Moon. I doubt there'll be much rape involved. Though if you want to play rough . . ." Magic rose, surging around him, glowing to Elena's senses. Mystical energies twisted bone and muscle, sending a wave of golden fur across his skin. When the forces finally died, something not even remotely human towered over Elena, almost seven and a half feet of golden fur, massive muscle, and razored claws.

Fangs gleamed as he grinned at her, and his pointed ears brushed the ceiling. "Now, you're welcome to shift, too," Stephen said, in a deep, growling voice that sounded nothing like his own. "I'd be more than happy to demonstrate just what little chance you have against me in a fight." He spread his fingers, making his claws flex. "Though it's safe to say you won't enjoy the demonstration nearly as much as I will."

Elena backed away, silently cursing both him and her father. At least they'd made her decision easier. If Stephen would do something like this to her—a woman he was supposed to marry—*anybody* was fair game. He had to be stopped, whatever it took. Even if it meant risking the life of an innocent man. "Where's your Chosen sense of honor, Stephen?"

"Where's yours? Your Alpha gave you an order, and you refused to obey."

Her Burning Moon temper exploded. "*It's my body.* I have a right—"

"To *nothing!*" Stephen roared back. "You are not some human female who can put on a pretense of equality! You're a Direwolf. You obey your Alpha. And as of tonight, that's me."

She bared her teeth, refusing to cower. "*You're not my Alpha!*"

A clawed hand flashed out and wrapped in the tough blue

fabric of her polo shirt, jerking her closer. "I say I am. And I say we're going to fuck. Now. Tonight. Tomorrow. Every damned day for the rest of the month until you're pregnant!"

And this will be the rest of my life, Elena thought. *Being bullied by this vicious prick simply because he's bigger and stronger. By God, I don't think so.* "No!"

Stephen shoved his fanged muzzle inches from her face. "You've got a choice, bitch. Either we can pretend we're civilized and do it like humans, or I do you as a Direwolf until you bleed. It's fine by me either way!"

"How about none of the above?" Magic poured over her in a hot, foaming wave, searing muscle and bone as it twisted and reformed her body. But not into Direwolf form.

Elena became a wolf.

Stephen had obviously assumed she'd Change to Direwolf. When she became so much smaller, he lost his grip—exactly as she'd hoped.

Elena hit the ground and darted away as he snatched for her, cursing.

"What the hell do you think you're doing, bitch?" Flexing his clawed hands, he stalked her. He could disembowel her with one swipe. Given his mood, she wouldn't put it past him.

Fear iced her veins, but she ignored it as she danced around him, snapping at his muscled calves like a dog teasing a bear. He grabbed at her, but she was low-slung and nimble on her four legs, and he missed.

With a taunting flick of her tail, she headed for the French doors and their wrought-iron grillwork. He followed, snarling like a chainsaw.

Stopping directly in front of one door, Elena feinted a lunging snap at his balls. *Come on, you big ox. Take your shot.*

"Oh, cunt, I'm going to enjoy putting you in your place!" He drew back a huge fist and swung at her with all his considerable strength. She ducked. His punch grazed the tips of her pointed ears and slammed into the door, which exploded outward from the force of the blow. Glass flew and iron shrieked, the sound competing with Stephen's shocked yelp of pain.

Bet that hurt, dumbass. With a triumphant bark, Elena sailed through the opening, dashed across the balcony, and leaped neatly over the railing. Stephen, trapped in the mangled remains of the grill, could only howl in frustration as she changed forms and ran to the Ferrari in the driveway.

Just in case, she'd left the car unlocked and the keys in the ignition. Now she started the engine and floored the Ferrari down the drive.

"Elena!" Stephen roared after her. "Come back here, or I swear, I'll rip out your guts!"

She ignored him. She didn't have much time to find Lucas Rollings.

CHAPTER 2

*E*lena barreled down I-26 as fast as she dared, flicking constant glances in her rearview mirror. No sign of Stephen's big black Hummer. Maybe she'd lost him the last time she'd doubled back, though how he could miss a candy-apple-red Ferrari was anybody's guess.

A green highway marker drew her attention. Ten miles to Harrisville, South Carolina.

Ten miles to safety.

She scooped up the ragged newspaper clipping from the passenger seat and darted it another glance. Candice was right—Lucas definitely looked as if he could set Stephen back on his heels.

The question was, did Elena have the right to ask him to do it? Stephen didn't play around, and he was obviously out for blood even before he knew Lucas was in the picture. Once he did . . .

Take two Alpha males, add a female in her Burning

Moon, and you had a prescription for bloodshed.

Dammit, Elena thought, disgusted with herself, she was a descendent of Wulfgar. If she had half the guts she was supposed to, she'd leave Lucas out of it and find some way to take care of Stephen herself.

Trouble was, Elena was simply no match for an Alpha. For one thing, she didn't have the combat skills, despite her earlier success. Stephen would mop up the floor with her, and he'd do it with no compunction whatsoever. Even aside from the effects of the Burning Moon, she'd disobeyed her father, the Alpha of the Livingston clan. In Stephen's eyes, she deserved whatever he did to her. Most of the Chosen, male and female alike, would agree.

The rest of the Direkind might have a different attitude, but they also wouldn't involve themselves in Chosen business. The Direkind's aristocracy kept to themselves and policed themselves, and those of the lower classes kept their muzzles out of it.

Hopefully, Candice was right and Lucas would feel differently.

Elena drummed her fingers restlessly on the wheel. What if Lucas turned out to be too *much* a concerned Alpha? What if he refused to accept the role she had in mind for him and sought to dominate her as Stephen had? The last thing she needed was another male trying to force his will down her throat.

One problem at a time, Elena. If Lucas tried to give her a hard time, she'd find a way to deal with him, too. She was through being a victim.

A flash of movement in her rearview mirror. Elena shot it a look and breathed a curse. Something big and black, coming up fast from behind.

Stephen's Hummer.

"Dammit," she swore, and stomped on the gas. "Dammit, dammit, dammit."

Elena swerved around an aged blue Geo Prism barely doing the speed limit, then flashed past an eighteen-wheeler. The Hummer shot after her with a sinister roar.

Bloody hell, she'd hoped to have time to approach Lucas before Stephen caught up to her, but it looked as if that wasn't going to happen.

Her only chance now was to head for the Harrisville Police Department and pray the presence of all those humans would give Stephen pause. It was strictly forbidden to use Direkind powers around humans. Disobeying that taboo was grounds for execution.

Zipping into the left-hand lane, Elena floored the Ferrari, which responded with a deep growl of power. Daring a glance in her rearview mirror, she saw the Hummer lumber after her.

"Bastard," she breathed, before jerking the wheel to the right. The Ferrari bolted across the right-hand lane and down the Harrisville exit ramp, barely missing the bumper of the eighteen-wheeler. The Hummer's brakes shrieked an instant later. Elena winced, hoping he hadn't triggered an accident. Stephen's Direkind reflexes would keep him out of real trouble, but the humans around him wouldn't be so lucky.

She listened as she turned left onto Heron Avenue. No crash, thank God, but no sound of the Hummer's engine either. With any luck, he'd overshot the exit and would have to backtrack.

With a sigh of relief, Elena dropped to a more sedate speed and headed for the police department. She really couldn't afford to get pulled over.

She'd barely gone two blocks before she looked up to see the Hummer in her rearview mirror.

Oh, hell.

Fifteen minutes later . . .

Lieutenant Lucas Rollings strode from the Harrisville Police Department with a sense of grim satisfaction. There was nothing like snapping the cuffs on a killer.

Joseph Bishop had gone sheet white when Lucas had confronted him with the evidence that afternoon. The case against Bishop was steel-trap solid, right down to the blood stains in the car trunk and his DNA under his wife's fingernails. The son-of-a-bitch had known he'd be lucky to avoid the death penalty for Mary Bishop's death. And Lucas intended to make sure he paid with his—

"Back off, Stephen!" The female snarl jolted Lucas from his thoughts. He jerked his head around. In the parking lot twenty yards away, a slender woman struggled with a tall, blond man beside a red Ferrari. A huge black Hummer was parked directly behind the sports car, blocking it in.

Lucas took in the situation with a single experienced glance. *Oh, hell. Stalker. This could get ugly.* He started toward them.

The man cooly drew back a hand and slapped his captive hard across the face. Red hair flew as she cried out in pain.

"Hey!" Lucas roared, breaking into a run as the man grabbed her shoulders. "What the hell do you think you're doing?"

"Get lost," the stalker snapped, without looking around. "This is none of your business."

"I'm the police, jackass. *Let her go!*" He stiff-armed the man back just as the woman tore free.

"Forget it, Stephen," the victim growled. "I'm not going anywhere with you." Her voice was much deeper than it should be, rumbling at a register more animal than human. Yet her face was delicate, fragile, like her lithe, long-legged body.

The blond pressed closer despite Lucas's restraining hand, grabbed her by one wrist, and started hauling her backward toward the Hummer. She threw herself back, trying to dig in her sneakered feet.

"Are you nuts, asshole?" Lucas slammed a hard blow against the man's elbow. It should have broken the bastard's grip, but he held fast and kept going, completely ignoring Lucas. "Let her go!"

"Stay out of this!"

Lucas grabbed him by the collar of his expensive shirt and slammed him into the hood of the Hummer.

"You touch that girl one more time, and . . ." He broke off in mid-sentence. Beneath the scents of toothpaste, the man's expensive cologne, and the woman's shampoo lay a familiar scent. A blend of forest and fur . . .

Deep inside Lucas, something stirred in ancient recognition. Oh, God. *Werewolves.* Both of them.

To make matters worse, the female's scent was also laced with pure sex. Lucas could feel his own body responding, his cock twitching and lengthening as it went hard as a rifle barrel.

Sweet Jesus, he realized, *she's in werewolf heat.*

Lucas had never encountered a Direkind female during her Burning Moon. It had only been a few years since he'd been Bitten, and there were no other werewolves in Harrisville.

Still, Ray Johnston had told him enough about the fuzzy facts of life to make clear he'd just stumbled waist-deep into serious shit. The Burning Moon was going to play merry hell with everybody's temper—including Lucas's. That big blond male was going to want a fight.

And considering the bruise he could see blooming on the girl's patrician cheek, Lucas was in the mood to give it to him.

"Lucas Rollings?" The redhead's throaty voice jolted him out of his preoccupation. He met her gaze to find her staring at him with a kind of desperate hope. "Are you Lieutenant Lucas Rollings?"

She knew him? Comprehension dawned. *She came here looking for me.*

Their eyes locked in an instant of startled mutual awareness. Hers were a deep, vibrant green, like spring leaves. Something in them was so intensely female, his body responded with a silent masculine rumble he felt all the way to the bone. It went beyond the Burning Moon, beyond simple chemistry. It was . . .

Magic.

And judging from the way her eyes flared wide, she felt it, too.

But that was ridiculous. He didn't believe in love at first sight. Not even the fuzzy kind. Even if the wolf in him was almost purring in anticipation. . . .

"Elena, you *bitch!*" Stephen reared in his grip.

Before he even knew what he was doing, Lucas clamped a hand around the Shifter's jaw and shoved him back against the Hummer's hood. "Back. *Off!*"

He wanted to rip out the fucker's throat.

The air filled with the ripe scent of blood. Lucas realized his nails had lengthened into claws, digging into the other man's skin. *What the hell am I doing?* he thought, shaken.

Get a grip, Rollings! He sucked in a deep breath, fighting to control the wolf clawing for the surface. *Not now. Not here.*

"Lucas Rollings, my name is Elena Livingston, and I seek your protection."

Lucas's eyes widened as he looked up from his captive to meet the woman's green gaze. Her face was almost bloodless except for the bruise slowly purpling on her cheek, but her eyes were level and determined.

She's formally asking me to become her champion. Ray had told Lucas that his size and attitude would make him an Alpha male among the Direkind, which meant the elderly, females, and children might ask him to defend them. Lucas had memorized the highly stylized etiquette of an Alpha champion, but he'd never expected to actually use it.

"Elena!" Stephen stared at her, incredulous. "What do think you're doing?"

She ignored him like a queen. "This male has threatened and abused me, and I beg your protection." There was no pleading in her gaze, just steady courage. Her face was delicately boned, nose straight and slim, mouth full, pink-lipped. And those eyes . . .

"Elena!" With a powerful wrench, the blond tore free of Lucas's hold. His voice dropped to a deadly whisper. "If you involve this mongrel, I'll kill him."

Lucas whirled to face his opponent, feeling his muscles coil into knots as he fought the need to Change and kill. Instead he throttled down his rage and gritted the ceremonial words, "Elena Livingston, I will defend you with my last breath."

"You *are* a fool." Stephen lunged at him. Lucas blocked his swinging fist and hit the Direwolf hard enough to rock his head back. The Shifter snarled, baring lengthening fangs.

Was he stupid enough to Change in the middle of the Harrisville Police Department parking lot? In broad daylight?

"No, Stephen!" Elena snapped. "Not here!"

"Hey!" Feet slapped the pavement. Lucas threw a look over his shoulder and mentally cursed as four uniformed cops ran toward them. That's all this situation needed to truly go to hell—humans seeing something they shouldn't.

Stephen froze, his cold eyes flicking toward the officers. Impotent fury flashed over his face before he took a step back. "We *will* settle this," he hissed.

Lucas glared back. "Not tonight."

"What's going on, Lieutenant?" The officers fanned out and surrounded them, studying Stephen with narrow-eyed hostility. "This guy giving you trouble?"

"Yeah. He just assaulted this woman right in front of me." Lucas turned toward Elena. Just the sight of her bruised cheek was enough to make his outraged instincts snarl. "Do you want to press charges?" *Say yes.* He wanted to lock his rival up for a few hours—long enough to find out what the hell was going on and figure out what to do about it.

"Elena!" Stephen growled. "If you do this, you're going to pay for it."

She didn't even flinch. "Yes, I want to press charges. I want him to go to jail."

"Oh, you stupid little bitch."

"That's enough!" Lucas grabbed Stephen by the shoulder and whirled him around. For a moment, he was tempted to slam the man's head into the hood of the Hummer. Instead he jerked a set of handcuffs from his pocket. He hoped the other officers didn't notice his hand was shaking with the intensity of his rage.

The werewolf stiffened, obviously considering fighting him before thinking better of it and allowing himself to be cuffed. Evidently he wasn't insane enough to violate the Direkind taboo against using their abilities in the presence of humans.

Still, Lucas could literally smell his fury, pungent and acrid against the springtime scents of the flowers in the department's flowerbeds.

"You all right, ma'am?" one of the officers asked Elena. "You want to go to the hospital?"

"I don't think that's necessary."

Lucas met her gaze again—and felt again the heat surging between them. Trying to ignore it, he turned to hustle Stephen toward the department's entrance.

He'd never felt like this before. What the hell was happening to him?

CHAPTER 3

*E*lena followed Stephen and Lieutenant Lucas Rollings through the police department's corridors. Her cheek ached, and she could feel her lower lip swelling. Minor injuries, particularly compared to what Stephen no doubt had in mind. The bruises would heal as soon as she transformed. But for the time being, they were just what she needed to make sure her would-be husband spent the night in jail. The longer they could keep him locked up, the better.

For one thing, she was willing to bet Stephen would challenge her new champion the first chance he got. Though Elena suspected it was inevitable, the idea filled her with a surprising dread.

She remembered the moment when Lucas had looked at her. Elena had known her share of men over the years, and yet she'd never felt such stark, instant attraction. His eyes had stared into hers, dark and male and elemental, recognition and hunger flaming up in them.

What's more, something ancient and female in her had purred in response. *It was just the Burning Moon,* Elena told herself firmly. *Just pheromones and biology.*

It doesn't mean anything.

While one of the uniformed officers booked Stephen, Lucas escorted her up a set of stairs to the detectives' division. Like those she'd seen in cop shows, it was a big, open room, filled with desks, filing cabinets, computers, and ringing phones. Unlike the television version, however, the light was much brighter, and dark blue cubicles surrounded the desks. Several detectives worked on paperwork, questioned suspects or witnesses, or talked on the phone.

"I just have a few questions," Lucas told her, gesturing her to a chair beside one of the desks. Elena settled into it as he sat down behind the desk and booted up his computer.

She watched him, taking in the sight of those big hands moving over the keyboard with speed and competence. Stirring in her chair, she remembered his claws growing, pressing into Stephen's throat, muscle flexing in his strong jaw. His powerful shoulders had bunched under the dark blue fabric of his suit coat, and his muscular backside had worked with the effort of keeping his enemy pinned.

Elena crossed her legs and swallowed.

He glanced at her as he opened a program file. Just one quick, dark glance, yet she felt it in the pit of her stomach. She recrossed her legs.

Lucas was definitely handsome, but not in the polished, Chosen mold. Instead, there was something a bit rougher in the width and angle of his cheekbones and the long hawk swoop of his nose. His upper lip had an intriguingly sensual curve, and his lower was suggestively full. It looked bitable, that lip. Tempting.

His eyes were dark, deep-set under thick, dark brows, and his short black hair curled as though inviting female fingers to set it to rights. When he asked her for her identification, his voice was deep, with a masculine rumble that seemed to suggest whispered intimacies in the dark.

Get a grip, Elena, she told herself. *It's your Burning Moon.* Her body was deep in its yearly rut, producing a flood of hormones that urged her to mate while driving every male around her to a dangerous sexual pitch. Even humans felt it, though they had no idea they were reacting to the pheromones she produced.

Lucas, however, knew perfectly well what was going on. A blend of masculine awareness and acute discomfort lit those dark eyes of his, as if his Direwolf instincts battled his sense of duty.

Some primitive part of her enjoyed that. The rest of her was appalled.

She wasn't supposed to feel like this. It was one thing to regret using him. But this intense . . . attraction wasn't part of the plan. It made her feel out of control, and she'd been out of control more than enough as it was.

He started asking questions, and she answered mechanically—her name, her address, Stephen's name and address. Typing her answers into his computer, Lucas didn't appear to recognize either surname. Which might just be an act for the humans' benefit, since they were the two most powerful Chosen families in the South. If nothing else, there was always plenty of gossip going around about the Livingstons and the Bradfords.

Then again, Harrisville was hardly a center of Direkind

culture. The three of them were probably the only werewolves for miles.

"So Mr. Bradford considers himself your fiancé?"

"He and my father have some kind of agreement. But I haven't said yes, and I don't intend to."

"Do you live together?" As she stiffened, Lucas explained, "If you share a residence, I can charge him with domestic violence under South Carolina law. Otherwise it's assault and battery."

"No, we don't live together. I've got my own place in Atlanta." Or she had, until her father used his illness to guilt her into moving back into the family mansion. If she'd had any idea what Richard had in mind, she'd never have come anywhere near Charleston.

"What brings you to Harrisville?"

You. Which was not an answer that belonged in his report. She shrugged and lied. "I was passing through. Stephen followed me, so when I spotted your department, I pulled in. I was hoping he'd leave me alone, but he didn't."

Lucas frowned, his mouth pulling into a surprisingly sensual line. "Assault and battery is a misdemeanor in this state. The most he could get is thirty days in the county jail, and it's doubtful a judge would even sentence him to that much. It's a lot more likely he'll just have to pay a two-hundred-dollar fine. Which means he'll be able to sign a personal recognizance bond and get out of jail in four hours or so."

Damn. She'd hoped they'd keep him locked up at least overnight. She badly needed a break before she took Stephen on again.

"But since he attacked and threatened you in a police department parking lot in front of a cop, I can argue that he's dangerous. I'm going to request a formal bond hearing, with the Solicitor's Office sending a prosecutor to argue for a higher bond." The Solicitor's Office was the South Carolina version of a District Attorney, handling all state prosecution for a given area. "Now, since it's Friday night after five, nobody will be available to do that until Monday morning. That gives us a little time to discuss this and decide what to do."

All weekend. She had all weekend to put her plan into action. "Thank God." Taking a deep breath, Elena met his dark gaze again. "So, what now?"

He shrugged. "I'm going to have to talk to Mr. Bradford, get his side for the report. Then after that, I'll escort you to your hotel."

"Actually . . ." Elena dropped her voice to a pitch she was fairly sure none of the humans could overhear. "A hotel isn't exactly what I had in mind."

"No?" Heat leaped in his eyes, rich with masculine anticipation. Her own body warmed in response.

"No." Elena swallowed and added hoarsely, "I'd rather go home with you. I'd feel . . . safer."

"Safer?" A dark smile curved his lips. "Are you sure?"

She found herself smiling back at him.

"If you touch her, I'll kill you," Stephen Bradford said.

Lucas looked up to meet the Direwolf's icy gaze with one just as cold. "You want me to add threatening a public official to the charges, Bradford?"

The man's nostrils flared like a furious wolf's. "Hiding behind that badge buys you only a few hours at most. My lawyer . . ."

". . . Is shit out of luck, because I just spoke to the Solicitor's Office, and they don't have anybody available to present the case until Monday."

"Coward!"

"That's rich, coming from you. What are you, 210, 220? Elena weighs 120 tops. Bet hitting her made you feel real manly, didn't it?" Good thing the detective's division had emptied out for the night by the time he'd brought Bradford up for questioning. They didn't have to worry about being overheard. Leaning forward, Lucas locked eyes with the Direwolf. "You want to take me on? Name the time and the place. I'll be more than happy to teach you how it feels to be on the receiving end of a fist."

"I'm not a schoolboy, mongrel. I don't exchange punches. We fight in Direwolf form until one of us goes down and doesn't get up." Bradford showed his elegant teeth. "Unless you want to back out?"

"Oh, no. I fully intend to send you to that big doghouse in the sky."

The Direwolf's patrician nostrils flared. "My second will be in touch with yours—assuming you've got one." His tone indicated doubt that Lucas had any friends at all, much less one willing to stand for him in a duel.

"I've got one." Knowing Ray Johnston, he'd be happy to help. Ray hated the Chosen anyway. They'd need a judge too; Ray would know which Charlotte clan official to call. "We'll see you and your second after the bond hearing Monday."

"In the meantime . . ." Bradford gave him an threatening glare and dropped his voice to a lethal whisper. "Don't get involved in whatever scheme Elena's hatching. She's a descendent of Wulfgar, and her father won't stand for her bearing any whelp of yours."

Lucas stared at him. "What the hell are you talking about?"

"You." Bradford curled his lip in revulsion. "And her."

Jesus. More weird werewolf shit. "First, I just met the woman an hour ago. We're not exactly going to be hopping into bed, Burning Moon or no Burning Moon. And second, in the unlikely event she did get pregnant, what could her daddy do about it—force her to go to a clinic?"

"You are ignorant, aren't you?" Outright contempt curled the Direwolf's mouth. "Mongrel."

"At least I don't beat women in parking lots like a drunken redneck." Lucas's mother had been on the receiving end of more than one parking-lot beating. God, he hated guys like this.

"I barely touched her!"

Lucas curled his lip. "Funny how blue-blood were-wolves spout the same shit as every other abusive asshole I've ever locked up." *And every one of my so-called "step-fathers."* Sue Rollings's taste in men had seriously sucked.

"This is not the same thing!" Bradford sat back, visibly reining in his rage. His tone leveled into patient condescension. "Elena has a duty to obey her clan Alpha—who is also her father—but she ran away instead. Richard Livingston told me to bring her back. And that's exactly what I'm going to do."

"Elena's twenty-seven years old, and she's an American citizen. She doesn't have to obey Daddy anymore, and she sure as hell doesn't have to obey you."

"You don't understand—she has a responsibility." Bradford leaned forward again as his cold blue eyes began to shine with a fanatic's fervor. "Those of us who are Chosen live by traditions of duty and honor that go back centuries. Without those traditions, we're no better than the humans."

"News flash, Bradford—you're *not* better than the humans. Most humans don't beat the shit out of people just because they're smaller and weaker."

"Don't be such a sanctimonious ass. All Elena has to do is transform, and whatever piddling injuries I gave her will instantly heal. And if she'd start showing a little respect for her bloodline, I wouldn't have to hurt her." Bradford studied him. His eyes suddenly narrowed. "You don't even know who Wulfgar was, do you?"

"No, and I don't care. 'I wouldn't have to hurt her'? Do you have any idea how many times I've heard that line? You're a real prick, you know that?"

Bradford's jaw flexed, but otherwise, he ignored the taunt. "Wulfgar was our Arthur. He was the first among heroes, Chosen by Merlin himself to drink from the Grail and become Direkind. And since her father is dying, Elena is the last of his bloodline. Even you must see she should mate with her own kind."

"I'm an American, asshole. I don't believe anybody's blood is better than anybody's else's." Lucas smiled tauntingly. "But I do know inbreeding when I see it."

The Direwolf stared at him, those cold eyes all but glowing in rage. "I'm going to kill you."

"Not even on your best day." With a vicious gesture, Lucas saved the report and hit print. "It's time for you to go to jail, Stevie. You can spend the weekend thinking about how much I'm going to enjoy ripping out your throat."

CHAPTER 4

"You know, boy," Ray Johnston's voice drawled in his ear, "you got a real gift for gettin' yourself in a shitload of trouble."

Lucas snorted and stopped the Crown Vic at a red light. He'd called his friend on his cell the minute he pulled out of the police department parking lot. "I can't help that all you fuzzy bastards are insane." Looking into his rearview mirror, he saw Elena's Ferrari behind him. She was supposed to follow him back to his house, though he had no idea what he'd do with her when he got her there.

"You think we're bad?" Ray demanded. "The Chosen are nastier than all the rest of us put together. And the Bradfords and the Livingstons are the most stone-cold ruthless of the lot. Not good men to piss off, my friend."

"What the hell was I supposed to do? He was beating that girl in the parking lot of the police department!"

"Yeah, that sounds like Bradford." His friend sighed.

"And getting roped into serving as her champion sounds like you."

Since the night five years ago when Ray had made Lucas a werewolf, the two men had become close friends. Ray had even served as his Wolfmaster, teaching him everything he needed to know about Direkind.

Good thing, too, because almost everything Lucas had ever heard about werewolves was pure crap. They weren't allergic to silver or wolfsbane, and they didn't need the full moon to change. And it was Merlin the wizard who'd created them, not some curse-casting gypsy.

As for the ravening killer idea—well, last week Lucas and Ray had gone to Jennifer Rosemond's ninth birthday party. The little girl barely remembered her kidnapping at all, having been out cold for most of it.

Now, if only the current mess would end that well.

"What can you tell me about Elena?"

"Not much. I've just heard her address meetings of the Southern Clans a time or two," Ray said, referring to the Direkind council that governed the southeastern werewolf clans. "She's something of a rebel—wants to end some of the more medieval Chosen customs, which doesn't go over well with the other aristocrats. I always figured she was a little too idealistic for her own good. Sounds like I was right."

Lucas frowned. "How much danger is she in, Ray?"

"Not as much as you, son. Did I hear you say she's in her Burning Moon?"

"Far as I can tell. Every time I take a breath around her, I get a hard-on."

"Yep, that's the Burning Moon, all right. Either way, you'd better keep it in your pants. She's way out of your league. You lay one fuzzy hand on her, her daddy'll cut it off."

Lucas flicked a look in his rearview mirror at the Ferrari,

still trailing behind. "Yeah, I kinda figured that," he said, and changed the subject. "You think you can find us somebody to officiate over the duel?"

"I'll give Don Jennings a call. In the meantime, keep it zipped, you hear me?"

He snorted. "Believe me, I'm not dumb enough to do anything else."

Lucas pulled into the carport of his rented house and got out to watch Elena whip the Ferrari in behind him. Even stopped, the car looked as if it was speeding.

Ray's right—she's definitely out of my league.

Then she got out of the car, and it was all he could do not to moan. Long-legged and slim-hipped, with high, sweet breasts, her hair catching flame in the light of the setting sun, Elena Livingston looked like every dream of sex he'd ever had. Even the bruises on that pretty face made her more appealing, like a woman who needed saving. A woman he could actually touch.

Now you really are dreaming. She's Chosen. She'd never let you lay one peasant finger on that pure-blooded Dire-wolf body.

Ray had told him all about the Chosen as part of his Dire-wolf indoctrination. They were the closest thing the Dire-kind had to aristocracy—direct descendents of the very first werewolves created by Merlin himself. Everybody else came from Bitten like him—poor bastards some Direwolf had fanged. Since the bite spread the spell called Merlin's Curse, whoever got bitten soon got furry.

The Chosen, on the other hand, considered themselves superior because their ancestors had been selected by Merlin. Proud of their bloodlines and highly secretive, they were bound by a web of complex traditions and blood relationships. They definitely did not mix with the likes of Lucas Rollings.

Great. Just what he needed: a weekend of sexual frustration followed by a a fight to the death with a jealous Direwolf.

As Lucas watched, Elena walked over and looked up into his eyes. Despite her apparent boldness, he thought he detected discomfort on her lovely face.

"I guess you're wondering what's really going on," she said softly. "Given that I couldn't tell you the full story back at the department."

"The question has crossed my mind." He gestured her ahead of him and tried not to inhale her luscious sex-and-sin scent.

She preceded him toward the house's entrance. "I need your help."

"And you'll get it. Bradford's already challenged me to a duel on Monday." Lucas reached past her to open the kitchen door for her.

"That's only part of it. I need you to get me pregnant."

"What the hell kind of game are you playing with me, lady?" Lucas stopped dead in the carport and stared at her, his handsome face darkening with offended anger.

Elena sighed. "I'm not playing, Lieutenant. Believe me, all of us are in deadly earnest." She raked a frustrated hand through her hair. "Look, could we just go inside and talk?"

He hesitated, then gave her a short, sharp nod. Well, at least he hadn't ordered her off his property.

Relieved, she stepped inside, finding herself in a small, sunny kitchen. For a moment she paused as the past several hours suddenly caught up to her. Her head ached, and her face throbbed. Her swollen eye was seriously throwing off her vision. She probed it delicately and winced.

"Want to Change?" Lucas asked gruffly. "The explanation can wait until you heal."

"You don't mind?" When he shook his head, Elena called her magic and threw her body into wolf form. No sooner was the transformation complete than she returned to human again.

Her legs always felt rubbery after Changing so many times that close together. She staggered over to his kitchen table and fell into one of the seats with a sigh of weariness. Gingerly, she touched her face and found it healed.

"Well, that looks a hell of a lot better," Lucas said.

She shrugged. "One of the mixed blessings of being a Chosen female. Our Alphas don't think it counts if you can heal it with a quick transformation."

He frowned, leaning a lean hip on the butcher block countertop. "Do all the Chosen go in for domestic violence?"

Elena grimaced. "Not all of them, but it is considered one of our 'traditions.' "

He curled a lip. "I thought the Direkind were supposed to be heroes."

"We are."

"Since when is there anything heroic in beating up somebody you outweigh by a hundred pounds?" He sighed and rubbed the back of his neck. "You want something? A Coke? A beer? I think I've got a couple of steaks . . ."

"A Coke would be welcome." Her stomach rumbled, reminding her just how long it had been since she'd eaten. "And I wouldn't turn down a meal, either."

He nodded and turned to the refrigerator. She stood and joined him, reaching for the Coke he offered her.

Their fingers touched. Just like that, awareness popped

and crackled between them like an electric line gone suddenly live. Heat raced over her skin.

Desire leaped in his gaze.

She tore her eyes away, popped the top, and took a sip. "Want me to set the table?"

Silence thrummed a moment, heavy with sexual awareness. "Sure." Lucas turned to get two steaks out of the freezer, then popped them in the microwave to thaw. "Glasses and plates are in the cabinet over the sink. Silverware's in the drawer by the dishwasher."

As she filled two glasses with ice, Elena decided to continue her explanation. It seemed wiser to give them both a chance to regain control. "For the record, the Chosen are the only members of the Direkind who are that patriarchal. Everybody else has pretty much the same attitude toward domestic violence as you do."

"So why are the Chosen the only ones still living in the Dark Ages?"

"The usual—money, power, and the willingness of everybody else to look the other way." She toasted him with her Coke. "But I mean to change all that—with your help."

He lifted a brow. "Which includes getting you knocked up?"

"Actually . . . yes."

Another vibrating silence. She found herself staring at his lush mouth. He took a step toward her . . .

The microwave dinged.

As if jolted back to normal, Lucas turned to get out the steaks and transferred them onto a broiler. "What's so important about having my baby?"

Elena blew out a breath. "It's complicated."

He shot her a dry look. "Anything to do with the Direkind usually is."

"Well, this is Direkind politics, which makes it even more convoluted. To begin with, the Chosen maintain seats on all the Clan councils, right on up to the Council of Clans for the entire planet. Which makes the laws we all have to abide by."

"Okay, I get that." He reached up and loosened his tie, then unbuttoned his collar.

Elena found herself staring at the hollow of his strong throat. With an effort, she dragged her attention back to business. "Well, unlike all the other officials, the Chosen's representative on the Council of Clans isn't elected—the seat is hereditary. For the past fifteen hundred years it's been held by a direct descendent of Wulfgar himself. . . ."

"The werewolf King Arthur?"

"That's him. Arthur and his knights were Celts; Wulfgar and his Direkind warriors were Saxon. It was Merlin's way of making sure the two groups didn't get too chummy." Like the myths about werewolves, Arthurian legend bore little resemblance to reality. Merlin had turned Arthur and his people into the Magekind—vampires and witches sworn to protect humanity from itself. Apparently being a little paranoid, the immortal wizard had also created the Direkind and ordered them to make sure their cousins didn't start abusing the very humans they'd been created to protect.

"And you're a descendent of this Wulfgar?" Interpreting her lifted brow, Lucas shrugged. "That's what Stephen said, between warning me to keep my mongrel mitts to myself."

"Stephen always was a charmer. But he's right. My father holds Wulfgar's seat now, but he's dying."

"I'm sorry to hear that." He frowned, studying her.

"So am I, though we've never been particularly close, I'm afraid. I was always a great disappointment to Dad."

Lucas got down a couple of plates, then started forking

the steaks onto them. "I can't imagine you being a disappointment to anybody."

She gave him a crooked smile. "One too many X chromosomes."

"Wanted a boy that bad, did he?"

"He had one. My brother didn't make it through his first Change." Elena shook her head, remembering the night she learned Robbie wouldn't be coming home. His magic had run rogue during his first attempt to transform, burning him alive. He'd been only seventeen. Two years later, Elena successfully made her own transformation. "Dad never forgave me for surviving when Robbie didn't."

"All of which means that when your father dies, you get his seat."

"Nope. Still too many X chromosomes."

Frowning, Lucas handed her a plate, then sat down with his own. "But women serve on the Council of Clans."

"Not in Wulfgar's seat. I told you, we Chosen are big on tradition. The only way a woman could hold that seat is as a custodian for a minor son."

"And you want me to give him to you. How do you know you won't have a girl?"

"It doesn't matter whether I do or not. Once I'm pregnant, I can legally declare myself emancipated from my father's control in favor of the new bloodline I just started. And once I'm emancipated, I'm no longer considered female under the Traditions, because I'll be the head of a household. Basically, an Alpha."

Lucas stared at her, a line of confusion between his straight dark brows. "That makes absolutely no sense."

"Yeah, well, that's the Traditions for you. Fifteen hundred years of accumulated rationalizations designed to benefit various people with a whole lot of money. Which, once I'm on the Council, I plan to methodically dismantle. Especially when it comes to the part about Chosen women being subordinate." She picked up her knife and cut into her steak.

"I hate to mention this, but there are eleven people on that council. What makes you think you can swing the votes to change anything?"

"There is a coalition of female council members who think it's time we abandon some of the Traditions. Or at least quit turning a blind eye to abuse. My father has always fought them, but if I took his place, I think we could get the rest of the council to go along."

"Bet your daddy would just love that. Does he know that's what you intend?"

Elena forked up a bite and chewed. It was surprisingly tender. "Oh, yeah. That's why he's so determined to marry me off to Stephen before he dies." Gesturing with her fork, she explained, "See, if Stephen gets me pregnant, he can assume the seat. So they're both determined Stephen's going to get me pregnant." She remembered the sadistic hunger in the man's eyes. "Whether I like it or not."

A muscle flexed in Rollings's jaw. "You saying he'd rape you?"

"He tried. Earlier today." She cut another bite. "I got away."

"I'm definitely killing that son of a bitch."

"Feel free."

"One thing I don't get—why me? I mean, there must be plenty of Chosen men who'd . . ."

"Be happy to take Wulfgar's seat? Oh, yeah."

"But you're not worried I will?" Comprehension dawned. "Because I'm Bitten."

Elena swallowed with effort, guilt turning the bite to sawdust in her mouth. "You'd have to be Chosen to hold it."

His dark eyes narrowed. "So basically, I'm a bodyguard and dick in one easy-to-use package."

She swallowed, forcing herself not to flinch at the anger in his gaze. "You're the only werewolf in the tri-state area who won't look the other way while they do whatever the hell they want to me."

"Oh, I doubt I'm the only one. I know a lot of werewolves who aren't assholes." Lucas threw down his fork. "But I am single, nasty enough to kick Bradford's ass, and *here*, so I guess I'll have to do."

Elena's muscles slowly uncoiled. "So you'll do it?"

"Fuck your brains out, knock you up, and fight a seven-foot werewolf on your behalf? Oh, hell, why not?" His smile was bitterly vicious. "I'm feeling chivalrous."

CHAPTER 5

"For the record, I don't like this either." Elena leaned forward, those big, green eyes meeting Lucas's earnestly. He wondered again if he was being suckered. "I realize I'm taking advantage of your decency, and I'm putting you in danger. But the Chosen can't be allowed to simply go on acting like medieval lords with a legal right to beat the serfs."

Yeah, all that sounded like a cause he was willing to fight for. Maybe even die for. A childhood spent watching his mother dodge one fist after another had given him a serious hate for abusive pricks. Which was why he'd become a cop to begin with.

But he hated being used.

What really got him about all this, though, was the nagging sense of disappointment. Becoming a Direwolf had complicated the hell out of his life. The keen senses and increased strength came in handy in his line of work, but lying had become a way of life. He hadn't been seriously involved with a woman since he'd been Bitten because, under Dire-kind law, werewolves only married other werewolves. If he fell in love with a human, he'd have to Bite her to give her Merlin's Curse. Which was a hell of a way to treat someone you love. And he hadn't met any Direkind females he wanted to get involved with.

He'd been willing to put up with all that, though, because he'd believed the Direkind the good guys—protecting humanity behind the scenes. Finding out their aristocracy beat their wives shattered that happy illusion.

"You know what I don't understand?" he said, sitting back in his seat to study Elena. "How could you beat a woman you're Spirit Linked to?" Ray had described the psychic link he had with his wife. They experienced one another's emotions, shared each other's pleasures. It had sounded damned tempting, even after Ray had told him the death of one partner would kill the other. "Seems like it would literally hurt you as much as it did her."

"It would. Which is why Chosen couples rarely link." Elena grimaced. Even that expression looked good on her lovely face. "Our males consider it a sign of being hen-pecked. Besides, our marriages are usually born more of dynastic concerns than love."

"And who the hell would risk dying for somebody you married for her money?"

"Exactly. I'll admit, I always dreamed of Spirit Linking with my husband." She smiled and dropped her head back, all that fiery hair shifting around her cameo face. "What would it be like, to know that kind of perfect love? I'd almost be willing to risk death to find out."

What would it be like to share that love with her? He shook off the thought. *You're a combination dick and body-*

guard, remember? She's not going to fall in love with you, moron. "How *does* the Spirit Link thing work, anyway?"

Elena shrugged. "I gather you touch your partner as you Change, then blend your magic somehow. Apparently it strengthens your powers considerably."

Damn, it did sound tempting. "Not the kind of thing you'd do with somebody you didn't love, though."

She gave a delicate little snort. "Hardly."

An unpleasant thought occurred to him, and he frowned. "Do Chosen males treat the kids as badly as they do their wives?"

"Oddly enough, no. My father never lifted a hand to me until I became a Direwolf." She sighed. "The taboo against child abuse has to be strong, because somebody like Stephen could do so much damage. Particularly since children can't transform and heal." The ability to shift only came at age seventeen or so—the Direkind version of puberty.

"That taboo's pretty strong in mainstream American culture too," Lucas pointed out, "but that doesn't stop anybody."

"But it's not an automatic death sentence if they catch you at it. Which it is, among us. Our child mortality rate is appalling as it is, with a fifth of all kids not making it through their first Change. If we tolerated child abuse on top of that . . . well . . ."

What kind of life had she lived? Lucas wondered suddenly. It was easy to picture her as a pampered little girl, treated like spun glass. Only to hit puberty, and find she meant nothing to the men around her but a walking womb. No wonder she was willing to do anything to change the system she was trapped in. "The transition from child to Direkind female must come as a shock."

"It's that way for everybody."

"But especially for Chosen girls, I'll bet. One day you're Daddy's little girl. The next, he's coming after you with claws."

"Not every day. Not all the time." Elena stood and moved to the window. Night had fallen while they'd talked. There was a thick stand of trees beyond the privacy fence that circled the yard, their leaves edged in moonlight. She found herself longing to Change and simply run. Lose herself in those dark woods. "Eleven months out of the year, he didn't much care what I did. It was only during my Burning Moon that he got paranoid." She shrugged. " 'We've got to keep the bloodline pure, Elena.' "

"You're twenty-seven," Lucas pointed out. "Why hasn't he already married you off?"

"After I graduated college, I figured out how to avoid drawing Daddy's attention. I moved out, I found a job, and I didn't get involved with anybody unsuitable. He was heavily involved in Direkind politics, so he let me go my own way." Elena pulled the curtain back farther, staring out into the darkness. "And my father's health has been good, up until this past year. He's seventy-six now, and his magic is beginning to go. Once you can't transform anymore . . ." She shrugged. Transformations tended to ward off the worst of the damage inflicted by age. But when the magic failed, a Direwolf's health tended to deteriorate fast.

"He must have been in his forties when you were born."

"Right. He was ten years older than my mother."

"What about your mother? You haven't mentioned her."

Because it still hurt. "Mom ran her convertible up under an eighteen wheeler at sixty miles an hour. The collision took her head off." There were some things even the Direkind couldn't heal. "It was right after Bobby died. I always wondered . . ." Her eyes began to sting, and she blinked fiercely.

He studied her with quiet sympathy. "Losing your mother and brother together like that must have been rough. How old were you?"

"Fifteen. That was right about the time Daddy started . . ." She gestured. ". . . pulling away." Her eyes started to fill in earnest. "Sorry. Burning Moon hormones." She blinked hard and reached up to rub her aching back.

"Shoulders hurt?"

Elena gave him a tired smile. "Being a werewolf isn't a protection against tension."

Lucas flashed her a dry smile and rose from the table. "Just the reverse, in fact." He reached for her. She started to pull back, but he took her gently by the arms and turned her around. "Allow me." Big, warm hands came to rest on her shoulders, fingers digging in gently. "You *are* tense. Some of these knots feel like Ping-Pong balls." He found a particularly tight one and went to work on it, thumbs circling and stroking.

Elena let her head fall back with a groan of pleasure. "You're good at that."

"Being a cop is pretty high-tension too. Which is why . . ." He leaned down to her ear and whispered, ". . . there's a hot tub on the back deck."

She looked around at him, intrigued. "Is there?"

Lucas shrugged. "When you spend your time wrestling bad-tempered bad guys into jail cells, sometimes you need a good soak."

Elena hesitated. "I don't have a swimsuit."

His smile turned wicked. "Would you believe me if I promised not to look?"

"Should I?"

He laughed, the sound rich and very male. "Probably not."

She slitted her eyes, enjoying the warmth of his hands. "I think I'll risk it."

She'd touched him. Pissed as he'd been—and Lucas had been pretty pissed off—Elena Livingston had gotten to him.

Brooding, he stared out across the moonlit back yard toward the stand of trees beyond the house. He'd changed into his swim trunks while she went to clean up. Now he found himself wondering what the hell he was doing.

Well, other than waiting for hot sex with a woman who seriously turned him on.

And why not? Lucas was about to fight a duel over her with a murderous son of a bitch who'd been a werewolf a hell of a lot longer than he had. He'd be lucky if he didn't get his head handed to him on the end of a rusty pocket knife.

Hot sex was the least she owed him.

So he had no problem with the sex. It was the rest of it that gave him psychic whiplash.

There he'd been, pissed, nursing the ugly suspicion that Elena had played him, when she'd started talking about losing her mother and brother. Not to mention that prick daddy of hers. Those big green eyes had gone so sad, so lonely.

And Lucas's entirely justifiable anger suddenly hadn't seemed to matter at all.

Pussy.

Then like an idiot, he'd offered to rub her shoulders. Her back had felt so delicate under his hands, with those slim muscles coiled into knots of tension he knew must hurt like a son of a bitch. He'd started rubbing his thumbs over those knots, and she'd made that sweet, throaty moan in her throat.

Lucas had looked down and seen the pretty mounds of her breasts in that shirt, and he'd gotten so violently hard, he'd expected his zipper to bust.

So now they were going to have sex. Only in his case, he was afraid it'd be a little too close to making love.

Elena, on the other hand, was going to be working very hard at getting knocked up as part of a wild-ass gamble for all her personal marbles. He'd give the girl one thing: she didn't lack guts.

Man, he liked that about her.

You really are a fuckin' idiot. Lucas thumped his fist on the deck railing in irritation. He was going to screw around and fall for the little blueblood werewolf, despite knowing perfectly well she'd walk right out of his life.

And why shouldn't she? He wasn't Chosen. Hell, he was Bitten.

As Lucas had discovered over the last few years, most Direkind females viewed first generation Bitten with considerable wariness. For one thing, if one of the Bitten did something dumb and somebody decided he weren't fit to be Direkind, his local clan could take out an order of execution on him. No smart girl wanted to get mixed up with a guy who was halfway to a dirt nap.

Which was yet another reason Lucas could count the dates he'd had in the last few years on one hairy paw. No wonder his libido was all but drooling at the thought of Elena Livingston and her Burning Moon.

Pussy was a wonderful thing.

Too bad he had the ugly feeling this particular kitty was

going to end up treating his heart like a catnip cat toy. He could almost feel her little needle teeth getting a good grip.

Dumbass.

Wrapped in a towel, Elena walked out on the back deck. And stopped dead as her Burning Moon hormones hummed in approval.

Lucas stood with his back to her, staring out over the yard. He wore a pair of red swim trunks, an obvious nod to her modesty. His back was breathtaking—a broad, well-muscled sweep from wide shoulders to a narrow, delightfully taut ass. His legs were long and powerful, dusted with dark hair, and his big feet were bare.

Elena's mouth went dry, and she swallowed, clutching the towel around herself.

"Better get in," Lucas said without looking around. "I don't know how much longer I can pretend to be a gentleman."

She laughed and dropped her towel, then stepped over the side of the hot tub. As promised, the water was delightfully warm and bubbling, and she sighed in pleasure as she sank down on one of the bench seats running beneath the surface.

He turned, his gaze hotter than the water as he looked at her. She was suddenly conscious of the pale upper curves of her breasts rising over the bubbling water.

Lucas started toward her, and Elena forgot her own modesty in favor of staring at him. The view from the front was even better. His pecs were wide, solid plates of muscle, and he was so lean, his abdominal muscles lay under his skin in sculpted ridges. When he braced his arms on the tub lip to boost himself over, thick biceps and triceps worked and shifted. Settling into the bubbling water with a sigh, he extended both long arms along the edge of the tub. Moonlight silvered them as he let his head fall back. "Man, I needed this. It's been a bitch of a day."

"And I made it quite a bit bitchier," Elena said softly. "I'm sorry."

"It wasn't intentional."

"No, but that doesn't change the fact that you're taking a big risk for me. And I'm grateful."

He shrugged in a lift of those breathtaking shoulders. "Comes with the job."

"Fighting Stephen isn't your job, Lucas."

"Somebody's got to do it." He spoke without opening his eyes. "The man's an asshole. I hate assholes."

She laughed despite herself. But as she sat watching him relax in the bubbling water, she realized he really could die in Monday's fight. Lucas was a big man, yes, but Stephen was no stranger to dueling; he had the advantage there. And a fight between Direkind males could be unimaginably vicious, in part because they could heal most injuries simply by transforming.

On the one hand, that meant Lucas could survive anything except a broken neck, decapitation, or ripping out his heart, as long as he could transform. But it also meant he'd suffer a lot more pain than a human would, because he could keep going when a human would simply die.

"You're thinking about this too much." He'd opened one eye to look at her.

"Just realizing I have no right to drag you into this."

He sighed and lifted an arm, inviting her to slide in next to him. "Come here."

Elena hesitated, then scooted across the tub to settle into the curve of that brawny arm. She rested her head against his wet, muscular chest, enjoying the hard heat of him.

"When I was a kid, my mother had a whole lot of lovers

just like Stephen," he told her softly. "They beat her and they beat me. We got into the habit of going to a different ER every time so none of the doctors would realize she wasn't walking into doors, and I wasn't just falling off swing sets."

She lifted her head from his chest, staring up at him in shock. "Oh."

"Yeah. There were times I'd have given my left nut if she'd had the balls to call a cop."

In a flash, Elena pictured him as a thin, big-eyed child, bruised and nursing his rage. "How could she stand by while they hurt you?"

"She'd convinced herself she was either helpless or that we both deserved whatever they did to us. Depended on her mood which theory she went with." He laughed, the sound short and bitter. "When I was sixteen, she threw me out for kicking her latest boyfriend's skinny little ass. I was already six-one and a wide receiver on my high school football team."

"And not in the mood to take any crap."

"Not really, no. I bunked on my friends' couches until I turned eighteen and could enlist in the Marines. Did my tour, came home, and became a cop."

"What happened to your mother?"

"Lung cancer. Six years ago, before I became a werewolf." Lucas met her eyes and gently cupped her cheek. "The point is I know what it's like to be a victim. I know what it's like to be willing to do absolutely anything not to be hurt anymore. I know how fear sits in your stomach and goes acid until all you want to do is throw up."

"Yeah, I guess you do," she said quietly.

"I also know it wasn't easy to come to a stranger for help. Much less ask him to get you pregnant. I admire you for that." He stroked a lock of hair back out of her eyes. "So you have nothing to apologize for."

Elena blinked hard, feeling her eyes begin to sting. "Thank you. You don't know how much that . . ."

Lucas leaned forward and took her mouth. It was a slow kiss, just a light brushing of lip on lip at first, almost chaste. Elena sighed and opened for him. He made a soft, growling sound and deepened it, his mouth possessive and hungry as his tongue slipped between her lips in a teasing, wet stroke. He tasted of steak and beer, a rich, thoroughly male combination that suited him.

Deep inside her, something tight and frozen began to thaw, to bloom. She moaned and tangled both hands in his hair. He rumbled something and hauled her against him. Elena caught her breath at the feeling of his firm, hair-dusted chest crushing her naked breasts.

This remarkable man was hers, if only for the moment. She could touch him, hold him. Pretend they shared something more than a weekend snatched from the teeth of violence.

The Burning Moon burst into full heat, running like lava through her veins. She had to have him.

Gasping with need, she tore free of the kiss and let her head fall back. Lucas's warm, skilled mouth found the line of her jaw, tasting, biting softly, sending chills of delight racing over her skin.

Then one big hand discovered her breast, cupping it boldly.

"Oh, God." She sighed.

He rumbled something, thumb and forefinger stroking the tight peak, coaxing it even harder, each caress sending another jolt of pleasure through her nervous system.

Dazed, she met his eyes. He was watching her, his gaze direct, predatory. His lips looked kiss-flushed. "Has anybody ever told you your breasts are perfect?"

She swallowed. "They are?"

"I love the way they fill my hands." He looked down at the soft globe he cupped and petted. "Your skin is like satin."

As if unable to hold back any longer, Lucas slid an arm around her waist and arched her back over it. Her nipples broke the water's surface, hard as cherries in the moonlight.

He covered one peak with his mouth, a sudden, delicious envelopment in wet heat. Then he started suckling, slow, deep, each sweet pull of his lips sending a pulse of raw pleasure through her nervous system.

"God, that feels good." Biting her lip, Elena closed her eyes and let herself float in sensation—the water bubbling around her sensitive skin, the strength of his arms holding her, his mouth, gentle and greedy at once. She let herself go completely limp, surrendering to him.

Lucas's free hand slipped between her thighs, gently exploring. He found her nether lips and traced his fingers over the soft hair covering them, then gently parted her.

The first stroke of that strong finger into her core arched her back with a jolt of thick, luscious pleasure. Crying out, she bucked against him.

Lucas lifted his head from her breast to watch her pleasure. "That's right," he said softly. "Let go. Give it to me." His thumb found her clit, strummed over the tiny erection to draw out another molten swirl of delight. A second finger joined the one inside her, pushing deep, then scissoring apart. Tormenting her deliciously.

With every stroke of his fingers, every swirl of his tongue around her nipple, another pulse of pleasure rolled through her. Until finally she was writhing, maddened with it, so close to coming, so desperate for the release her body craved.

He lifted his head from her breast to watch her, enjoying her pleasure, her desperate yearning.

"Lucas," she groaned. "Please!"

Another taunting stroke. "I like the sound of my name on your lips. Say it again."

"Lucas!"

"You're close, aren't you, baby?"

"Oh, God, yes! Please, Lucas!"

"Oooh, yeah." And he thrust hard, deep, simultaneously circling his thumb over her clit.

Her back arched, bowing ferociously as she cried out, the orgasm sweeping her up and throwing her high. Sweet, endless pulses of it that went on and on.

Until, at last, they subsided, leaving her panting and spent.

Dazed, she looked up at him.

His gaze was intensely satisfied, possessive—and hungry.

And she realized he was far from done with her.

CHAPTER 6

*E*ven as Elena's slowing heartbeat sped up again, Lucas set her back on her feet, then caught the edge of the hot tub and vaulted out.

He met her gaze with a smoldering stare. "I want to look at you when I take you."

She swallowed, feeling inner muscles clench. "All right."

"I wasn't asking permission." He reached over the side of the tub and caught her in his arms, lifting her out as if she weighed nothing at all to him. Which she didn't, given his Direkind strength.

Swinging around, Lucas carried her to a red-stained wooden chaise lounge, then lowered her to the thick cushion.

He straightened and stood looking down at her a moment, his gaze hungry and possessive. That look would have insulted her coming from anybody else, yet from Lucas, it felt . . . right. Not to mention wildly arousing, particularly combined with the thick tent in the front of those trunks.

She smiled up at him, eying it. "Is that a rocket launcher in your pocket, or are you happy to see me?"

Lucas grinned. "I think the actual quote was 'pistol.' "

Elena gave him a lusty smile and her best Bogie drawl. " 'That ain't exactly a snub-nose, schweetheart.' "

"You sure about that? Maybe you need a closer look." He reached for the waistband of his trunks.

She caught her breath in anticipation.

Lucas slid them down slowly, a wicked half-smile quirking his lips. The head of his shaft appeared over the lowering waistband, fat as a plum, then the thick shaft with its long, veined underside. Finally his balls, full and tight with arousal in their nest of dark curls.

He bent with surprising male grace and pushed the wet trunks the rest of the way off, then kicked them aside. Straightening to his full height, he caught his erect cock in one hand. Long as his fingers were, it was a handful even for him. Setting his big feet apart, he angled the curving shaft upward, stroking its length as he cupped his balls in the other hand, displaying himself shamelessly. "What do you think?"

"I think modesty is not your best thing." Her voice sounded embarrassingly hoarse.

He laughed. "Honey, I'm an Alpha. We don't do modest."

Elena blinked, watching a gleaming droplet roll from one tiny male nipple, down the sculpted ridges of his ribs to the top of one strong thigh. "What do you do?"

"Whatever we can get away with." He stepped closer and sat down on the edge of the chaise. Bracing a strong arm on the cushioned back, he leaned down toward her mouth. "Speaking of which . . ."

Elena reached for the kiss eagerly, hungry to taste him again. She hadn't been mistaken about that mouth. His lips really did feel like satin, and his tongue stroked between hers with a connoisseur's skill. Still kissing her lazily, he cupped one breast, caressing her, teasing her already hard nipple until it began to ache again.

The Burning Moon driving her in concert with her own curiosity, Elena started touching him. Her fingers traced the great slabs of muscle covering his chest, her nails tracing through the cloud of dark, soft hair that covered them. Circling his tongue with hers, she followed the silken trail downward, over the intriguing ridges of his belly. Down to his cock, jutting urgently against her hip. She wrapped her fingers around it and was delighted to note her thumb and index finger didn't quite meet. Dreamily, she gave him a slow stroke, back and forth. He growled against her mouth, the sound feral.

By the time he pulled away, they were both breathing hard.

For a long moment, they stared into one another's eyes, feeling the raw need pulse between them. The moment was so intense, she felt driven to crack the tension with a joke. "Definitely a rocket launcher."

Lucas's laughter boomed as he pulled away and knelt at the foot of the chaise. "Wench! Just for that . . ." Grabbing her hips, he hauled her ruthlessly right to the edge, then spread her wide, his palms warm on her thighs. She caught her breath, startled and delighted, as he buried his face right between her legs.

The first stroke of his tongue felt as if it would blow the top off her head. She arched, gasping. "Lucas!"

"Yes?" Another wicked, teasing stroke. He spread her with two fingers and lifted his head, tilting it to one side as he studied her. "Pretty little puss." Lucas gave her another long, slow lap, then swirled the tip of his tongue around her clit. Fire spiraled in its luxurious wake.

Elena squirmed. Panted. Remembered the feeling of that promising cock filling her hand.

She wanted it in her. Every inch, filling her all the way up. *"Lucaaas!"* Tossing her head on the cushion, she groaned in need.

"Mmmmmm?" He was making all kinds of extravagant, wet noises now as he teased her juicing flesh. Every time he flicked her clit with his tongue, a little pop of flame darted up her spine.

"Would you please quit teasing me and fuck?" She blinked at her own voice. It was an octave lower than it should be, all but rumbling with her Burning Moon.

"Getting a little impatient, darling?" Something entered her, and she jolted, belatedly realizing he'd slid a finger between her desperately wet lips.

"God, yes!" She pumped her hips, grinding down on that promising digit. Big as it was, though, she wanted something a whole lot larger. "Dammit, Lucas, you're making me insane!"

He reached up her body and found one nipple. Gave it a teasing twist. "You might consider begging."

Elena panted and wrapped both hands in his hair. "I thought you were a nice man!"

His chuckle was just slightly sinister. "You thought wrong."

"Lucas, dammit!" She transferred one hand from his hair to a brawny shoulder and dug in her fingers.

He jerked. "Hey, watch the claws!"

"Now!" It was an outright Burning Moon growl. She realized distantly she was one deep breath from Turning.

"Well, if you insist."

And he pounced.

There was no other word for it. He simply bounded from

the foot of the chaise and landed on top of her with a low, dark growl of his own. Rearing up, he grabbed her under one knee, jerked her thighs wide, and aimed that thick, upcurving cock with the other.

Elena lifted her head to watch hungrily as the round head brushed her sensitive lips, then nosed its way inside. Bracing himself on one muscled arm, he rolled his hips.

And drove that thick cock deep in one hard thrust.

It filled her completely in a delicious rush. Though Elena was tight, she was also very wet, and the powerful surge of his hips pushed him in to the balls.

She yowled.

He felt incredible. Thick, hard—almost too much so— each thrust shooting an explosion of pleasure into her ravenous body. With a wordless cry of need, she wrapped both legs around his working backside and coiled her arms around his shoulders.

Teeth clenched with effort, she started grinding up at him, desperate to shoot them both to the peak she could feel just out of reach.

God, she felt incredible. Those slick inner muscles of hers milked his cock with every thrust. He panted like a wolf, hunching against her, half wild with feral hunger.

She stared up at him, her green eyes glittering and savage in the moonlight, her lips pulled back from her teeth. Teeth that, unless he was mistaken, had lengthened into fangs.

Lucas was just as close to Turning himself. His fingernails were damn near claws, and he had to hold her carefully to avoid puncturing that delicate skin.

He wanted to slow it down some more, but Elena

wouldn't let him, rolling her body fiercely against his, her sex so slick and hot as it gripped him.

Muscles began to pulse deep in her core, rippling along the length of his shaft. Lucas gritted his teeth and fought to hold on, but she felt too wet and tight and good. Her beautiful eyes went dazed and vague, and she threw her head back, sending all that red hair spilling over the cushion. "Lucas," she gasped, and screamed. *"Luuuuucaaas!"*

The sound of his name combined with the luscious feel of her sex and the warm, wet satin of her straining body. His back jerked into a bow as fire boiled up out of his balls and down his shaft in sweet, burning pulses of pleasure. He bellowed, coming, pouring himself into her.

Giving her everything he had.

So they writhed together, sweating flesh and straining effort, and pleasure so great it was blinding.

Until at last it was over, and they collapsed into one another's arms, panting and wet. He drew her closer and lay his head against her pretty breast, listening to the slowing thunder of her heart.

His arms were trembling. He could feel the muscles in her thighs jerking where her legs were wrapped around his waist. And his softened cock was still clasped in her sex.

"Man." Lucas groaned.

"Umm. Yeah." She unwrapped one of her arms from his shoulders. It fell to the cushion. With a sense of satisfaction, he realized her hand was shaking.

Good. At least he wasn't the only one.

Carefully, reluctantly, he withdrew from her. He frowned. He was actually a little sore. She'd feel it even more. "I didn't hurt you, did I?"

"God, no."

With an effort, Lucas levered himself off the chaise and braced his legs. His knees were shaking. He laughed. "Damn, girl, I think you killed me."

She blinked up at him slowly, her cameo face bathed in moonlight. "Murder-suicide, maybe." Groaning, she sat up, drawing his attention with the sway and bounce of her lovely breasts.

"Want to wash off in the tub?"

"Nope." She swung those long, lovely legs over and stood up. "I want all that lovely sperm just where it is."

Lucas laughed and walked over to the railing, where he'd left two thick towels hanging. "Well, this is a first. Normally the last thing I want is to get my partner pregnant." He handed her one, then took the other for himself.

Slowly, she started drying herself off. Despite her denials, she moved as if she were a little sore. Looping his towel around his neck, he took hers from her unresisting hands and began toweling her off.

Elena stood still in the circle of his arms, her eyes drifting closed as she let him minister to her. The top of her head barely came to his shoulder.

That observation triggered another wash of protectiveness. He wrapped the big towel around her like a child, then used his own to work on her hair.

When he finished with her, she watched sleepily as he dried himself off. Resting one hand on the small of her back, he urged her toward the door. "Come on, Elena. Time for bed."

With a wordless murmur, she went where he directed.

CHAPTER 7

Lucas found Elena a brand-new toothbrush still in its package—a souvenir of a recent trip to the dentist—and let her borrow a brush and a hair dryer.

His generosity was rewarded when she bent at the waist and flipped her red hair over her head to give it a brisk brushing. The sight of her pretty breasts bouncing with the motion was almost enough to rouse his sated cock.

Once they'd cleaned themselves up for bed, he led the way to his bedroom. The bed was a massive four-poster he'd found in a secondhand shop, a big pine monster he'd bought solely because it was long enough to accommodate his six-foot-five-inch frame.

He watched her check out the picture on his bedside table. It was the only photograph he had of him and his mother, a stiff Christmas shot taken twenty years before at Kmart. He'd been a sullen twelve, while Sue Rollings looked far too thin and far too old for her age. Her closed-lip smile was intended to hide her crooked, cigarette-stained teeth. Her hair lay in a straight, gleaming black curtain around her shoulders. It had been her one beauty, her one vanity.

His mother had been a victim for every man she met. If Sue had been in Elena's shoes, it would never even have occurred to her to fight Stephen at all. She certainly wouldn't have taken a chance on running all the way across the state to ask for help from a cop she didn't even know.

Elena's long, elegant fingers touched the cheap metal frame. "Is this you and your mother?"

"Yeah. Not exactly blue-bloods, are we?"

She gave him a sudden wicked grin. "Personally I prefer my blood red." Standing on tip-toe, she wrapped her arms around his neck and drew him down for a kiss that curled his toes. By the time she let him up for air again, his cock was twitching with interest. She gave her upper lip a flirtatious flick of the tongue. "And hot."

"You're definitely good at heating mine." He blew out a breath.

"I do try." With a light laugh, Elena turned and slid between the covers. She turned onto her back, all that glorious hair of hers spilling over his pillow like a river of copper and flame. Green eyes met his. "Come to bed."

He joined her under the comforter. By rights, he should be wiped out after all that sex, yet he felt oddly keyed-up. Waiting for the other shoe to drop.

Waiting for her to realize she really was too good for him.

After all, she drove a Ferrari and was a descendent of a warrior king. He'd grown up in a trailer park, alternately beaten and ignored by a series of part-time fathers.

Compelled for no reason he could name, Lucas said, "Stephen was right, y'know. I am a mongrel."

"Stephen was, as always, full of shit." She rolled over

against his side, sliding a long, slender arm around his chest. Her head came to rest on the hollow between his shoulder and the swell of his right pec, spilling a wealth of silken hair across his side. "Good night, Lucas."

Damn, she felt good there.

Ten minutes later, he followed her into sleep.

Elena woke early, as she always did.

She found herself lying half across a warm, sculpted, hair-dusted chest, which rose and fell in sleep. Lifting her head, she stared down into Lucas's strong face with its regal nose and arrogant chin. Black lashes lay on his high cheek-bones like dark feathered fans.

Her right hand, draped over her waist, brushed the head of his erection. She lifted her head to enjoy the view. He'd kicked off the covers during the night, so now he lay gloriously revealed. Big as the bed was, his shoulders still seemed to take up most of the mattress. His tanned skin looked golden in the sunlight pouring in through the half-opened curtains, and his legs were long and powerful.

Careful not to wake him, she traced her nails through the ruff of hair on his chest. *You're a dangerous man, Lucas.*

All her life, she'd dreamed of a man like him. Then again, she supposed every red-blooded woman in America had dreamed of a man like Lucas Rollings—body by God, face of an archangel, a protective streak a mile wide. Who wouldn't want somebody like that by her side?

But there was more to him than great abs and an Alpha male growl. She remembered the vulnerability in his eyes when he'd described his abusive childhood. He'd gone out of his way to assuage her guilt and convince her he admired her for her battle against Stephen and her father.

When she thought about it, that little confession of his was pretty unusual all by itself. Most Alphas would rather eat glass than admit they'd ever been anybody's victim. It ran against the whole persona.

Lucas was definitely not your typical Alpha. Which was a good thing, because she'd had more than enough typical Alpha behavior in her life. The last thing she wanted was another male giving orders. She thought she could trust Lucas on that front.

Yet despite his flashes of tenderness, he had a definite edge. She wouldn't want to piss him off, that was for damn sure. He'd never lay a hand on her in anger, but she strongly expected he had a tongue that could make a girl limp.

Elena grinned wickedly. Come to think of it, his tongue had already left her pretty limp. The man had a seriously talented mouth.

Speaking of which, he was probably going to be hungry when he woke up. The least she could do was cook him a nice breakfast.

She rolled out of bed, hoping he had something edible in that big refrigerator of his.

Lucas woke to the smell of frying bacon—and even better, the scent of fresh coffee. His mouth began to water, and his stomach growled.

After pausing just long enough to dig out a pair of jeans and drag them up over his hips, he headed for the kitchen.

Elena stood at the stove wearing only one of his T-shirts and a pair of panties. She looked up from the cast-iron skillet full of scrambled eggs, a smile curving that full-lipped mouth. "Good morning, gorgeous."

"Good morning to you, too." He eyed the center island, where a pile of bacon steamed on top of a plate covered with paper towels. Selecting a strip, he found it crisp and perfect. He looked at her and munched. "This is really good. Where'd you learn to cook like this?"

Elena smiled as she started transferring the eggs onto another plate. "My mother loved to cook. It always outraged Dad—he kept asking why we had a chef when Mom insisted on cooking all the time—but it made her happy. I learned from her."

On the opposite side of the kitchen, bread popped from the toaster. Lucas went to collect the slices and toast a couple more. "So what's on the agenda today?" Opening the jar of jelly she'd put on the counter, he gave her a hopeful grin. "More sex?"

She grinned back at him. "After a quick trip to the mall. I literally don't have a thing to wear except what I got here in."

"You really don't need clothes. I like you just fine naked."

"Nice try, but no cigar. We're going shopping."

"And *then* more sex?"

"You really have no shame, do you?"

"Hey, I'm a guy." A thought made him sober. "I wonder if last night's activities . . ." He broke off, suddenly imagining a little girl with Elena's flaming hair and leaf-green eyes. The image sent a surprising shaft of yearning through him.

You're just the sperm donor, dumbass.

She cocked her head, considering the question. "No, I'm not pregnant yet." A smile teased the corners of her mouth. "Maybe later."

"Wait—you can tell?"

"Yeah, my scent hasn't changed. And it would, within a couple of hours of getting pregnant." She carried the plate of eggs to the table and sat down. "It's part of Merlin's spell. Which is a good thing, because otherwise none of us would ever carry a child to term. Shifting causes miscarriages."

"Ouch. We'll just have to make sure you don't shift, then."

Elena gave him a teasing grin. "Well, not right after sex, anyway."

They spent the morning at the Harrisville Mall, selecting a couple of pairs of jeans and three cute tops. Elena rewarded Lucas for his patience with a trip to Victoria's Secret, laughing at his mock leer over the lacy panties and bra she bought. She even added a red barely-there teddy to her purchases, mostly to watch his eyes glaze.

"Oh, man," he moaned, as they strolled from the store. "I'm getting visions of you in that teddy, sprawled across the hood of the Ferrari."

She grinned at him. "Perv."

"Yep, that's me." He gave her a toothy grin. "Want to play Little Red Riding Teddy and the Big Bad Wolf?"

"Sure. But which one of us gets to be the wolf?"

He eyed her. "Well, I sure as hell ain't wearing the teddy."

"Oh, come on! You'd look just fabulous . . ."

She was grinning at him when it suddenly struck her just how long it had been since she'd had such a good time with a man.

CHAPTER 8

$\mathcal{L}$ucas managed to keep a stranglehold on his libido through most of the shopping trip, though the sight of Elena prancing around in various tight outfits played hell with his self-control.

But as he drove them back home, breathing her pheromones in the close confines of the Crown Vic, he could feel himself starting to lose it.

God help him, she smelled like distilled sex. Shooting her a glance, he reached down and adjusted himself, trying to relieve his zipper's bite.

Lucas looked at her again—and found her gaze locked on his crotch. A blush burned on her high cheekbones. Licking her lips, she looked up and realized he'd caught her. Her green eyes widened still more.

"I want you." The words came out rough, growling. He sounded even more ragged than he felt.

The corners of her mouth twitched. "I noticed."

Despite his need, he found himself smiling back. "Tease."

Another of those quick, darting looks. "I hate to admit it, but I enjoy teasing you."

Damn, but he liked her. "Better watch it. You know what happens to little girls who tease the Big Bad Wolf." Lucas gave her his best feral grin. "They get eaten."

Her eyes lit in challenge. "Only if you can catch me."

He whipped the car into the driveway and pulled into the carport. "Oh, I can catch you."

Elena threw her car door open and shot him a challenging smirk over one shoulder. "Prove it."

And then she was off and running.

"Hey!" Hurriedly, he threw the car into park and jumped out. "Where the hell do you think you're going?"

But she was already halfway across the yard. He vaulted over the Crown Vic's hood and shot after her. His longer strides helped him gain on her, but not quite before she made the woods.

No sooner had she reached the concealment of the trees than he sensed the rise of magic as she Changed.

All he saw then was the red flag of a wolf tail, rapidly pulling away.

"Oh, no you don't!" Lucas growled, and shifted himself. Magic poured over him as he ran, twisting muscle and bone until he was four-legged himself.

Elena's scent was even more powerful to him in this form, wrapping around his lupine balls, teasing him to desperate hunger. He lengthened his stride, fiercely determined to catch her.

To prove to her she couldn't outrun him.

The long red blur that was Elena grew closer. Lucas gathered himself and leaped, meaning to take her down . . .

Even as he flew toward her, she veered away, leaving him

to hit the ground frustrated. With a soft, determined growl, he charged after her. He saw her fanged jaws gape in a canine grin as she ducked away. He spun. She zigzagged. He headed her off, then feinted one way. She changed direction—and ran right into him as he leaped in front of her. They tumbled together as he tried to pin her with his greater weight.

For a moment he succeeded.

Until Elena changed, shifting back to human. She started to leap to her feet, but he shifted himself, caught her by one slim ankle, and tumbled her to the leaves.

"Got you!" he crowed, and pounced.

"Dream on!" she panted, trying to squirm out of the arm he'd looped around her narrow waist.

"Give it up, Elena!" He wrapped both legs around her thighs, pinning her.

"Hey, let go, you big jerk!" She kicked and wiggled, but he had a good grip now, and no intention whatsoever of releasing her.

At least, not until he had her naked.

Grabbing the hem of her knit shirt, he tugged it up over her head, then attacked the front clasp of her bra.

"Brute!" She aimed a mock swat at his hands as he flicked the cups aside, leaving her pretty breasts bare.

"Yep, that's me," he purred in her ear, cupping one soft mound. "A big, nasty brute. You, on the other hand, are small, sweet and . . ." Gently, he pinched her hardening nipple. ". . . edible."

Toying with the little peak, Lucas reached for the snap of her jeans with his free hand.

She jerked against his hold, though he could smell her arousal. "Cut that out!"

"No." Flicking the snap open, he unzipped her fly, then

slid his hand down over her silken belly and under the waist-band of her panties. "I caught you, and you're mine." Lowering his head to one of the straining cords of her throat, he raked it gently with his teeth. "And I'm not letting you go."

Elena swallowed hard as Lucas's broad, warm palm slid down between her thighs. A finger sought between softly furred lips. "Mmmmm," he purred in her ear. "You're wet."

And he was hard. She could feel that thick cock of his pressed against her ass. She shivered in anticipation, remembering how it had felt last night, driving into her.

He was so damn big, so damn male. It occurred to her she'd never have another man like him. . . .

That exploring finger circled her hard clit, triggering a hot, clenching pleasure. Elena let her head fall back with a helpless moan.

"Nice, huh?" Lucas rumbled, tugging her nipple as he simultaneously thrust that exploring finger deep in her clenching sex. "Just think how my cock is going to feel."

Oh, she was. The sensation of it pressed against her butt was maddening. If anything, the memory of last night's impassioned lovemaking only intensified the need.

Elena writhed, trying to break free again—but not to escape. She wanted to wrap her fingers around that thick cock, to taste him on her tongue, salty and hot.

She wanted to hear him moan.

He tightened the grip of his legs, suppressing her struggles with no particular effort. "Stop that." Another milking squeeze of her nipple.

"I want to touch you!"

"Too bad." He released his grip on her legs only to grab the waistband of her jeans. Before she could attempt another escape, he started dragging her pants and panties down over her legs.

Finally, he tossed them aside, leaving her completely naked.

He, on the other hand, was still dressed. Something about being nude while he wasn't struck her as deliciously erotic.

She tried to turn over and face him, but he grabbed both her wrists in one hand and pinned them to the ground. Elena yanked, trying to free herself, but Lucas just let his weight press down over her, flattening her in the dry leaves.

"Lucas!"

"Shhhh." With his free hand, he explored her backside, kneading the firm flesh. "You know, you've got a really delicious ass."

She licked her dry lips, enjoying his wickedly skilled touch. "Yours isn't so bad either."

"Thank you." Two fingers found her opening and started working their way inside. "But since I'm the one on top, that's a little irrelevant."

Elena shuttered her eyelids, savoring the sensation of his hot, slick strokes. Every entry sent a cascade of pleasure into her core.

The sensation was intensified by the way Lucas's big cock pressed eagerly against her ass. She found herself rolling her hips upward, silently demanding to be entered, to be filled by that huge shaft.

God, he made her hotter than she'd ever been in her life.

Lucas fought for control as Elena rolled her lush little body against his. His cock was aching, begging to bury itself in her tight, slick sex. Every breath he took carried her lusciously erotic scent.

He withdrew his fingers and reached for his fly, liberating his aching cock. It sprang out, rock-hard at the prospect of hilting itself in her heat.

No, not yet, Lucas decided. He needed to work her a little more, get her even hotter. He tumbled her onto her back and started to lower his head between her thighs.

"No," she gasped. "Let me do you, too."

That was not an offer any red-blooded male was likely to turn down. Releasing her, Lucas turned head-down along her body, so his cock jutted over her mouth as he dipped his own head between her thighs.

Elena tasted delicious, all salt and slick femininity. But before he could settle in to enjoying her in earnest, she caught his cock and angled it down, then engulfed its plum head in her mouth.

Lucas stiffened with a gasp as she swirled her pointed tongue over the head of his cock. A drop of pre-come appeared, and she lapped it up with a long, slow pass. He squirmed, feeling his lust spike.

Then she sealed her lips over his shaft and sucked so hard he threw his head up with a shout of pleasure.

Damn, he was never going to last if she kept that up. Carefully, he drew away from her.

"Oh, no you don't!" She grabbed for him again.

"Oh, yes." He grabbed her by the shoulders and flipped her over. "I do."

Then he grabbed his shaft, aimed it for her cream-slick opening, and started thrusting his way in from behind. Elena groaned as he slid into her inch by inch, her snug flesh gripping his shaft.

Finally his balls rested on her butt, and he paused, reaching around to recapture her wrists in one hand. Lucas slid the other beneath her body to cup her breast again.

Then, enjoying every thrust, he started fucking her. Despite his clawing hunger, he was determined to take it slow, so he clamped a chokehold on his libido.

It wasn't easy. Her sex welcomed him with tight, wet heat, and she groaned, rolling her backside up at him. "Take me, Lucas," she gasped. "Harder!"

Maddened, he braced his weight on his arms and began to fuck deep into her slick grasp, grinding his hips, giving her exactly what she wanted.

He felt his orgasm gathering like a hot storm, ready to break at any instant.

Every time Lucas slid inside her, it felt as if he was reaching halfway up her throat. And Elena loved it.

As turned on as he'd had her last night, this was even more intense. The sensation of being pinned under him like this, the rasp of his blue-jeaned thighs against her bare legs, the grip of his fingers around her wrists—it was all so deliciously arousing. She felt completely overwhelmed by him, by the sheer, hard strength of his body and the ferocity of his demanding lust.

Yet even as his body dominated hers, he caressed her nipple with one hand, using tender delicacy. Somehow the contrast made her even more hot. She groaned, throwing her head back against his shoulder, savoring the sensation of that big cock screwing its way deep.

As if her cry of arousal was a signal, Lucas started pumping harder, faster, grinding mercilessly deep in her sex. Elena felt her interior muscles begin to pulse and clamp. She tossed her head and gritted her teeth at the stark, hot rise of her orgasm.

"Yes," he growled in her ear. "That's it. Come for me. Come *now*!"

"God!" Her climax exploded, heat and pleasure pumping through her veins until she writhed with it.

As she convulsed, Lucas drove to the balls and stiffened with a roar, spilling deep within her.

Dazed, Elena lay panting in the leaves, breathing in the smell of growing things and sex and Lucas. Her lips curled into a delighted smile at the combination.

"Damn, girl," he rasped in her ear. "You're killing me." Carefully, he drew free from her sex. "But I think I'll die happy."

"Me, too." She grinned and stretched, suspecting her expression was more than a little smug. "You are really . . ."

He stiffened against her. "Shh! You smell that?"

"What?" Alarmed, she looked around as he jerked away from her.

"Somebody's coming." He grabbed her shirt and bra and tossed them at her. "Get dressed. Now!"

Frantically, she started dragging on her clothes. Even as she fastened her bra and pulled her shirt down over her breasts, the breeze blew into her face. Oh, hell, she knew that scent!

"It's Stephen!" she gasped, and grabbed for her jeans. "But it's only Saturday. I thought you said he wasn't supposed to get out of jail until Monday?"

"Apparently I was wrong." Lucas was on his feet, staring in the direction of the scent. He sniffed, testing. "And he's got company. There are at least five other men with him."

Elena jumped to her feet and zipped her pants. "And one of them is Daddy."

CHAPTER 9

As Elena watched, Lucas Changed into his Direwolf form.

"You going to shift?" he asked her, his voice deep and growling.

She started to nod, then froze in horror as realization struck. "I can't! I may be pregnant."

"Okay, I'll handle it."

"But . . ."

He flashed her a level gaze. "It's what I'm here for, Elena."

But how could she just stand by while he fought for his life? She could get pregnant again, but if he died . . .

Before Elena could decide what to do, five Direwolves emerged from the clearing. She recognized four of them as her father's security team. One of them held her father cradled in his arms like a child, while another carried the old man's wheeled walker.

Stephen stalked along in the lead, his ice-pale eyes blazing with triumph and anticipation. He was already in Direwolf form.

"What are you doing out of jail?" Lucas's big hands curled into fists.

Stephen's jaws gaped in a vicious lupine grin. "Seems someone at the jail mislaid a little paperwork. I'm out on my own recognizance."

Elena swore. "You bribed them."

"I don't play to lose, Elena."

"This was not . . . well done of you . . . Elena," Richard Livingston panted as one of his guards unfolded his walker. The other sat him down in its seat. Richard wrapped his painfully thin hands around its handlebars and glowered at her. "I don't appreciate . . . being forced to leave my sickbed to . . . reason with you." Only a couple of years ago, he'd been a big, fit man, with a hawkishly handsome face and thick silver hair.

Losing his magic to age had weakened him. Unable to Change, Richard's body had grown vulnerable to illnesses it did not have the immune system to fight. He seemed to have aged in the three days since she'd last seen him, his skin grown translucent and yellow.

Pain shot through Elena at the sight of his frailty, but she forced herself to glare. "And I don't appreciate your betrothing me to this abusive creep, Dad." She bared her teeth at Stephen, who was moving closer. "What's more, I'm not marrying him."

Stephen sniffed the air. "Brave words, considering you don't seem to be pregnant."

"Oh, she easily could be," Lucas drawled, with a taunting display of teeth. "Considering what we just finished doing. I understand it takes a few hours for the scent to change."

Stephen growled in a vicious chainsaw snarl of warning. "I told you to keep your hands off her!"

"I don't take orders from you, Stevie." Lucas flexed his claws. "But if you want that duel now, I'm ready to go."

Ice-blue eyes narrowed. "Duels are for equals, mongrel. And you're certainly not my equal."

Lucas coiled into a crouch. "Well, we're agreed on that, since you're a gutless pussy."

"This is not necessary," Richard husked, raising his voice over Stephen's enraged growl. "Your attempt to help my daughter was laudable, Lieutenant." He stopped to pant. "I'd hate for her . . . machinations to result in . . . something regrettable."

"Are you threatening me?"

"I would . . . prefer not to involve my . . . security team in this." Richard broke off and coughed into his fist. Blood flew in his spittle. He fumbled for a handkerchief and wiped his mouth. "You would be wise . . . to walk away."

"You go to . . ."

Elena was concentrating so hard on the confrontation between her father and Lucas that she didn't notice Stephen creeping closer until a blur of gold flashed out of nowhere. The impact staggered her.

Agony exploded in her guts, tearing a shriek of shocked pain from her mouth.

"Elena!" Lucas roared, whirling and grabbing for her as she bent double with a high, helpless shriek.

Numbly, she stared at the blood streaming between her arms, which she'd instinctively wrapped around her middle.

Stephen laughed. "So much for the mongrel's theoretical brat."

From a great distance, she heard Lucas raging, "You gutted her, you bastard! I'm going to tear your fucking head off!"

Pain ripped at her with crocodile teeth. Her magic rose before she knew what she was doing, flaring over her, reforming muscle and bone. Even as she shifted to Direwolf, she grieved. Now she'd never know whether she'd carried Lucas's baby.

The moment she was whole again, Lucas let her go and lunged for Stephen's throat. Furious, she met her father's horrified gaze over their roars of combat. "You listen to me, Richard," she snarled, refusing to call him her father. "I will *die* before I marry Stephen Bradford."

Whirling, she charged toward the brawling Direwolves.

Richard must have given some order. One of the bodyguards ran to help Stephen, while another grabbed for Elena. Cursing them all, she raked at him with her claws even as he smashed her to the ground.

Lucas sank his fangs into Bradford's forearms and clamped down hard, intent on breaking bone. The rich man howled and struck out with his claws. Lucas blocked the strike and ground down. Damn, but it felt good to finally cut loose against one of those abusive little pricks.

"Get him off, get him off!" Bradford writhed and kicked, his clawed feet raking Lucas's calves. Lucas didn't care, too intent on doing damage. An image flashed through his mind: the terror and agony on Elena's face when Bradford had laid her open.

Something crunched at last. Bradford yelped.

Before Lucas could savor his triumph, something slammed into his head. His jaws loosened as stars shot behind his eyes. Somebody grabbed him from behind and hauled him off Bradford, spinning him into a right cross that filled his mouth with blood. Lucas staggered, distantly aware that Bradford had taken to his heels.

A black-furred werewolf who must have been one of the bodyguards lunged for Lucas's throat, intent on finishing him off. Lucas ducked the charge, planted a shoulder in the shifter's gut, and let him roll over his back. The man hit the ground hard. In the moment he was stunned, Lucas buried his claws in the bodyguard's belly, raking him mercilessly as he yowled in agony. Shifting into wolf form, the man scrambled away, narrowly avoiding having his throat ripped out.

Elena howled in rage and frustration. Forgetting the bodyguard, Lucas whirled. She was struggling with another black-furred werewolf as her father watched. Lucas growled and started for them.

Before he took another step, a blur of dark brown slammed into his side, tumbling him off his feet. Fangs sank into his shoulder, shooting fire through his flesh. Lucas twisted and managed to rake his claws across the other's long muzzle, forcing him to release his hold. Growling, he jolted forward, a second swipe of his claws leaving the werewolf's ears a bloody ruin. The bodyguard retreated with a yelp.

Spotting another shifter lunging for him, Lucas scrambled to his feet. Blood matted the fur of his left arm from the bite in his shoulder, and his legs burned viciously from Bradford's raking claws. Despite the pain, he bounced on the balls of his feet and decided he could afford to put off changing form a little longer. The transformation to wolf would heal his injuries, but it would also leave him smaller and more vulnerable against his Direwolf enemies.

Besides, Changing too many times could make his power

turn on him. He had no desire to burn to death in a pyre of out-of-control magic.

"Give it up, cop," one of the three bodyguards growled as they closed in on him again. To Lucas's satisfaction, one was limping and another was almost as bloody as he was. "She's not worth dying for."

Lucas bared his teeth. "Yes, she is." He flexed his claws and eyed the three men, looking for an opening. "But do you really want to die for Bradford?"

The brown-furred Direwolf shrugged. "We're not outnumbered, asshole." He charged.

Lucas pivoted aside, blocking the bodyguard's attack, but a second saw his chance. Talons darted at his throat. Lucas ducked, but the first guard kicked a clawed foot into his gut. Pain screamed through him, and he staggered. He felt blood spill, along with something wet and soft.

Oh, shit, Lucas thought. *That doesn't feel good at all.*

Something into his muzzle, knocking him backward onto the ground. Bradford roared in triumph. Suddenly the blond bastard was there, crouching over him, wrapping a big clawed hand around his throat.

Fuck. I'm screwed now.

"Stop fighting me, Miss Livingston," George Ross gritted in Elena's ear. He had both massive arms wrapped under her arms, hands cupped behind her neck in a full Nelson. "You're going home, and you're going to do what your father tells you to do."

Elena barely heard him. Her horrified gaze was locked on Lucas, who was writhing in Stephen's murderous hold. He was bleeding from dozens of wounds, while Stephen's fur wasn't even marked. Apparently her former fiancé had managed to heal his injuries while Lucas was fighting the bodyguards.

We're losing, she realized, despairing. *There's no way Lucas can fight off all four of them. He's going to die.*

In a single white-hot flash, Elena remembered the taste of his mouth, the feel of his strong body moving against her. Remembered his deep, roguish laughter, his smile, the male heat in his eyes. He'd made her feel more alive in the past few hours than she'd been in all the hollow years that came before.

Lucas, all that strength, all that heroism, all that wicked humor—gone.

No. Rage flooded her, washing away fear and despair with its white-hot burn. Stephen and her father weren't going to get away with this. She'd let them trap her into living half a life for fear of what they'd do to her, but this was it.

They weren't taking Lucas away.

Twisting in the bodyguard's grip, Elena released her clawed grip on his wrist and drove her hand backward. He jerked in shock as she wrapped her clawed hand around his genitals. "Let me go," she growled, "or I'll rip them off. You'll heal, but it'll hurt. A lot."

"Shit! You little bitch, you'd better . . ."

"Have it your way, George," she growled, and raked.

He screamed, his grip going lax. She tore free as the bodyguard fell, gagging, to his knees. Even as George transformed to heal his injuries, Elena raced toward Stephen, who was struggling to control Lucas. Her foe turned toward her . . .

. . . and she kicked him right in the muzzle. Stephen's head snapped back, and he lost his grip on Lucas, who promptly shifted to wolf and scrambled free.

As all three bodyguards lunged for them, Elena threw herself over Lucas's furred body.

They had one chance, and one chance only—*if* he'd agree. Curling herself tight around him to protect him from the werewolves, she gasped, "Spirit Link with me!"

Spirit Link? Lucas's astonished question emerged as a lupine whine. In wolf form, he didn't have the vocal cords to speak.

"Get off him, Elena!" Stephen snapped. His voice was ugly with excitement.

"Please, Lucas!" she whispered. "I can end this! Trust me!"

If she was wrong and they killed him, Lucas thought, the link would kill her. But if he didn't do it, they'd kill him— and Elena would be at Stephen Bradford's mercy for the rest of her life. Beaten and abused just as his mother had been, all that fierce spirit slowly dying.

Hell no.

Bradford's voice, approaching. "Get off him!"

"I'm changing!" she whispered in his ear. "Help me!" Magic began to boil around her.

Furiously, he gathered his own and let it spill over him. Simultaneously, their bodies started glowing, shifting form, wolf and Direwolf vanishing into the magic. For a heartbeat, neither had a form at all. . . .

And their minds touched.

He could feel her, her strength, her fear, her intelligence, her desperation, and her courage. In that moment, he knew her as he'd never known another person in all his lonely life.

And she knew him.

Oooh, she breathed in his mind—not a thought so much as pure, sweet wonder.

And he shared it.

Touching her mind was like laying naked in warm sunlight after a cold winter. His spirit unfurled with a hungry desperation, enfolding her and bringing her close.

Just as she enfolded him. *Together. . . .*

Finally, a voice said deep inside him. *This is what I was looking for all along.*

You.

There were tears in his eyes. Lucas blinked, and realized he had eyes again. Elena's slender human arms were curled around his big Direwolf body, as if still trying to protect him.

Until she was jerked violently away. With a roar of fury, Lucas surged to his feet.

"Enough of this," Bradford snapped, glaring at him as he held Elena by one slender arm. "Kill him!"

"No!" It was Richard, his voice trembling. "They glowed when they changed! I saw them. Elena . . ."

"Yes." Her grin was vicious. "We're Spirit Linked. Which means if you kill him, I die, too. And so does Wulfgar's line." She curled a lip. "And so does your chance at Wulfgar's seat."

Bradford's eyes widened in horror before he recovered enough to sneer. "You're lying. There's no way you'd chain yourself to this mongrel."

"There's nothing mongrel about him." She turned to her father, her chin lifted. "He's more than worthy to sire Wulfgar's descendents. Certainly a hell of a lot more than this maggot you dug up."

"They're bluffing," Bradford snapped at the bodyguards. "Kill him."

"Better call them off, Richard," Elena warned.

The men took a step toward Lucas. He tensed, preparing to fight. Regardless of the odds, he was going to have to take them all down. Otherwise Elena didn't have a prayer.

"No!" Richard gasped. "No, she . . . she means it. I know my daughter. She . . . doesn't bluff."

The bodyguards hesitated, surprise in their eyes. "Are you sure, Mr. Livingston?"

The old man slumped against his walked. "I'm . . . sure. I don't want to . . . die with her hatred."

Stephen stared at him with astonished rage. "You gutless old bastard! We had a deal!"

"It's done, Stephen!" In his anger, Richard actually managed something close to a snap.

"Not yet!" Fangs bared, Stephen sprang toward Elena, one clawed hand lifted for a killing blow.

Lucas grabbed the Direwolf as he lunged past, wrapping one arm around his neck in a choke hold and jerking him to a stop. "Oh, hell no, you don't!"

Gagging, Bradford tried to tear free, claws raking Lucas's forearm. "Let me go, you son of a bitch! We're not done!"

"Actually, we are." Ignoring the pain of his savaged arm, arm, Lucas wrapped his other hand around the werewolf's muzzle. "And Elena won." He wrenched the Direwolf's head violently to the side.

Something snapped.

Lucas let Bradford's body fall. It collapsed in a heap, his head at an unnatural angle.

Lucas met Elena's eyes and opened his arms. She came into them without hesitating, wrapping her own around his furry chest.

He lowered his muzzle to the top of her head and rested it there as he held her. It seemed he could feel the glow of her spirit through the link, warm as sunshine. He closed his eyes in relief and gratitude.

"Shit," one of the bodyguards muttered.

"Oh, yes," Richard said hoarsely. "You did Link, didn't you?"

Lucas looked up to see the longing in the old man's eyes.

"My bitterest regret is . . . I didn't link with your mother," Richard told Elena, who lifted her head at the quiet words. "If I had . . . maybe she wouldn't have died . . . the way she did. And I wouldn't be alone . . ." He broke off and began to cough violently into his red-spotted handkerchief.

Without another word, his bodyguards moved to help him. As Elena and Lucas watched, one picked him up while the other collected his walker.

"What about Mr. Bradford?" the third bodyguard asked.

"Take care of him," Richard said, his voice quavering weakly. "You know . . . the proper procedure."

"Somehow I don't think we want to watch," Lucas whispered to Elena. "Let's get out of here."

She only wrapped her arms tighter around him and nodded. She'd started to shake.

Together, leaving the bodyguards to their grim job, they walked out of the woods.

Neither of them spoke to her father.

CHAPTER 10

*N*ow that it was over, Elena felt shell-shocked.

Lucas had snapped Stephen's neck like a twig. Yet if he hadn't, her so-called fiancé would have killed her.

"It's funny," she said over the sound of the shower as Lucas adjusted the water temperature. He'd led the way to the bathroom the moment they'd entered the house, as if knowing exactly what she wanted. Which, given the link, he probably did. "I knew Stephen was a vicious little bastard, but I never realized he'd try to kill me if he didn't get his way."

Lucas shot her a look. "Classic abuser behavior, sweetheart. 'If I can't have you, nobody can.'"

"Yeah, I guess that does sound like Stephen." Brooding, she leaned against the wall to pull off her jeans and panties. Looking up, she realized he was stripping too and paused to enjoy the mouthwatering view.

He eyed her as he tossed his shirt into the wicker clothes

hamper. "It bothers you that I killed him." Elena opened her mouth to deny it, but he shook his head. "That's okay, it bothers me, too. Not that I had a choice—it was the only way to protect you. But still . . ."

"You've never killed anyone before." She blinked. "It's odd. I'm not reading your mind, exactly, but I seem to . . ."

". . . feel what I'm feeling." He shrugged his broad shoulders and stepped into the shower. She followed him under the warm spray. "I can tell this is going to take some getting used to."

Elena looked up and met his dark eyes. "Do you regret linking with me?"

"No," he said quietly. "I'm glad. And not because it was the only way out."

"But we've only known each other a few hours."

Lucas cupped her chin in his palm and tilted it upward until he could meet her eyes. "And when we Linked, we touched each other more profoundly than a couple who have been married twenty years. I *know* you, Elena. Maybe I don't know what your favorite color is, or whether you like anchovies on your pizza, but I do know the core of your spirit." His voice dropped, going even deeper and more resonant.

Big hands cupped her breasts. Caressed. Teased. Her nipples stiffened against his palms, until her head fell back. Lucas pulled her full against him with a soft, masculine rumble of hunger.

Elena let herself melt into his hard body, savoring his strength. His thick erection nestled against her belly, a silent testimony to his need. She almost purred at its satin heat.

A wicked thought slipped into her mind, and she grinned against his mouth.

He smiled back, lifting his head to gaze down into her eyes. "What are you planning, wench?"

"A little experiment." She went to her knees in front of him and watched his eyes go wide. Gently, she ran her hands up his wet belly, watching the water bead and run, enjoying the spray beating gently on her shoulders.

She closed one hand around him and leaned in, extending her tongue for a slow lick, tasting the tiny drop of his arousal. He rewarded her with a deep groan and leaned his back against the shower wall.

Angling the big shaft upward, she eyed its elegant contours before tracing the tip of her tongue up the sensitive ridge on its underside. Through the Link, she felt a luscious echo of the sensation. Intrigued, she pulled his length downward and engulfed him in her mouth for a fierce, hot suckle. The blast of pleasure that followed made her shudder in delight.

It was suddenly very clear why men loved blow jobs.

A strong hand came down to cup the back of her head, long fingers threading through her wet hair. She bent her head and gently drew one of his balls into her mouth. He swayed, and she smiled, knowing his legs had gone weak.

Her own were shaking a little too.

Enjoying the delicious blend of familiar act and alien pleasure, Elena settled down to sucking him in earnest. His heartfelt groans told her how thoroughly he approved of her little experiment.

Until neither of them could take any more.

"Damn, woman, you're driving me insane!" He bent and dragged her hungrily into his arms. With a soft, satisfied laugh, Elena wrapped her legs around his lean waist as he turned off the taps and pushed open the shower door. She kissed him as he carried her into the bedroom and lowered her to the bed.

"We're going to get the mattress wet."

"I'll turn it over," he told her, and covered her mouth in a fierce, demanding kiss. As their tongues dueled sweetly, his hand slid between her legs, a finger probing gently. He growled in approval at what he found. "You're creamy."

"You have that effect on me."

"Good." He spread her legs wide and aimed himself for her core.

His first hard thrust froze them both in astonishment at the sensations pouring through the Link.

"Oh, man," Elena breathed, her eyes flaring wide as she felt both her own pleasure and his.

Lucas blinked. "That's, ummm . . ."

"Oh, yeah. Do it again."

Another thrust, slower this time. "Damn," he said. "I'm not going to be able to last."

"That's okay," she gasped. "I won't either."

Lucas grinned. "What the hell." And he plunged deep. Elena gasped, stunned at the sensations of his cock filling her sex and her sex gripping his cock.

Just like that, the Burning Moon reawoke, drowning them both in flame. Lucas started lunging, grinding his hips in the cradle of her legs even as she pumped up at him. Each thrust carried such sweet, blinding pleasure that it stoked their mutual lust even higher. Desperately needy, they rode together, panting, straining. Loving the feel of each other's bodies, entranced by sensation and need.

Elena's climax took her by surprise, a glittering erotic storm that tore a cry from her mouth. Lucas echoed it a moment later as her pleasure shot him to his own.

"I love you!" Elena cried, as the burning feedback of climax shot through them.

"Yes!" he roared back. "Yes, God yes, I love you!"

And both of them knew it was true.

• • •

They lay collapsed in one another's arms, sleepy and sated, their bodies still buzzing with the aftermath. Lucas rolled over with her and arranged her half on top of his still-damp chest. Still panting, Elena lay like a rag doll, feeling utterly wrung out.

She'd have to call her father, she thought sleepily. Hanging on to her anger no longer seemed worth it. Not when there was such a wonderful new life ahead of her and Lucas. After that, there'd be Wulfgar's seat to claim, and the uphill battle that would follow as she went to work on dismantling the Traditions and freeing the women of her class. A few days ago, the thought would have intimidated her, but now she knew she was more than up to the challenge. After all, she had Lucas Rollings on her side.

What more could any woman want?

Lucas laughed in her ear. "The Chosen don't have a prayer."

She lifted her head and grinned at him. "Not against us."

BETWEEN the MOUNTAIN and the MOON

Virginia Kantra

◐

For someone who is always
"obstinately, perfectly herself."
Be careful on the trail, sweetie.

◐

CHAPTER 1

*H*er parents were right.

Cait MacLean adjusted the cinch on her backpack, hoping to distribute more of its weight to her hips. A couple of weekend camping trips were no preparation for the Appalachian Trail. Ten days out of Springer Mountain, Georgia, her bones ached, she had blisters on both heels, and the moleskin bandages she'd applied to protect her feet had balled at the bottom of her socks.

The slanting afternoon light fired a stand of purple rhododendron, their pink blossoms vivid against a background of somber fir trees. Cait glanced back at Josh, trudging silently behind her across the rough flank of the mountain, and pointed.

But Josh didn't look. He wouldn't even meet her eyes. Maybe he was cold. Or concentrating on his footing.

Or maybe he was still sulking because she wouldn't have sex with him last night.

Cait sighed. Four of them had started the trek: Cait and her roommate Jill, and Jill's boyfriend, Tyler, and Tyler's buddy Josh. But just south of Bly Gap, Tyler twisted his ankle, and Jill went off trail to take him home, promising to meet up with them in Hot Springs. Which meant for at least the next two weeks, Cait was stuck with Josh and his conviction that now they were alone, they should be sharing a lot more than the cookstove and the two-man tent.

Cait resumed her dogged progress up the slope.

She had considered dropping off the trail. But Jill claimed she would feel terrible if Cait changed her postgraduation plans because of Tyler's accident. More than a hike, this trip was Cait's chance to prove to her parents—and herself—she was an adult now, capable of tackling life on her own.

She straightened her shoulders against the weight of the pack. So, okay, her plan sounded pretty dumb now that she was actually putting one foot in front of the other, like something she would have dreamed up in middle school, like a mistake. A six-month mistake. But it was *her* mistake, and she was committed to it. Her family took commitments seriously, which probably explained Josh and sex.

Cait smiled wryly. Or rather, Josh and no sex.

The last rays of afternoon touched the ridgeline, and a shelter humped into view. Cait drew a relieved breath. At least he wouldn't pressure her tonight.

She lengthened her stride, eager to shed her pack and her own thoughts for a while in the company of other hikers.

But as she approached the three-sided shelter, her steps slowed. Instead of the dozen or more bodies she expected, there were only three sprawled on the wooden platform: a really big guy, a really small guy, and a tall, seated figure in the shadows.

"What are you waiting for?" Josh asked behind her. "An invitation?"

Cait hesitated. Violent crime was rare along the trail. But something held her back, like her father's hand or her mother's voice. She'd read stories . . .

Josh bumped past her. "Come on. It's getting dark."

Dark and cold.

At least this shelter boasted a fire pit. You couldn't build a fire just anywhere along the trail. If she wanted to get truly warm tonight . . . Anyway, Josh was with her. His determination to couple up annoyed her, but it would also protect her.

Reluctantly, she followed him under the metal roof. A circle of lamplight pooled on the rough timbers.

The little man looked up from his . . . whittling? Pale curls of wood decorated the floor by his boots. A knife flashed in his hand. "Welcome. I'm Goodfellow."

The big guy, with a head like a bullet and a build like a bear, grunted. "Ursus."

Josh let his pack thump to the floor. "Diogenes," he introduced himself. He jerked his thumb toward Cait. "Wildcat."

Cait flushed. She understood the tradition of trail names, the impulse that drove the pilgrims and dropouts to shake off their old identities and choose new ones. But she thought Josh's chosen name—Diogenes, the philosopher, the cynic—was pretentious, and she hated the name he had bestowed on her. She was five-seven, for God's sake, with her father's lanky build and her mother's brown eyes. Hardly a wildcat. Every time Josh used the name, she felt less like some sleek native of these mountains and more like his sex kitten. Maybe that's what he had in mind.

"Just Cait," she corrected hastily. "Caitlin."

Josh glowered.

The little man grinned, revealing small, pointed teeth.

Cait blinked. "Diogenes, eh? And is it one honest man you're seeking by lantern light?"

Josh puffed his chest, pleased by the recognition. Cait kneeled to unstrap the cookstove from her pack.

"Aren't all travelers on the trail seeking something?" Josh asked grandly.

"Or running away," the third man put in quietly from his corner.

His voice, deep and unaccented, flowed over Cait like warm water. Flustered by her reaction, she yanked harder at the strap.

Josh frowned. "Who are you?"

"Rhys."

Not a trail name, she thought, tugging. The strap yielded as the third man, this Rhys guy, unfolded from his corner and strolled forward into the light so that she saw him, really saw him, for the first time.

Her jaw dropped. Well. *Wow.* He was . . . handsome was too weak a word, and beautiful sounded too pretty. But he *was* beautiful, with a face that could have been painted by Da Vinci, all bold lines and secrets, and a body like a Greek statue. His eyes were the color of old gold coins, his hair was long, dark, and shiny, and his clothes—black jeans, black jacket—were fitted and clean.

Cait was suddenly conscious of her straggling blond braid, her clunky boots, her sweat-drenched layers of clothing.

"You're not a thru-hiker, are you?" Josh asked.

In the closed society of the trail, thru-hikers, hikers attempting to complete the two-thousand-mile trek from Georgia to Maine between spring and first snowfall, were its scruffy aristocracy.

But Tall, Dark, and Clean-Shaven didn't seem abashed by

Josh's attempt to put him in his place. If anything, he looked amused. "No."

"Where are you from?"

Like freshmen during new student week or strangers in a bar, hikers followed predictable conversational patterns: *What's your major? What's your sign? Come here often?* But under Josh's question, Cait heard an unfamiliar note of challenge.

Rhys smiled faintly. "Around."

Josh scowled.

Cait straightened. No way was she standing here while they pissed on trees or pawed the ground or did whatever men did to mark their territory. "I'm getting water."

Rhys turned his beautiful, golden eyes on her, and her insides contracted. She opened her mouth to breathe. "There's a stream," he said. "I'll show you."

Cait felt an instant's qualm. Forget beautiful. She didn't go off into the woods with strangers. She looked at Josh, expecting him to say something like, *Let me get it* or *I'll come, too.* But all he said was, "Good. I want some tea."

Well, at least he'd be within shouting range.

She grabbed the canteens and marched—stomped, really, her mother always told her to watch her temper—into the woods. Rhys didn't stomp. He glided through the trees like Uncas in *The Last of the Mohicans.* Cait slowed, setting her feet with care among the rocks and leaves.

She heard water before she saw it, like the gurgle in the pipes when somebody showered upstairs, muffled but close.

Rhys eased through a break in the bushes, still doing the Native American guide thing, and squatted beside a fallen log. Between slick rocks, a narrow stream pushed its way through tree roots and over stones rippling with moss.

He extended his hand. "Give me your canteen."

Cait tugged the strap over her head. "I've got it. Thanks."

He drew back so she could squeeze in beside him. Wedged above the rushing water, she barely had space to kneel, and precious little room to maneuver. Her hip pressed his thigh. Her shoulder brushed his arm. The scents of earth and water, green and growing, sharp and secret, rose and enveloped her.

Her head swam.

She looked up, struggling for breath. Rhys watched her, his pupils large and dark in his odd gold eyes.

Tearing her gaze away, Cait plunged the canteen into the stream. The cold shock cleared her head. She filled both canteens before adding purification tablets to the water.

"You don't need to do that here," Rhys said.

She screwed the caps back on. "Better safe than sorry, my parents always say."

"Do you always do what your parents tell you?"

She winced, his words chafing like the boots against her blisters. Not his fault he'd touched a sensitive spot, she told herself. Or theirs. Her parents *loved* her. And she loved them. It was only recently she'd found that love a little . . . restricting.

"Pretty much," she admitted. "Until now."

He raised his eyebrows. With his dark hair falling into his face, he looked like every mistake her mother had ever warned her about, every bad boy her father had ever chased away from their door. "Until . . . now?"

"This trip," she explained. "They didn't want me to come. They thought it was dangerous."

"They were right," he said.

Cait's throat constricted. But she wasn't letting herself

get played by some stranger on the trail, even if he did look like a Greek god.

She stood, slinging the water bottles across her body. "I can handle myself."

His eyes gleamed. "Lucky for you."

She searched for a snappy comeback and found her mind blank. She had to fall back on dignified silence, which wasn't nearly as satisfying.

Rhys smiled a cool, exasperating smile and practically sauntered back to the shelter.

Well, damn.

Cait followed.

While Josh scanned the news and notes scribbled in the shelter's log book, she coaxed water to a boil and prepared their nightly meal of ramen noodles. Nobody else cooked anything—maybe they had eaten already?—but the bearlike guy scrounged branches from the surrounding woods, and Rhys kindled the fire.

The little man stood, shaking his wood shavings into the flames.

"Oh," Cait exclaimed, delighted. "You carved a flute."

He made a queer half-bow and offered it to her. She ran her fingers in disbelief over the smooth, delicate instrument. She had watched him ply his knife for the past half hour, but the piece he held appeared as fine and finished as wood turned on a lathe.

"Can you actually play that thing?" Josh demanded.

Goodfellow regarded Josh with beady black eyes like a bird's. "Maybe. And will you be paying the piper, then?"

"The price isn't his to pay," Rhys said from his corner.

Goodfellow cocked his head. "More's the pity."

Cait refused to be sucked in by the undercurrents swirling

through the shelter. "It's lovely," she said, handing the pipe back to Goodfellow.

He tucked it away in his jacket—a shaggy leather jacket, with the fur turned to the inside. She stared. And was that a feather in his hair?

"Are you . . . Is it Cherokee?" she asked.

He chuckled. "Could be, could be. The old ways are still alive in these hills. The Cherokee knew that."

"But can you play it?" Josh repeated.

Goodfellow's eyes brightened with firelight or malice. "I can play, boy-o. But you might not like my tune."

"I'd love to hear you play," Cait said.

Honestly, what was the matter with Josh? They had to spend the night with these people. Couldn't he at least try to get along?

Josh shrugged. "Suit yourself. I'm turning in."

He retreated to his sleeping bag to unlace his boots, leaving her alone with the other three men in the circle by the fire.

Two weeks until Hot Springs, Cait reminded herself. She could put up with anything for two weeks.

"Goodnight," she called.

Let him cool off. She intended to warm up by the fire. Dragging her own sleeping bag over to protect her butt from the cold ground, she sat and hugged her knees.

Goodfellow blew on his fingers and then, softly, on his pipe. The flute made a sleepy, contented sound, like birdsong at twilight. He grinned at her, his eyes alight and wicked. Cait smiled back, charmed. Uneasy.

He played, a breathy, droning, soothing song, never wavering more than six notes up or down the scale, the tune rising and falling as naturally as the wind or the flames of the fire.

Cait blinked. Smoke wreathed Goodfellow's head and

twined around the flute. On the other side of the stone circle, red light slid greedily over Rhys's long body. The fire danced in his eyes. The music swirled, lulling, drugging. It filled her lungs. It caught her thoughts and spun them up and out like sparks against the night sky.

Her breathing slowed. She was warm. Very warm. She should take off her jacket.

The flute's tempo quickened with a throb like a drumbeat that gradually took over the rhythm of her heart. In the fire, images flickered, joined, and combined. Her limbs felt heavy. Her feet were restless. Her blood ran hot.

She wanted to leap and sway like the dancing flames, like the lovely, naked figures in the fire. She stood, combing her curly hair loose from its braid with her fingers. Out of the blaze a dancer rose to partner her, tall, long-legged, lean-hipped, moving with the heat and energy of the fire. Dazzled, she could not see his face. She could not stop her feet or resist the rhythm that crackled and flowed around him. It trapped her, twirled her as the pipe called, faster, wilder.

Caught in the music, lost in sensation, they twined and writhed together. He was so warm, his dancer's body hard and fluid. Heat radiated from him, from his skin and his golden eyes. Familiar eyes, she thought. *Rhys.*

She glowed. She burned. Shaking back her hair, she swayed around him, rubbed against him. Warmth infused her cheeks and flooded her veins. She was melting inside, trembling and molten, quivering on the brink of . . .

Her thoughts stumbled.

Trembling on the point of . . .

What the hell was she doing?

Cait opened her eyes. She stood alone in front of the fire wearing jeans and a T-shirt. The shifting flames mocked the sudden, shocked stillness inside her. Her arms were bare and cold, her feet leaden in her hiking boots.

All three strangers stared at her: Rhys with dark intensity, Goodfellow almost with pity, and the man called Ursus with a look that made her shudder.

Her mouth opened, but no sound came out. What was she doing? What had she done?

Mortified, shaken, she stooped and groped blindly for her jacket. Her face burned. Her body throbbed.

Rhys swept up her jacket and offered it to her.

"Thank you." She thrust her arms into the sleeves. She couldn't look at him, at any of them. Her breasts still felt heavy. Sensitized. Her knees trembled.

"Are you all right?" His voice was politely impersonal.

She shivered. Was she? What had just happened? Her mother's cautions about date rape crowded the back of her mind. She wondered, with a flash of horror, if she'd been drugged. But all she had eaten was the food she had prepared and some dried fruit from her backpack.

Cait straightened her shoulders. Maybe the wooziness she felt was only an effect of the fire, the result of smoke inhalation and fatigue.

"Fine," she said. But as she turned from the fire, she stumbled as if she'd been drinking.

"Let me help you."

"No!" she said sharply. Too sharply. Her reaction wasn't his fault. But she was still aroused and unbelievably uncomfortable. If he touched her now . . .

She couldn't think of that. She didn't want to think about it.

"I'm good, thanks," she said.

Goodfellow chuckled. "Good won't always protect you."

"Protection enough," Rhys said. "This time."

Cait ignored them. She wobbled toward the shelter, dragging her sleeping bag with her. Keeping her back to the group by the fire, she struggled with the zipper before crawling inside. Josh never stirred, the rat bastard.

What had happened? She had never been much of a party girl. Her parents' love and watchfulness had seen to that, although Cait considered their worries mostly misplaced. But she'd been spectacularly drunk once or twice in college and had put her roommates to bed more times than she could remember.

This was worse.

Squeezing her eyes shut, she pretended to sleep. Her mind still burned with the after-images of the fire, and her body was restless. Her thoughts raced and scrabbled like the mice foraging for food in the corners of the shelter. Her dreams, when they came, were suffused with tongues of flame and twists of smoke and lots of red, glowing, naked skin. Despite her fatigue, Cait slept fitfully and woke sweating.

The ground was cold and hard and the sky the color of iron when she peeled her eyelids open. Josh snored beside her. She held very still, as if she could somehow hold the day at bay. She didn't want to see the amusement in Goodfellow's eyes or the menace in Ursus's. She didn't want to face Rhys—who had featured in her seething, fevered dreams—at all.

But when she finally, reluctantly, turned her head, the other travelers were gone.

CHAPTER 2

*T*he tatters of Cait's dream clung like cobwebs through the morning, leaving her uneasy and out of sorts. Tea hadn't helped. Hiking didn't help. The sky pressed down, heavy and cold. The rocks rose up, hard and inhospitable. And Josh was in a mood again.

"Josh." Cait raised her voice. "Hey, Josh."

Since breaking camp, they had tramped four hours without once stopping or seeing another soul. She was glad they hadn't caught up with the others, with Goodfellow and Ursus and Rhys. But . . .

"I need a break," she said.

Josh didn't turn around. "We can't stop. I want to reach the next shelter before it snows."

Cait squinted through the bare trees at the gray sky. Had the weather discouraged all traffic on the trail? "Snow? In May?"

"May first. We're in the mountains, Wildcat. Elevation four thousand feet. It could definitely snow."

She ignored his patronizing attitude. "I still need a break. A potty break," she added before he could argue.

"Well, hurry up," Josh said.

Like she wanted to hang bare-assed over a six-inch hole in the ground one second longer than she had to.

She eased her pack from her shoulders, setting the frame on the ground, and grabbed her roll of toilet paper and the shovel.

The tall pines close to the trail offered little privacy. Cait walked farther than she wanted to before she found a sheltered spot behind a big boulder.

She was zipping her jeans when she heard an approaching rustle like a large animal or another hiker. Hastily, she buckled her belt and reached for the shovel.

"Josh?"

Silence.

She peered through the screening bushes at the bare, brown slope. Nothing. A crow cawed and launched noisily from a tree.

"Is anyone there?" she called, feeling foolish.

No answer.

Which was a good thing, she told herself staunchly. Picking her way through the coarse, matted undergrowth, she rounded the rock, and came face to face with a bear.

Cait shrieked.

Not a bear. A man with a bear's bulk and menace, a bear's shaggy coat and heavy jaw. Her heart pounded as she recognized the dark beard and gleaming eyes of the big hiker, Ursus.

"Sorry. You startled me," Cait said.

Ursus's little eyes fastened on her face. He didn't say anything at all.

An hour ago she had hoped she would never see Rhys

again. Now she wished he would show up. "Are your, um, friends with you?"

Ursus shifted from side to side without speaking. She was now officially, totally, creeped out.

"Well." She edged to her right, but she didn't quite have room to pass between the rock and the tree. "Josh is waiting for me. I'll see you on the trail."

The big man didn't budge.

"Josh?" She raised her voice. "Josh!"

Ursus lunged like a charging bear. Cait screamed and swung the shovel. It connected with a force that jarred her shoulders, and Ursus bellowed and grabbed the handle and wrenched it from her grasp. Her arms stung. Her hands burned. She screamed again and spun around to run.

He clawed at her arm, jerked her jacket. His breath scorched her cheek. Fear rose, blinding, bright. She couldn't see. She couldn't think. She had to get away.

Tearing free, she flung herself forward and ran, her pulse pounding like a rabbit's. She blundered through bushes and around trees, her heavy boots striking and sliding on rocks and leaves.

Ursus roared and lumbered after her.

The trail. She needed to find her way back to the trail, to Josh and safety.

But every time she turned, her pursuer veered to catch her, to cut her off. Roots tripped her ankles. Branches whipped her face. Her legs were tired. Her lungs labored, the cold air scraping her throat and stabbing her chest like knives. She had no breath to scream. She barely had breath to run. But she floundered on and on, driven by will and panic and the sound of crashing behind her.

The ground reared up, and she fell, hard, knocking the air from her lungs. Cait sprawled, clutching twigs and leaves between her fingers, her heart buzzing in her ears and black spots dancing before her eyes. The wood tilted and spun crazily as she gasped and prayed. *Oh, God, oh God, oh God . . .*

Gradually, the silence seeped into her senses.

No crashing. No grabbing. No roaring. Only the occasional rustle of a squirrel and the smell of leaf mold tickling her nostrils.

Cait breathed in and out as her heart drummed and the forest floor settled and was still around her. In. And out. Where was he?

Where was she?

Cautiously, she levered herself on her elbows and raised her head.

Nothing.

She crawled to a sitting position, taking careful inventory of her scratched hands and bruised knees. No broken bones, no twisted ankles. She was only breathless and shaken and scared. She scanned the silent, empty woods.

Scared and lost.

The first flakes fell as the shadows deepened under the trees. Cait felt the snow's kiss on her cheek, cold and soft as dread, and shuddered.

She needed to keep moving to stay warm. But the longer she walked, the more difficult it would be for her rescuers to find her. Where the hell was Josh? Why hadn't he heard her shouting? Why didn't someone—anyone—come?

She had been hiking for what felt like hours, terrified she was wandering in circles. Hadn't she passed those standing rocks before? And that stump looked awfully familiar.

Tears pricked her eyes. She willed them away, straining

for a glimpse of the white and blue blazes that marked the trail and its connecting paths. Still nothing. She raised her pocketknife and dug her initials into a tree to guide whoever might come after her.

Too bad she didn't have any bread crumbs to drop. She was starving.

Her hands shook as she returned the knife to her pocket.

Her maps and compass were in her pack, back on the trail. She climbed uphill toward the ridge line, trying to orient herself by the uncertain gray light. But every time she congratulated herself on her progress, the landscape shifted like a giant carpet shaken out and laid down in a new direction.

The trees crowded around her, dark and unfriendly. Their branches whispered and snickered together, and the shadows played tricks on her eyes. She kept turning her head to stare. A white blob of a face under a pointed red cap was only an odd fungus growing on a tree. Two menacing eyes resolved themselves into knot holes on a gnarled trunk. Cait couldn't resist the feeling that the trees were *moving* just beyond the corners of her vision, herding her downhill.

Which was ridiculous. Maybe she was losing her mind. Not that going crazy would make dying of exposure any easier.

"Help!" She had yelled herself hoarse. Her throat ached with tears. "Hello?"

The forest swallowed her voice. Snow fell, big, wet, white flakes that clung to her hair and melted on her face like tears. Cait closed her eyes in despair.

She wanted her mother.

She wanted to open her eyes and find that this hike through hell was all some horrible dream. Her parents had been right. She only hoped she lived long enough to tell them so.

Straightening her shoulders, Cait opened her eyes and saw, flickering between the dark tree trunks, the red glow of a . . . fire?

Her heart pushed into her poor, abused throat. She blinked. The glow was still there.

Hardly daring to hope, she forced her heavy legs onward, slipping on wet leaves, grabbing at branches for balance. A path opened before her, as if the wood itself yielded her passage. Rocks and roots smoothed out of her way. Or maybe it was only her eagerness that made the going seem easier.

The smell of wood smoke curled through the trees. Cait sniffed. Somebody was cooking something over that fire. Her stomach rumbled. The last thing she'd eaten was a bowl of gluey oatmeal nine hours ago. Maybe whoever built the fire would be willing to share their dinner?

A rock face loomed out of the twilight, lighter than the bare, black trees, darker than the sky. The fire crackled at its base, protected by an overhang. Maybe she wouldn't die of exposure tonight after all. Cait approached, feeling positively . . . Okay, cheerful was too strong a word. But she was definitely upbeat.

Until she recognized the tall, broad-shouldered figure feeding a stick to the dancing flames.

Rhys.

The air whooshed from her lungs. It was like falling all over again, first the blow to her chest and then the forest whirling around her while she fought for breath.

She must have made a sound, a gasp, a whimper, because he looked up and frowned. "Caitlin?"

She wanted to run. She didn't think she could move. The energy drained through the soles of her boots, leaving her lightheaded and swaying on her feet.

Rhys straightened and took a step toward her. "Are you all right?"

She tightened her hand on the little knife in her pocket. Like *that* would protect her. "Where are your friends?" she croaked.

He stopped, still frowning. "Friends?"

"Those . . . the people you were with. Goodfellow and—and Ursus."

Rhys paused before he answered. Taken aback? Or thinking up a lie? "They are not friends," he said at last, carefully. "I travel alone. As you do."

Relief made her wobbly. She wanted to believe him. Could she afford to trust him? Could she afford not to?

"Where is your companion?" he asked.

Cait opened her mouth and shut it again, because admitting she was lost and alone seemed like a really bad idea. But what could she say?

His mouth tightened. "Never mind. You look frozen. Come, sit down. Eat."

Cait bit back a hysterical giggle. *Come into my parlor, said the spider to the fly . . .*

She always figured the stupid fly got what it deserved. But what if the choice was between the tangled, sticky web and freezing to death in the wilderness? Could you really blame the fly for taking its chances with the spider?

"Okay," she said. "Thanks."

He had stacked wood under the overhang, out of the snow. He steered her to a log by the fire without actually touching her and seated himself at an angle, so she could keep an eye on him without having to stare directly into his face all the time. Sensitive of him. Or else really, really smooth. The fire beating at her exposed face and frozen toes made it hard to care. She hugged her arms, soaking in warmth, trying not to think about how she got here or what she was going to do next.

Rhys leaned forward, and she flinched. He gave her a long, measuring look before removing a heavy aluminum pot from the fire. Okay, so she was a little jumpy. She'd had a bad day, damn it.

She watched him ladle the whatever-it-was from the pot into two bowls. Why two, if he was traveling alone? Unless they'd been sold as a set. All his gear had that shiny, fresh-from-the-showroom look, as if he had more money than experience. He knew his way around a campfire, though. The stuff in the bowls smelled delicious. After almost two weeks on the trail, Cait was sick of noodles and granola.

"Thank you," she said again and dug in.

She identified onions and potatoes, carrots and barley. She poked cautiously at a mushroom cap, remembering the red-and-white fungus on the tree. But it tasted good. She noticed Rhys didn't eat much. He didn't talk much either, but that was okay. She was too hungry to make conversation.

The stew warmed her from the inside out. She nodded, lapped by the heat and lulled by the hiss and pop of the fire. Perhaps she even dozed, because the next thing she knew Rhys was taking the bowl from her hand, saying in his smooth, deep baritone, "You must sleep now."

Uh oh. She struggled back to consciousness. "I, um, don't have my sleeping bag."

He studied her with his beautiful, golden eyes. "You are lost."

Lost and alone in the woods with Tall, Dark, and Mysterious. She didn't need her parents to warn her that was a dangerous combination.

She stuck out her chin. "I ran into a little trouble on the trail. I'm meeting up with my friends at the next shelter."

"At the next shelter," Rhys said, not quite making it a question.

She resisted the urge to squirm. "That's the plan. Is it far?"

"Not far, but difficult to find. I could take you there tomorrow."

If he were planning to rape her, murder her, and dispose of her body tonight, he wouldn't talk about tomorrow, would he?

"That would be great," Cait said. "So I guess we should, um . . ."

"Sleep," he suggested, a gleam in his eyes that could have been amusement. She hoped it was amusement. "We will be cramped in one sleeping bag, but you will be warm."

Cait ignored the flutter under her breastbone. "Or we could stay up and talk a while."

"Talk."

She wished he wouldn't repeat everything she said. It sounded even more inane the second time around.

"Yeah. Generally I like to know somebody before I crawl into bed with him. . . . That was a joke," she explained, in case he didn't get it. In case he got the wrong idea. "Tell me about your family."

"I have no family," he said in this very flat voice.

Okay. Good to know he didn't have a wife and kiddies tucked away somewhere (and never mind why), but what about parents? Brothers and sisters?

"Then we can sit around the campfire and tell ghost stories," she said.

"Do you know any ghost stories?" Maybe she'd imagined that end-of-subject tone, because he definitely sounded amused now. A current of laughter ran under his dark voice like a stream in the earth.

"Actually, no. My mom didn't like me reading anything supernatural. Which is funny, because she's a librarian and totally against censorship, you know?" Cait shifted on her log. It steadied her to think about her parents: her cheerful, practical mother; her calm, strong father. "She read to me, though. *Little House on the Prairie*, *Anne of Green Gables*. But no woo woo stuff, no ghost stories or even fairy tales."

"She is unimaginative," Rhys said.

Cait found herself jumping to her mother's defense. "Not unimaginative. Just . . ."

Scared.

It was a disconcerting thought. An old memory surfaced of the day her mother discovered *The Faerie Queene* was required reading in Cait's sophomore English class. Cait didn't recall the story itself that well—something about a knight and a lady and lots of enchantment and honor and violence—but she remembered her mother's reaction.

"She's just protective, I guess. Maybe she was afraid they'd give me unrealistic expectations." Cait shrugged. "Or nightmares."

"She may be wise. Dreams have power," Rhys said.

He really talked like that, as though he wasn't used to expressing himself or English was his second language or something. It should have sounded hokey. But remembering her erotic dreams of the night before, dreams in which he had played a starring role, Cait blushed. "Yeah."

"Would you like me to tell you a story?" he offered unexpectedly.

Cait was grateful to be rescued from her embarrassment. "A ghost story?"

"A folk story. Although I think it has sufficient—what did you call it?—'woo woo.'"

She laughed. "Bring it on."

Rhys stared into the heart of the fire and then took a deep breath. "There was ere now a Pooka—"

"What's a Pooka?"

"I'm telling you. It's . . . Well, it looks like a wild black horse. A pony."

"Why don't you say pony, then?"

"Because it's not a pony. It's a . . . it's something else. Do you want a story or not?" Frustration edged his tone.

Cait grinned, unrepentant. "Yes, please. Sorry."

So he told her the tale of the Pooka, who would invite you to mount for a ride and then throw you into a ditch or off a cliff. She listened, enthralled, to his dark, liquid voice. His stilted, slightly formal speech only added to the magic of his tale.

He would have been a big hit at the preschool story hour at her mother's library.

"Do you know any more?" Cait asked when he was done.

He nodded and launched into another story, about the small brown Oakmen in red, pointy caps who turned the axes of careless woodsmen to chop off their own legs, and of the will-o'-the-wisp who led travelers astray to drown, and of the Wild Hunt that harried the damned across the sky.

Cait was whirled up in the world he described. Carried away by his voice, she heard the nasty snickers behind the trees, smelled the despair of the decaying bog, cowered at the clamor of the Hunt. His world was magical. Vivid. Evocative. And all his stories ended in death or disaster, at least for the people involved.

No wonder her mother hadn't liked them.

"Don't you know any nice stories?" Cait asked at last, torn between amusement and dismay.

Rhys gave her a sidelong look. "The *sidhe* are not nice.

They just . . ." For the first time since he started his tale, she saw him struggle for words. ". . . are," he finished finally.

Are what? Cait wondered.

"Who are the shee?" she asked.

"The people of these hills."

"That makes sense. It sounded Scottish."

His eyebrows lifted. He did it beautifully. He must practice in a mirror.

"The word," Cait explained. "Isn't it Scottish? This area was settled by the Scots, a long time ago."

Rhys shrugged. "Whoever crawls on the surface, they are the same mountains."

"What do you mean, the same?"

He leaned forward to add a log to the fire. Sparks flew into the night. Beyond the overhang, snow drifted down, heavy white flakes that clung to the trees and melted in the draft of the fire. "Longer than your long ago, these hills were a single mountain range that stretched over half of the earth. In time, the lands drifted apart and an ocean came between. But the mountains remember. In their bones and in their heart, they are still the same."

"What are you, a geologist?"

He shook his head. "No. But I have studied . . . certain things."

"So you're a student."

He smiled faintly, with a gleam like moonlight on the snow. "Sometimes."

Cait exhaled in frustration. Talking to him was like trying to catch a fish with your bare hands. "I just graduated," she said. "This trip is my present."

Some present. Although now that she was safe and fed and sitting by a warm fire with a hot guy, it almost matched her mountain fantasy.

"You said your parents didn't want you to come."

A hot guy who listened. Cait was impressed.

"They didn't." She grinned. "It's more like my present to myself. I'm supposed to start graduate school in the fall. I just wanted some time to clear my head and figure out what I want to be when I grow up without all the parental pressure, you know?"

Rhys was silent so long she was afraid she had offended him.

Cait bit her lip as realization struck. "Oh, God, I'm sorry. I forgot you don't have any family."

His mouth twitched. Was he annoyed or amused? "Not like your family. But I understand perhaps better than you think."

"I doubt it," she said gloomily. "Not unless your father changes the oil in your car every three months and your mother ends every phone call by reminding you to take your vitamins."

"I haven't seen my father since I was eight years old."

Sympathy wrenched her. *Eight?* Poor kid. Poor baby. She wondered how old he was now. He had the grace and arrogance of a young man, the smooth complexion and shining hair of a child.

Rhys met her gaze, and the glitter in his eyes stopped her breath in her throat.

Not a child, she acknowledged.

"Sorry," she repeated.

"Don't be," he drawled. "It was a long time ago."

Cait couldn't imagine her own childhood without her father's steady, loving presence. "So you're just . . . over it?"

Rhys's face was cool and smooth as marble. "Yes."

Right. Maybe he believed what he was saying. She did not. She tried again. "You know, it's only human to miss him. To care."

He gave her another of those dark, unfathomable looks. She didn't want to be attracted to him, damn it. It made an already awkward situation unbelievably uncomfortable.

"What?" she demanded.

He shook his head. "It's not important. We can talk again later. You must be tired after all you've been through."

And how did he know that? she wondered. Sure, she'd admitted running into trouble, but she hadn't breathed a word about Ursus.

On the other hand, Rhys wasn't stupid. And she *had* practically fallen asleep in her soup.

He smiled, still gazing deep into her eyes. "You should rest."

In the one sleeping bag. His sleeping bag.

Her heart pounded against her ribs while her brain scrolled glorious, hot red, high definition images of all the things she was pretty sure she hadn't done with him last night.

She wasn't out of the woods yet.

In more ways than one.

CHAPTER 3

*R*hys burned.

He lay swaddled by the sleeping bag, facing the fire, trapped by the weight of the woman who curled with her back to him. Every contact between their bodies seared him: the shy brush of her feet, the tickle of her corkscrew hair, the thrust of her shoulder blades.

She was so warm.

He hadn't expected that, hadn't known he could be moved by something as simple and profound as the stutter of her breathing or the scent of her unwashed hair. *It's only human to care . . .*

But he wasn't human. He hadn't let himself be human since he was eight years old. Or even half human. Caring was out of the question.

Restlessly, she stirred, her round buttocks bumping his heavy sex. She froze.

"Relax," Rhys said, his lips moving against her hair. "I can't do anything you don't want me to do."

"That's what I'm afraid of," she muttered.

He grinned reflexively before his smile faded. He didn't want to like her. It would make what he intended much harder.

Lying beside him, she pulsed with life and energy, solid and smooth as an egg, firm and ripe as a peach. Juicy. He wanted to turn her over, spread her wide, and sink into her living, giving heat.

He clenched his jaw, staring over her head at the dancing flames. Not yet.

She had to trust him, she had to want him, or there was no pleasure in possession.

Or revenge.

"Did you sleep well?" Rhys asked in his smoke-and-velvet voice.

They were lying spooned together—*close* together, Cait registered with the part of her mind that seemed to be working—in his sleeping bag. Beyond the overhang, snow glinted on the rocks and trees. The morning smelled crisp, cold, and delicious. Rhys smelled musky, male, and even more delicious.

Cait didn't even want to think about how she must smell or what she was feeling and certainly not about what she might actually do next.

In the romance novels her mother loved, the virginal heroines were always swept away by passion into the embrace of dark and dangerous strangers. Cait had never been swept away by anything. But she admitted to a trickle of curiosity and, deeper, more insidious, the slow welling of desire.

She was twenty-two years old. Wasn't it time she took this particular step into adulthood?

Step, hell. This was a giant stride, a leap of faith. What if she misjudged and fell flat on her face?

"I'm fine," she said cautiously. "Why, did I snore?"

Or thrash? Or . . . Oh, God, maybe she drooled in her sleep.

"No." He sounded amused again. "You just seem tense this morning." His thumb brushed her cheek, his touch light as a snowflake. Cait trembled. Catching a strand of her hair, he smoothed it carefully behind her ear. "You're all stiff."

She cleared her throat. "So are you," she pointed out.

That *was* his erection nestled against her bottom.

His soft laughter stirred the hair on the back of her neck and reverberated in the pit of her stomach. "I know something we can do about that."

She held her breath.

His arm came around her, warm and heavy. She closed her eyes. *Don't breathe, don't think . . .*

Don't stop.

A zipper rasped, loud in the stillness. The weight lifted from her abruptly. Cold air rushed in.

Cait yelped. "What are you doing?"

Rhys stood over her, smirking. "You should warm the stiffness from your body."

She curled on the open sleeping bag, hugging her knees to her chest. "What did you have in mind? A jog through the snow?"

Rhys hefted his small pack and held out his other hand. He had beautiful hands, strong and long-fingered. "Come."

Ignoring his help, she scrambled to her feet. "Where?"

He nodded toward a fissure in the cliff face behind them,

a smooth, narrow passage in the rock. She was glad she hadn't noticed it last night.

"That's not a cave, is it?"

He smiled without answering and disappeared into the side of the mountain.

Damn it. She didn't want to brave some spooky tunnel. In fact, the only thing she wanted less was to wait out here alone. Straightening her shoulders, Cait followed him into the dark.

Except it wasn't dark. Not completely dark. Gray light filtered from high overhead and glittered from winking minerals in the walls. It wasn't that cold either, despite the dampness in the air. Her boots scuffled on the gravel floor.

The way widened. The light and heat increased. So did the moisture. It clogged her lungs and ran down the walls. The passage twisted; opened. Steam drifted and swirled above deep, still pools ringed with stone. Water gleamed, dark with the shadow of the cliffs, silver with the reflection of the sky overhead. High above them, trees clung to the lip of the crevasse, their branches sparkling in a sheath of ice.

Cait caught her breath in wonder. "What are we doing here?"

Rhys ventured farther in, stepping from stone to stone until he reached a ledge along the opposite side of the gorge. "I thought you would appreciate a hot bath."

She would kill for a bath. Her bones ached. Dirt chafed her skin. But . . .

"I can't get my clothes wet. I don't have anything else to wear."

Rhys shrugged, setting his pack on the ledge beside him. "So take them off."

"No."

"Suit yourself." In one fluid motion, he pulled his shirt over his head.

She looked away.

He laughed.

Cait's head snapped around. She opened her mouth to say something really cutting, but the words died in her throat.

The sliding light caressed the strong planes of his naked torso. She stared, transfixed by the sight of his dark hair spilling against his smooth shoulders, his broad, bare chest, his sleek, muscled arms. Wreathed in steam, silhouetted against the rock, his pale skin glowed in the gloom. He looked like a statue tribute to male beauty, like some ancient temple god brought to sudden, aching life.

She inhaled sharply, the sound echoing off the high walls.

Rhys smiled, taunting her, and dropped his hands to his belt. .

She was beyond modesty. Beyond even pride. But she wrenched her gaze away, driven by simple self-preservation.

With her sight frustrated, her other senses yearned for him. She strained to follow the rustle of his clothing, the scrape of his boots, the clunk of his belt buckle. She heard his grunt of satisfaction as he entered the pool. Water lapped the rocks. Its faintly mineral scent filled her head and lungs. Under her clothes, she was hot. Sweating.

"It's safe now," Rhys said, his tone mocking.

Did he mean the pool? Or . . . ?

She glanced at him, standing chest-deep in iridescent water, silver, brown, and blue. She could see his face, a shadowed oval, and the perfect column of his throat and the lean grace of his arms. He had pulled some kind of soap from his pack. Its scent, sandalwood and clove, drifted over the surface, mingling with the steam. He rubbed the bar slowly across his chest. Lather broke and ran down his flat brown nipples.

Cait's mouth dried.

It wasn't fair he got to wallow naked in all that lovely hot water while she trembled on the edge. She didn't want to be an observer. She didn't want to be afraid.

Bracing her butt against the wall, she unlaced her boots and peeled off her socks. The moleskin bandages came with them. She tugged off her jeans, one leg at a time, holding on to the rocks for balance. The stone felt slick against her cold, bare feet.

"Sit," Rhys ordered. "Before you fall down."

His eyes were hot and intent.

Her heart beat high and rapidly in her chest. Her hands trembled. She fumbled with her bra beneath her T-shirt, sliding the straps down her arms and off. Stepping out of her panties, she sat gingerly at the pool's edge, feeling the full, shocking contact of warm stone on her naked bottom. The steaming water felt like heaven on her bare, battered feet. Her toes curled in pure pleasure.

She grasped the hem of her shirt. "Don't look."

Rhys raised his eyebrows.

Okay, he was going to watch. She swallowed thickly. She wanted him to watch.

She yanked her shirt over her head and slid off the boulder. Warming, soothing water rushed up her naked thighs and over her breasts. She gasped, her feet seeking the smooth, rounded stones at the pool bottom. Heat washed her, wrapped her, seeped into her. The water glided over her skin like silk, decadent, glorious. Her senses sprang to quivering life.

Rhys waded toward her. Cait held her ground as he stopped less than an arm's reach away. The reflective surface of the water shielded him from sight. She was acutely conscious of his nakedness. And her own.

His skin was smooth and flawless as a child's, but there was nothing childlike about his sleek, heavily muscled chest. Nothing innocent about the warm, lazy gleam in his eyes.

A different heat bloomed in her, opening under the water like an exotic sea flower, soft and strange, flowing, swaying with the pull of an unseen tide and the pulse of her blood.

She moistened her lips. "I've never done this before."

His brows arched. "Very few have. This place is not on any of your maps."

"No, I meant . . . I don't normally take naked baths with strangers."

Or have sex with them, either.

Her mind shied from the thought. But under the warm clasp of the water, her body accepted it. Welcomed it. Thrilled to it.

"I can't do anything you don't want me to do," he said again.

She wanted him to touch her. She longed for him to sweep her away, to relieve her of her decision and all responsibility.

Grow up, she told herself. She was done waiting for things to happen to her. For her.

It was time she made things happen for herself.

"I want to touch you," she said.

Something flickered in his golden eyes that wasn't mockery. He braceleted her wrist lightly with his fingers and put the bar of soap in her hand.

She clutched it. "What's this for?"

Stupid. It was soap. She was filthy. Obviously, he wanted her to wash.

He held her gaze. "Wash me."

Oh.

Oh.

Okay.

She ran the flat, slippery bar over his chest. He went utterly, absolutely still. Encouraged, she washed him with bold strokes above the water and tentative forays under it: his broad, smooth shoulders; his lean, muscled arms; his flat abdomen and silky thighs. His erection brushed her arm, full and hot, and he made a sound low in his throat. His eyes glittered. She paused, hands shaking, heart pounding.

"Caitlin." Just her name, in that dark, fluid voice, a command and a plea.

The blood rushed to her face. She touched him as she longed to, her fingers exploring under the warm water, tracing the smooth, blunt shape of him, testing his weight, his thickness, his unyielding stoniness.

The air grew humid and hard to breathe. She opened her mouth, and the scent of cloves and sandalwood filled her lungs, fogged her head, and lingered on her tongue.

"Now," Rhys said.

She looked at him, lost. *Now?*

In the depths of her mind, a thought, a warning, a remnant of caution darted and disappeared, lost in dark and hazy delight.

His lips curved. "It's my turn to wash you."

Oh, yes.

He slid the soap from her hand.

He was very gentle and very, very thorough. His soap-slick hands flowed over her, before, behind, between . . . Her knees wobbled. He nudged his leg between both of hers, supporting her, positioning her to ride his hard thigh as his palms glided up to close on her breasts. The pressure above, the friction below, made her crazy. She foundered, gasping with pleasure, drowning in sensation.

Swept away, after all.

• • •

Rhys clung to the sheer edge of reason by his fingernails. It was her fault. Caitlin's. She was hot and wet and eager, distractingly pink, delightfully awkward.

He wanted her.

Craved her.

And that was wrong.

She was supposed to crave him. He had leashed his own desires, smothered his feelings, and turned his considerable talent and technique to making her want him. To making her writhe and shudder. To making her twist and burn. To binding her to him.

But every time she gasped and floundered, flailed or grabbed at him, he felt himself slip another inch. She threw him off his rhythm. His heart pounded out of control. His blood thundered in his ears.

Cait arched and gulped, her curling hair sodden in the water.

She was messy, he told himself. A noisy, clumsy human.

And he yearned for her as he once yearned for his soul.

His hands shook. He forced himself to go slowly, penetrating her very gently with one finger, focusing on her pleasure, her arousal. He petted her, stroked her, over and over, torturing them both with exquisite restraint.

Caitlin sat up abruptly, water streaming down her back. "What are you doing?"

She was panting. So was he.

"Giving you pleasure." Only after he had brought her to peak after shattering peak could he risk losing himself in that hot, pink body.

Her face flushed. "I don't want you giving me anything."

His hand stilled. "What?"

"I'm not getting off while you watch. I want you in this with me."

"I'm here." He rubbed himself against her to prove it, clenching his teeth against the excruciating sensation.

She grabbed fistfuls of his hair and dragged his face to hers. "Then *be* here," she said, a demand and a plea. "Be with me."

He shuddered. "I can't. I don't—"

"*Do* it."

His control snapped and broke. His lust and his need sprang forward like unleashed beasts, snarling and clawing.

How could she? How dared she?

He pushed her hard against the rock and crashed into her with all the finesse of a boar in the underbrush.

She was ready, wet, aroused, but he heard her cry of shock or pain. His mind screamed at him. He was doing it too fast. Too hard. All wrong.

He couldn't stop himself. He had to . . . He needed . . .

His hips pumped. His vision blurred. Her hands tightened in his hair. Scored his back. She felt so good. So hot. Water sloshed over them both as he pounded into her, lost in urgency, in simple animal hunger. He was frantic for her, desperate for the slap of flesh on flesh, for the hot, tight clasp of her body, for the grunt of her breath against his cheek, in his ear. He was shaken, shaking, coming apart.

For a man whose survival depended on his lack of feeling, who prided himself on his exquisite control, it was over embarrassingly quickly.

• • •

She cried.

He should have expected that, Rhys told himself as he held her body and stroked her back. But he had never touched another human's tears, never known a mortal's grief. Even his own father . . .

He shoved the thought away.

Her tears leaked from the corners of her eyes, precious, hot, and harrowing. He licked them, pressing his cheek to hers, wracked, unmanned by the musky scent of her skin and the salt taste of her in his mouth.

"I'm sorry," he said against her temple, into her hair. "I'm sorry."

"It's all right. I'm all right. I asked for it." Caitlin raised her damp, flushed face. Her smile wobbled, twisting his insides. "Literally."

Rhys frowned. She shouldn't be making jokes. "I hurt you."

He intended worse than the brief, physical pain of penetration, but she didn't know about that. He didn't want to think about it.

Her fingers brushed the back of his neck, her touch soothing. That was wrong, too. He should be the one comforting her.

"Not really. I guess I just wasn't expecting it to be so . . . intense." She attempted another smile. "But I'm okay. It was okay."

Rhys's eyes narrowed. "Okay," he repeated.

She nodded. "For my first time. You know."

He didn't know anything anymore. All he understood was that she had shredded his control, violated his emotions, turned his world upside down, and for her it was just . . . *okay*.

She watched him, her brown eyes troubled. "It could have been a lot worse."

Defensive, mocking, he asked, "How would you know?"

She shrugged. "Girls talk. At least we weren't drunk."

Rhys scowled. He wasn't drunk. He had no excuse for his uncharacteristic loss of control.

And she . . . She was immune. Even in passion, Caitlin remained obstinately, perfectly herself. Instead of being reduced by sex and magic to a mindless, wordless, whimpering bitch, she made demands. Jokes. Excuses for him.

He couldn't stand it.

Puck, known to mortals as Robin Goodfellow, had warned her: *Good won't always protect you.*

But it had. It had.

Instead, *she* had destroyed *him*. Challenged *him*. Not merely sexually—he might have coped with that—but emotionally.

He could barely forgive her for that.

Or himself.

Bracing his hands on the stone by her head, he launched himself from the pool. Water lapped and sloshed. He welcomed the chill on his body. Naked, he pulled a blanket from his pack and turned to offer her a hand.

Caitlin climbed out awkwardly, her bare toes gripping the rock, gooseflesh prickling her arms and chest. Steam rose from her warm flesh. He didn't want to look at her. He wrapped the blanket roughly around her shoulders and then froze, staring down.

Pink smeared her white thighs. Blood. Her virgin's blood, streaked with water. Unthinking, he reached to touch her.

She smacked his hand away. "I told you I'm fine." She pressed her long legs together, pulling the blanket tightly around her. She sounded annoyed. Embarrassed. Not so immune, after all.

And she had cried.

Rhys met her brave brown eyes and felt a weight in his chest that might have been his heart.

If he'd had one.

CHAPTER 4

Cait emerged from the narrow ravine, scuffling in her untied boots, still clutching the blanket over her damp clothes. In a sudden shift of weather, the sun had appeared, making the snow sparkle and the trees blaze with melting ice. Vapor shimmered in the air.

Cait blinked. It was like coming out of a movie theater or the eye doctor's office. Everything looked brighter, sharper, clearer, every rock rimmed with shadow, every leaf illuminated with light. Even Rhys's already amazing looks took on an unearthly edge.

In this dazzling, light-tinged landscape, she felt small and cold and ordinary. Hitching the blanket around her shoulders, she shuffled toward the fire.

Rhys followed her silently, stooping to throw another log on the fire. The dying flames seized it greedily.

She cleared her throat. "Thanks. My hair's turning to icicles."

Rhys frowned. "You should dry it. You don't want to get sick."

"No," she agreed fervently.

WARNING: UNPROTECTED SEX IN FANTASY SETTINGS WITH MYSTERIOUS STRANGERS MAY RESULT IN HEAD COLDS.

AIDS.

Pregnancy.

Panic pressed under her breastbone like a knife. Oh, God, what had she been thinking?

All her life she'd been so smart, so careful . . . until Rhys. When she was with him she had no more inhibitions than a drunken coed at a frat party. Even now, she ached with awareness of him, his long-fingered hands and hard, lean body, his guarded, golden eyes and sensitive mouth.

She took a deep breath, to steady her nerves and her voice. "Although my mother says colds are caused by viruses, not exposure. So, as long as you're healthy . . ." She trailed off, looking at him expectantly.

"I am healthy. You will take no hurt from—" He paused. Some emotion flickered in his golden eyes and was gone too quickly to identify. "You will not get sick because of me. But you could get chilled."

"Healthy" was good, Cait thought hopefully. She could live with "healthy." She would prefer not to live with "pregnant," but she would deal with that when and if it happened. She ignored the crazy hammering of her heart, the unfamiliar soreness between her thighs. She was a grown-up. She would take responsibility for her actions.

She bundled the blanket around her wet head like a towel. "There. Satisfied?"

Rhys's gaze drifted over her, touching her breasts, her throat, her mouth. "No."

The rush of heat caught her unprepared. She was overre-acting. Emotional. Off-balance. Because it was her first time, she supposed.

She reached for the kettle, covering her awkwardness with action. "I'll make us some tea."

"Caitlin."

She squinted at the fire. Whatever affected her vision this morning shot dancing color through the flames. "What?"

Rhys knelt beside her. He tipped her face to his. His eyes were warm, his touch light and cool. "I have something for you."

She struggled for breath, for humor and normalcy. "Breakfast?"

His smile gleamed. "Breakfast, certainly, later. This now."

He bent and kissed her mouth.

Heat washed over her. Cait closed her eyes and leaned into him, needing his warmth, seeking the reassurance of him wanting her. But before the kiss could go anywhere, he left her kneeling alone by the fire.

She heard him rustling in his pack. Chilled and disappointed, she opened her eyes.

He turned to her. She was so focused on his face she didn't see at first he held something in his hands, something that glittered in the tricky light: an intricately woven, thick gold chain.

He held it up, and the sunlight ran along the links like fire. "For you."

For a moment she wondered who the hell hiked through the Appalachians with an expensive necklace tucked in his backpack. But the sun struck the worked gold, dazzling her, and the question faded.

"Wow, it's . . . beautiful." In her new, sensitive sight, the light dripped from the heavy links of the chain and blurred the edges like water.

"It's for you," Rhys said, and stooped to place it around her neck.

Cait rocked back on her heels, moving instinctively out of his reach.

He frowned. "Caitlin?"

She stared at the gleaming necklace in his hand like a mouse transfixed by a snake. The links pulsed with a light and life of their own. She shivered.

"Don't you like it?" Rhys asked.

How could she explain her aversion to his gift? She didn't understand it herself.

"I . . . It's too much. We hardly know each other."

Which made the fact that she'd had sex with him—"*Do it.*"—even more incomprehensible.

"It's a token," Rhys said.

Some token.

Cait stared at the sparkling, mocking necklace. The heavy gold chain resembled a rapper's bling or a . . . a dog collar. A very beautiful, very valuable, very decorative dog collar.

Her hand went to her throat. "I can't accept this."

"I want you to have it," Rhys said, kneeling behind her. "Let me fasten it for you."

She was tempted. All that gold carried weight. The necklace felt significant somehow, like a gift from a longtime lover rather than a trinket from a one-night stand. She wanted to think her first time meant something to Rhys. That she meant something to him.

But when the chain swung in front of her face, her hand reached of its own volition and grabbed it. "No! I want—" *What?* What could she possibly say without offending him? "—I want to look at it first," she finished weakly.

"You can look at it all you want," Rhys said, a bit grimly. "Around your neck."

Cait's hand tightened. The chain seared her palm. Her stomach clenched. "Not without a mirror."

His face tensed. And then he shrugged and released the necklace, leaving it dangling from her hand. "I can't force you, of course."

The knots in her stomach eased. Cait felt as if she had won some kind of victory instead of a silly dispute over a necklace. Of course he couldn't force her. She was overreacting again.

Her hand burned. She stuffed the chain into her jeans pocket without looking at it again.

Fortunately, Rhys didn't seem to notice. Or maybe he was simply too polite to comment. "You will at least accept breakfast," he said.

Relieved, Cait smiled. "I'd love breakfast. If we have time."

He gave her a blank look.

"Before we go to the shelter." Cait tried again. "You said you would take me to the nearest shelter today."

Rhys stared down his long nose at her. "You are in a hurry to rejoin your companion?"

Maybe he was jealous.

"Josh?" Somehow in the last twenty-four hours, Josh had gone from being an annoyance to being completely irrelevant. Cait shook her head. "No, but he must be worried about me."

"Then why hasn't he come looking for you?"

Cait shifted uncomfortably. Josh hadn't responded to her screams for help yesterday. She told herself he hadn't heard her, but . . . "I'm sure he reported me missing. There are probably rangers out looking now."

"If he notified the authorities, there would be search teams. And dogs," Rhys pointed out with depressing logic. "We would hear them."

"Maybe the snow slowed everybody down."

"The snow would have increased the urgency of the search. If there were a search." Rhys didn't exactly say *Fat chance,* but his tone implied it.

Cait frowned, troubled. She trusted him. He had rescued, fed, and sheltered her. They'd had sex, for heaven's sake. But she would feel less . . . *alone* if somebody else knew where she was. Or rather, that she wasn't where she was supposed to be.

"I still need to go," she said. "I don't want to risk Josh contacting my parents and freaking them out."

"Your parents . . . They would be upset if something happened to you." Not quite a question.

"I told you they were overprotective." She watched him take four small red-and-yellow apples, a loaf of bread, and a jar of honey from his pack. Her stomach rumbled. "I think it's because I'm all they've got."

Rhys quartered an apple. His knife had a bone handle with carved snakes twined around the grip. If she didn't look straight at it, the snakes wriggled in the corners of her vision. The illusion was almost enough to make her lose her appetite.

"They did not wish for other children?" Rhys asked in a perfectly normal voice.

She blinked and accepted a slice of apple. "They couldn't have any. Which is kind of ironic, because my mom was pregnant with me when they got married."

He lowered the knife. "They told you this?"

She swallowed. "No, I did the math when I was about ten. It didn't bother me. I mean, my parents are crazy about each other. Ever since they were in grad school. I did wonder why they waited fourteen years to make their relationship official, but maybe they just needed a little push." She shrugged and wiped her fingers on her jeans. "Maybe they didn't believe in marriage."

"Or maybe there was someone else."

She rejected the suggestion instantly. "Mom says Dad is the only man she ever loved."

"I meant for him."

The idea that her father could have had another lover seemed odd, disloyal, even, but Cait forced herself to consider the possibility for all of . . . oh, ten seconds. She had the impression—not from anything her parents said, more from the things they carefully *didn't* say—that her father had split for a while before they got married.

And then she shook her head. "You don't get it. You don't know my dad. He's Mr. Family Man. He would never do anything to hurt my mother. Or me."

"You are fortunate," Rhys said, and because of his peculiar, formal speech she couldn't tell if he was being sarcastic or not.

Maybe not. She remembered he hadn't seen his own father since he was eight years old. *I have no family,* he'd said.

Sympathy flowed through her. Impulsively, she reached out and patted him on the knee.

Rhys stiffened in outrage.

She couldn't feel sorry for him. He would not tolerate it. If she had the slightest idea who he was or what he had been sent to do, she wouldn't dare feel pity for him.

He could destroy her.

Her hand still rested on his knee. Her tanned, warm hand.

He looked from her ragged nails into her compassionate brown eyes and was lost. He couldn't do it. Not now.

She had touched him voluntarily. In kindness, not in lust. She had baptized him with her human tears, anointed him with her virgin blood. She had resisted his enchantment.

He could not destroy her now if his very existence depended on it.

Which, he reflected grimly, it might.

Her hand tightened. "What's the matter? You look . . ."

She paused, her kindness warring with her honesty, and he did not know whether to laugh or weep. How did a man contemplating his damnation look?

"Are you okay?" she asked.

He was offended.

He had been rejected before, of course. His father had hugged him sometimes, or ruffled his hair, but his mother never had. And when Rhys's father had chosen death over continued existence in the Queen's court, the eight-year-old had quickly learned his mother was impatient with grief and intolerant of tears.

But the adult Rhys had never been refused—anything— by a sexual partner before. He understood now the Queen's fury at a lover's rejection.

Not a good thought. Rhys got a grip. Not a helpful thought.

Not a thought he could explain to Caitlin or defend any longer to himself.

"I'm fine," he said. "But you are right. We should go soon."

There was a chance, if he got her away quickly, that his treachery would go undiscovered. Not a good chance. Ursus would have reported Caitlin had been successfully separated from her companion on the trail, and Puck—despite his occasional sympathy for humans—could not be trusted.

But the other *sidhe* were not Rhys's main concern. They would not question his command, and they had no reason, yet, to doubt either his power or his will.

Caitlin was his, by birthright. He had been chosen to bind her. He would be granted time to accomplish his task—even to enjoy it—before the others came.

Before the Queen came. The thought slid into his chest like a knife.

"You sure?" Caitlin asked, still concerned.

Her ignorance was her defense.

He forced himself to smile. "That we should go now? Yes. You don't want to worry your parents." He could not say the word without a slight bitterness. If not for her parents, she would not be in danger. Of course, she would never have been born, either.

The reminder goaded her to get up and moving. She laced her boots while he doused the fire. Rhys watched her clear away the remains of their breakfast, confident and awkward in her youth and her humanity, her wildly curling hair falling into her face; and longing for her flamed in him.

He had never forgiven his father for letting lust rule him, blind him, consume him, so that all he lived or hoped for was a smile from the Queen. When the smiles stopped, he had gone uncaring to his death, heedless of the son he left behind.

But now at least, perhaps, Rhys understood him.

He could not afford his father's weakness. He was his mother's son.

He slung his pack over his shoulder. "Come."

Caitlin cast a startled glance toward the overhang. "What about the rest of your stuff?"

He could hardly tell her the "stuff" she saw, chosen to impress and reassure her, was so much human trash to him. He had no need of it where he was going.

"I'll come back for it," he said.

As they hiked, the sun climbed. The snow retreated from rocks and ridgelines. Fog floated under the trees. The air filled with birdsong and the sound of rushing water. Ice tumbled down, revealing dark patches of fir and bare, wet branches.

Cait swung along, lifting her face often, drinking in the sun or the view or the moisture. "It's like a scene from a movie."

He had no idea what she was talking about. "A movie?"

She smiled at him. "You know, the one where the four children are fleeing the wolves through the snow, and the snow starts melting, and it turns to spring, and the whole time they're being pursued by the evil queen."

He stared at her, appalled, his heart pounding in his chest.

"You didn't see it," she guessed.

He managed to find his tongue. The evil queen . . . "No."

"It's based on some really famous children's book. Not that my mother ever let me read it," Caitlin added ruefully. "Too much woo woo."

"My mother," Rhys said with precise and terrible irony, "never let me read it, either."

Cait grabbed his arm. "Oh, look!"

Rhys tensed. He couldn't help himself. The *sidhe* did not touch except in the formal figures of the dance or the equally deliberate moves of sex. Every time Cait touched him, she breached the walls he'd learned to construct to protect the sniveling, abandoned, eight-year-old child within.

She pointed to a carpet of flowering trillium, its heart-shaped leaves poking through the melting crust of snow. "Isn't it beautiful?"

"Beautiful."

But he wasn't looking at the wildflowers.

Smiling, she turned and met his gaze. Her color rose, pink and warm and full of life.

The *sidhe* didn't blush, either.

He bent and saluted her with his lips—her warm cheek, her sunburnt brow. Her arms came around his neck. Standing on tiptoe, she kissed him back with undisguised enthusiasm.

She kissed him back.

Her response stripped him of finesse and control. He was suddenly shaking, desperate and clumsy as a boy beset by a succubus in the dark. Only the woman pressed against him was no greedy demon. This was Cait, sweaty and sweet, warm and real. Vulnerable.

He tangled his hands in her hair and heard—felt—her make a sound low in her throat. It vibrated in his chest. His cock swelled, hard against her leg. She wiggled against him, her arms tightening around his neck.

Yes, he thought. *Hold me. Kiss me. Let me . . .*

Shuddering, he tore his mouth from hers and buried his face against her throat. Her pulse drummed. Her hair waved against his cheek.

"Stay," he whispered, his lips against her skin. She tasted of salt. "Stay with me."

If she stayed, he would find a way to protect her. He would devote himself to her happiness. She would live forever and never want, never need, anything else. Anyone else.

"Here?" Cait asked.

He raised his head. She was smiling, the curve of her lips warm and amused, her eyes free of shadows.

Or comprehension. She did not, could not, know what he was asking of her.

"Don't you think eventually we'd get a little tired of the great outdoors?" she asked.

He shivered. She had no idea. And it was better that way. Safer that way for them both.

He brought her along the paths of his people back to the woods she had left behind. The air thickened with human contagion. Her world overlaid his like a veil, dimming its sparkle, deepening its shadows. Here, where the old growth trees thrust their roots deep in the earth and pierced the sky with their branches, the fabric thinned. Any tiny tear in her perceptions, and she could fall from one plane to another.

But ahead, Rhys could see the dull obscurity of the track cutting like a scar through the living landscape. The trail, conceived by mortal minds and built by human hands a mere seventy years ago, would protect her.

His own way forked.

Rhys stopped and pointed. "There, do you see? Your way is there, through the trees. The blue blazes will take you back to the trail. The shelter is only a few hundred feet to your right."

Caitlin faltered. "Aren't you coming with me?"

He clenched his jaw against temptation. He could not. This reality was all he knew, all he'd ever known. His ignorance terrified and shamed him.

"I have to go back," he said.

Her gaze was steady on his face. "To collect your things." He did not correct her.

"Well . . ." She sighed. "I'm meeting up with some

friends in Hot Springs in two weeks. If you change your mind."

He held himself rigid. Was it his imagination, or were the birds suddenly, strangely still?

"Or . . . or you could call," she said.

He willed himself not to say anything. Her tears and her blood constrained him. Maybe they bound her, too. If he called her, she might come.

And if she came, it would be to her doom.

Her gaze fell. "I don't even know your last name."

There was power in names. But he would give her his, to carry like a talisman back to safety.

"Rhys Danuson." Rhys, son of the goddess.

She smiled as if they'd just been introduced. "Cait MacLean."

The forest was quiet. Too quiet. Even the rush and drip of water seemed muted and far away.

"Yes," Rhys said, unthinking. "I know."

Cait's brown eyes widened. "How—"

The trees held their breath. The air around them shivered.

"Go," he said harshly. "Go now. Quickly."

But it was already too late.

CHAPTER 5

Cait stared at Rhys. Her heart ached like a bruise.

She was an adult. She accepted responsibility for her own choices. Just because they'd had sex . . . She heard her own voice demanding, pleading, *"Do it,"* and shuddered. Anyway, just because she'd given herself for the first time in a fit of lust or rebellion or adolescent curiosity didn't mean she expected Rhys to say he loved her.

But at least he could say, *I'll call you.*

He was looking over her shoulder. He wouldn't even meet her eyes.

" 'Go quickly'?" Cait repeated. "That's it? You can't do better than that?"

"Apparently not." The cold, clear voice, a woman's voice, rang from behind Cait—not loud, but as hard and scoured of emotion as a mountaintop. Rhys stiffened. "So, he disappoints us both."

Cait turned. And gaped. Whatever weird sparkly thing

had affected her sight must have affected her brain, too, because she was definitely seeing things.

At least, she hoped she was.

She wanted to believe the woman blocking the path to the trail couldn't possibly be for real. She was too tall, over six feet at least, like a runway model. Not thin, like a model, or young, but fierce and beautiful and outlandishly dressed in a long, full skirt the color of blood and a high, white collar that framed her face.

Her face . . . Cait gulped. Her face was cold and shining as the moon. Her eyes were black and hostile. And at her skirts, crouched like a dog, was the short hiker, Goodfellow.

Cait's heart hammered. Her gaze darted to the trees, searching for Ursus. But the woman wasn't the sort of person you felt comfortable taking your eyes off for long.

"Bind her," the woman commanded. Her voice echoed in Cait's head.

Cait blinked. *Uh* . . .

"I cannot. Not against her will," Rhys replied seriously, as if the woman had actually made a rational request.

As if . . . Cait glanced back at him, her stomach sinking. As if he *knew* her. Now that Cait saw them together, they even looked a little alike. Their height, she supposed, and their hair color, and something strong and proud and secret in their faces.

He disappoints us both.

Oh, no.

The woman drew herself up, so she looked even taller and scary, despite the Mardi Gras costume. Or maybe because of it.

She sneered. "I do not need you to instruct me, manling. You must bend her will to your desire."

Nobody sane, nobody real, talked like that. Either the

lady was crazy and Rhys was mixed up with these loonies, or Cait was losing her own mind.

And yet . . . Cait had a sick, growing conviction they were talking about her, Caitlin, about *her* will, about . . . Okay, she didn't have a clue what they were talking about. But her gut knew it was bad.

Goodfellow cleared his throat. "Perhaps with time, Lady . . ."

"It is not time he lacks," the proud woman said with crushing scorn. "It is stomach."

Speaking of stomachs, Cait's was making a serious effort to lose the tea and apples. Her head throbbed as if she had a migraine.

The woman's voice bored into her brain. ". . . deal with it myself."

Rhys answered.

Good, Cait thought, struggling to focus. He knew her. Let him deal with her.

Through the pounding in her skull, Cait heard, ". . . *your grievance"* and, ". . . *not her fault,"* and felt a spurt of gratitude.

"I will have what is mine," the woman said.

"She was never yours," Rhys said evenly. "Nor is she mine."

The woman pinned him with her coal black eyes. "You lie. I can smell her on you."

Cait winced. Okay, that was creepy.

Her head hurt. She wanted to cling to the idea that the woman was crazy. Scary, the way the homeless guy in the campus garden mumbling to himself was sometimes scary, but not actually dangerous. But what did that make Goodfellow? A fellow escapee from the asylum?

Cait shivered. And what about Rhys?

Goodfellow cocked his head, regarding Cait with bright, black eyes. "She does not wear the necklace."

The woman's laser beam focus switched to Cait. Cait froze, her heart beating like a rabbit's, the necklace burning in her pocket. Her hand crept to her throat.

Leave me out of this, she wanted to protest. But the words clogged in her throat.

"It does not matter," the woman announced at last with magnificent indifference. "My debt will be satisfied."

"The debt is her parents'." Rhys was rigid, his voice without expression. "Let the punishment be theirs."

Now, wait a minute . . .

The woman smiled. Not a nice smile. "Her fate is their punishment."

Cait tried to think through the jagged pain in her head. They were definitely talking about her fate. About *her* parents. Talk about crazy. Her parents were the steadiest, most boring people Cait knew. Her mother was a librarian, for crying out loud. Her father owned a garage. Any two people less likely to be involved in . . . involved in . . . But here her imagination quite simply failed.

Your parents . . . They would be upset if something happened to you, Rhys had said.

Her fate is their punishment.

Cait felt a small, warming spurt of anger. ("Too stubborn for her own good," her mother used to say, and her father would laugh and shake his head.) She was tired and confused and her head hurt and the man she had given her virginity to was talking about her as if she wasn't there with a seven-foot-tall scary psycho woman. But she wasn't standing by while they threatened her parents.

She took a step forward. "Look—"

The lady swung her savage focus on Cait. Cait met the full force of her black gaze.

And immediately wished she hadn't.

The darkness in those eyes yawned like a pit before her. Whoever, whatever, stared back at her from the lady's eyes wasn't crazy.

It wasn't human, either.

Black wasn't a color, it was the void, deep and treacherous as a shaft under the mountain, empty as space without moon or stars. Faced with that bottomless gaze, Cait couldn't think. She could barely breathe. She was being drawn in, sucked into oblivion.

Relax. The memory of Rhys's voice caught at her soul like an anchor. *I can't do anything you don't want me to do.*

She didn't know what she wanted anymore. The lady's gaze sapped her will, weighted her limbs, squeezed her lungs. Her resolution slipped. She trembled on the brink of falling.

The chain burned in her pocket like a hot coal against her thigh.

From somewhere, Cait found the strength to breathe, and then the courage to resist. She concentrated on the pain, using it, holding on to it to withstand the pull of that black, immortal gaze, to drag herself back from whatever edge summoned her.

Gradually the grip on her senses slackened. Cait came to, still staring into the lady's eyes.

The lady frowned in displeasure. "There is more of your dam in you than I reckoned. Well, no matter." She raised her hand.

Cait gulped.

Rhys jerked. "*No.* Mother—"

Cait felt herself teeter on another edge. *Mother?*

The lady barely spared him a glance. "I am the Queen. I will have payment of my debt."

Rhys's face was as white, as set, as hard as hers. Seeing the two faces, so close, so alike, made Cait's stomach lurch. "Then take me."

Slowly, the lady lowered her arm. The quiet pressed under the trees.

Sharp anxiety seized Cait. "What are you doing?"

Goodfellow coughed. "Majesty . . . Please. Consider."

"Take me in payment," Rhys repeated, never taking his eyes from the lady. His *mother*? "And let her go free."

"What are you talking about?" Cait snapped.

"So be it." The words dropped like stones. The air shimmered like the surface of a pond. The queen flung up her hand. "Live solitary, apart from all your kind. And die alone."

"No!" Cait yelled. "Wait! Stop it!"

She didn't even know what she was trying to stop. But *"die alone"* couldn't be good.

She threw herself toward Rhys. The sky cracked. The earth heaved. She flung her arms around his shoulders and felt him change, felt his bones shudder and lengthen, felt his skin roughen and erupt with fur, felt his muscles shift and bunch. She tumbled with him to the ground, sprawling on her knees as the cry from his throat stretched into a howl that hung on the air. For one horrible, hairy, confused moment, she clung to him, feeling the terrible *wrongness* of his shape without comprehending. Details flashed without registering. Hot breath. Bared teeth.

Flaming golden eyes in a snouted, furry face.

Cait screamed.

The animal (*"Wolf!"* her mind shrieked) in her arms scrambled desperately for freedom, his paws digging at her thighs, ripping her clothes, his claws scoring her arms, drawing blood. Pain welled, thick and hot as fear, blotting out thought. Fresh screams tore from her throat.

The wolf crashed away through the underbrush.

Cait was sobbing, bleeding, her mind bright and blank with disbelief. She staggered to her feet. *To follow it? To follow him?* The forest floor buckled, pitching her into darkness.

She lay stunned, her fingers clutching rotting leaves, her body sprawled in melting snow. Her brain buzzed like a fly caught in a web. She couldn't think. She couldn't move. A black haze wrapped her, tangling her mind, trapping her limbs.

"What will you do with her, then?" somebody asked close to her head.

"Nothing." The silver voice stabbed like a knife through the fog. "She's none of mine."

None of mine, none of mine, none . . . The words spread through the woods like ripples on water.

Take me in payment, Rhys had said. *And let her go free.*

No! Cait cried in her heart.

But she could not move.

Overhead, the trees whirled lazily with a sound like car tires on wet road. Time passed, measured in heartbeats and the pulse of pain. Cold seeped into her bones. Snow pressed her cheek. She couldn't feel her feet.

She tried again to move. To cry out. Nothing.

Alone, she struggled against the creeping cold, against the blinding, binding fog and the pull of the dark. Her parents would be really upset if she never came home. And Rhys . . . Her mind splintered into a kaleidoscope of fangs and fur and burning golden eyes. Her cuts throbbed.

Okay, she wouldn't think about Rhys. Not yet.

A rustle broke the quiet. Cait's heart pumped. A squirrel? The Queen?

The wolf?

She heard . . . Could that be voices? She wasn't that far from the path to the trail. Casual, normal, *human* voices, carrying through the woods.

Hope rose, a warm trickle against the cold. Cait fought to lift her head. A weak croak escaped her throat.

Encouraged, she tried again. "Here."

Better.

"Help!"

Better still.

Two hikers—male and female, middle-aged, with sensible gear and shocked, concerned faces—rushed forward.

"Oh my God, oh my God," the woman kept repeating.

I'm fine, Cait tried to reassure her through chattering teeth, but she was shaking too hard to speak.

The man helped her to sit.

"What happened?" he asked as the woman pulled a thermal space blanket from her pack.

Cait accepted the blanket gratefully, clutching its foil edges around her shoulders. She looked into their kind, pragmatic faces and her heart sank.

What could she possibly say?

"Your daughter is a very lucky girl," the doctor told Cait's parents. Her father, Ross MacLean, stood at the foot of Cait's hospital bed. Her mother, Janet, sat holding her hand. "She's going to be fine. You'll be able to take her home this afternoon."

Cait didn't feel lucky. Or fine, either. Depressed, uncertain, and confused was more like it. She had no context and no explanation for what had happened. She was glad her parents were here. But . . .

"She can't walk," Janet objected. "Shouldn't she stay another night for observation?"

"All of her symptoms—the stumbling, the slurred speech, the confusion—are a result of hypothermia." The young doctor spoke in an earnest, lecturing manner he'd copied either from his teachers or some doctor on TV. "Not surprising, given that she was lost all night in a snowstorm. Now that the IV fluids have brought her temperature back up, she should make a rapid recovery."

"What about her cuts?" Ross asked.

"You'll want to change the dressings once a day when you get her home. And she'll need to see her doctor to complete the series of rabies injections."

Cait winced. She didn't want more shots. But if she tried to explain she wasn't likely to get infected from a man who had been magically transformed into a wolf by his pissed-off mother, the doctor wouldn't just treat her for rabies. He'd lock her up as a loony.

Her father frowned. "You said she wasn't bitten."

"The rabies virus can enter through a scratch. And since we don't have the dog that attacked her to test it for infection . . ." The doctor shrugged.

"It wasn't a dog," Cait said.

They all looked at her.

She dropped her gaze to the white top sheet on her bed, sorry she'd said anything. "It was a wolf," she mumbled.

"That's impossible," the doctor announced. "There are no wolves along the Appalachian Trail."

"Actually, that might not be true," Janet said in her librarian voice. "Back in the nineties, the Fish and Wildlife Service attempted to reintroduce red wolves into Great Smoky Mountain National Park, but the experiment failed. The pups all died and the surviving adults were supposedly re-captured. But there might be one wolf left in the wild."

Live solitary, apart from all your kind, the Queen had in-toned. *And die alone.*

Cait stared at her mother, stricken.

Janet tightened her hold on her hand. "Honey? What is it?"

"Are you all right?" her father asked.

Cait pulled herself together. Her parents were her strength. Her support. How could she confront them? "I don't want to talk about it."

Her parents exchanged looks over the foot of her bed, drawing together, as they always did, at the least sign of trouble.

Rhys's voice haunted Cait. *The debt is her parents'. Let the punishment be theirs.*

What debt had he taken on? What had her parents done?

"You'll feel better when we get you home," her mother said with determined cheerfulness.

The young doctor scrawled on Cait's chart. "The nurse will be in later to remove the IV and go over your discharge instructions. Your things are in the locker. Any questions?"

None that he could answer. Cait shook her head.

"Well, then." He offered her his hand, clean, cool, a little dry. "Best of luck."

Cait had the feeling she was going to need it. Her heart pounded as the door closed behind him. Her mouth was dry.

"Do you want anything, honey?" Janet asked.

She wanted her life back. She wanted the confidence that had set her on the trail, the time when her parents' love was the bedrock of her life, the world where her mother kept all woo-woo stuff away and tall, terrifying queens didn't mate-rialize out of the woods to wreak magical vengeance.

But Rhys didn't belong to that world.

If she wanted Rhys, if she wanted to save Rhys, she had to leave that life behind.

She was afraid to question her parents, terrified their answers would shake the foundation of everything she knew and believed. Something had happened out there. She hadn't cut her arms and legs walking into a tree. But a tiny, persistent doubt niggled at her. She could have hallucinated. What if her parents had no idea what she was talking about?

Or . . . A knot formed in her chest. What if they did?

Cait swallowed. "Could I have my clothes, please?"

Her mother frowned. "Don't you want to wait for the nurse? Your IV—"

Cait tightened her hands on the sheet. If she didn't do this now, she might lose her nerve. "Can you just get them?"

Another look between her parents.

"Sure." Janet stood and retrieved a small overnight bag from the bottom of the room locker. "I didn't know what you would need, so I packed a little of everything."

Her mother's thoughtfulness tightened her throat.

"Thanks," Cait said. "But I meant my old clothes. In the locker."

"You can't wear those," Janet said.

"I know. Can I have them please?"

Janet opened the locker and laid the plastic bag that held Cait's wet, dirty, bloodstained clothes on the bed.

Taking a deep breath, Cait tugged the bag toward her. She needed proof her mind wasn't playing tricks on her, that she hadn't made everything up—Rhys, the Queen, the wolf—in some exposure-induced dream. With a quiver of distaste, she plunged her hand into the pocket of her jeans. Her fingers touched warm, smooth metal.

She hadn't hallucinated that.

Relieved, she drew the necklace from the bag and glanced at her parents.

Her faint, brief satisfaction died.

Her mother was as white as the sheets of the bed.

Her father's handsome face looked haggard and old. "When did you get that? Who gave it to you?" he whispered.

CHAPTER 6

*H*er father stared at the chain in Cait's hand as if he saw a ghost. She felt his recoil in her gut.

"May first," Janet said suddenly. She looked at her husband for confirmation or reassurance. "She disappeared on May first."

Ross nodded. "Beltane."

Cait shivered. She needed the answers her parents could provide. But every response raised fresh questions. How much did they know? And how did they know it?

Janet clasped her hands together in her lap. "You told me once the *sidhe*'s world intersects with ours at times and places when we're vulnerable. But why now? Why, after all these years?"

The *sidhe*. The people of the hills, Rhys had called them.

Ross's mouth was grim. "She couldn't touch us before. Not after you defeated her. But what better way to strike back at us than where we're most vulnerable?"

Realization widened Janet's eyes. "Through our daughter."

Our daughter. They were talking about her as if she weren't even here. Just like Rhys and . . . and his mother.

Frankly, she was getting tired of being treated like the only nonadult in the room. "Hello?"

Her father regarded the necklace coiled like a snake against the white sheets of her bed. "What are you doing with that . . . that thing?"

The light ran lovingly along the length of chain. Cait poked it with one finger. "I was hoping you, um, could tell me. What is it?"

"It is a *sidhe bràighde*," Ross said. "A binding chain. Did you get it from her?"

"Her, who?" Cait asked. But she knew. She knew.

"The Queen," Ross snapped. "Did the Queen give this to you?"

"N-no."

"Ross, honey." Janet touched her husband's arm. "Caitlin isn't wearing it. She's all right."

He glared. "All right? She's in the fucking hospital."

"But she's here. With us. She's safe."

Cait didn't feel particularly safe. Not with the cuts on her arms and legs still oozing blood and her father looking like thunder.

"She's safe *now*. Who gave this to you?" he asked Cait again.

She had never seen her steady father so upset. She'd never given him any reason to be upset. She was the girl who was home before midnight, who kept track of her drinks, her purse, and the car keys.

Cait could only imagine how her dad would react if he found out exactly what had happened out there in the woods. *Everything* that had happened.

"It was a gift from . . . from someone I met on the trail," she said.

"Male or female?"

"Male." She stuck out her chin. "His name is Rhys. Rhys Danuson."

Giving him his full name made their meeting seem more normal, more acceptable, as if Rhys were someone she could bring home to meet her parents instead of a trail hookup with a seriously scary mother and very bad karma.

But her father didn't appear reassured. "The *Queen's* Rhys?"

Cait's jaw dropped. "You know him?"

"Another lover?" Janet asked.

Ross shook his head. "Her son. By her favorite before me."

Cait's heart pushed into her throat. Rhys was the son of the fairy queen. The man she'd given her virginity to wasn't really a man at all.

And her father knew him. . . .

"When was this?" she demanded.

"A long time ago. Before you were born."

Cait struggled to do the math, but nothing added up. "So, Rhys was, what? Like, five?"

"When I first met him? Eight or nine. He was a young man when I left. The *sidhe* do not age the way we do," he added, forestalling her question.

Rhys's words burned in her brain. *I haven't seen my father since I was eight years old.*

"What about Rhys's father? Did you know him, too?"

"His father was . . . gone shortly before I got there."

Janet caught her breath.

Cait moistened her dry lips. "What do you mean, gone?"

"He died."

Unease formed an indigestible lump in Cait's gut. "So, he was . . . mortal?"

"Yes."

"Human?"

"Yes."

That was something, Cait thought. Wasn't it?

"What happened to him?" she asked.

"Does it matter?"

"Yes!"

Janet stirred in her chair. "Caity, honey . . ."

Her father still stared at the golden chain, his shoulders bent, his face drawn. Cait refused to feel sorry for him. She had to know. Rhys had sacrificed himself for her. She had to know why.

"Tell me," she begged.

Ross turned his back to the room and stared out the hospital window. "The children of the earth, the *sidhe*, are immortal. They are neutral in the war between heaven and hell that plays out in humankind. But their neutrality comes at a price."

Cait tightened her grip, clinging to the necklace like a lifeline. "What price?"

"Every seven years, they sacrifice a human soul to hell."

Sacrifice?

"How do you know?" Cait whispered.

Her father turned from the window, and hell was in his eyes. "Because I was almost one of them."

Cait felt her assumptions disintegrating like a sand castle caught in the tide. She had always looked to her parents for love, guidance, support . . . answers. Only her parents weren't the people she thought they were, and the answers she had relied on were making things worse.

And yet her father's responses made a horrible kind of sense.

Maybe there was someone else, Rhys had suggested.

I am the Queen. I will have payment of my debt.

"So, what happened to you?" Cait demanded. "Did you just get lucky or something?"

Janet made a choked sound of protest.

Ross dropped his hand to her shoulder. To comfort her? Or steady himself? "You could say so. Your mother saved me."

Cait looked at her safe, round, comfortable mother, with her sensible short hair and the crow's-feet at the corners of her eyes, and felt another assumption topple and slide away. "How?"

"I loved him." Janet reached up and squeezed her husband's hand. "I went to the fair folk on Midsummer's Eve and I . . . Well, after that, I wouldn't let go.

"Honey, we're so sorry," Janet said. "We never thought this would affect you."

Remembering their vigilance all through her childhood, Cait wondered if that were true. "Why didn't you *tell* me?"

Her mother gave her The Look, the one she used to hush noisy patrons in the library. "What could we have said? We didn't want to scare you. And we never dreamed the Queen would take revenge on us by sending her son after you."

"Did he hurt you?" Ross asked sharply.

The long scratches on Cait's thighs pulsed and burned. Her mind pulsed and burned. *Rhys licking the tears from the corners of her eyes, his cheek hot against her own, his voice whispering, "I'm sorry. I'm sorry. I hurt you."*

Her insides contracted.

"No," she said breathlessly. "No, he was—"

She recalled that moment by the fire when some unidentifiable emotion had flickered in his eyes. *You will take no hurt from—You will not get sick because of me.*

"He was very careful and—and kind," she said.

Janet's gaze was soft and penetrating. "Are you sure?"

Cait flushed, uncomfortable with what her mother might see. Or guess. "Yes."

"At least you're safe now," Ross said. "Thank God you escaped."

Janet leaned forward and patted her hand. "It's over."

Cait was safe, but she hadn't escaped, exactly. Rhys had saved her. And it was far from over.

Cait bit her lip, looking down. Her mother's hand rested on the hand that clutched the necklace. The links were warm against her palm.

This was one problem her parents couldn't fix for her.

She had to go back. To save him.

Her parents argued with her, of course, because they loved her and they were afraid. Her mother cried.

"You're not going," her father said adamantly. "You survived the last time. There's no guarantee you'll survive the next."

"You don't understand," Cait said.

"*I* understand. I was with the *sidhe* for fourteen years. They will destroy you, baby."

"Daddy, I have to try. Rhys sacrificed everything for me."

"Why would he do that?" Janet asked.

"Well, he . . ." Cait floundered. Confessing to her parents Rhys had been her first lover didn't seem like a good way to get her father on her side. "He felt sorry for me, I guess."

"Good for him," Ross said. "That doesn't mean you have to kill yourself for him."

"But I care about him."

"Any feelings you have for this . . . fairy, the Queen will use against you. You don't know what you're up against."

"So help me."

"No."

Cait cast desperately for an argument that would convince him. "You said you knew the *sidhe*. Maybe one of them could help."

Janet turned troubled eyes to Ross. "Do you think Puck might . . . ?"

"The minute she sets one foot off the trail, Puck will take her straight to the Queen."

"Who's Puck?" Cait asked.

Her parents ignored her.

Cait appealed to her mother, who could usually be counted on to see both sides of every argument. "I have to go."

"You can't," Janet said.

The Queen's words echoed in Cait's head. *There is more of your dam in you than I realized.*

"Why not?" Cait cried, exasperated and afraid. "You did."

"I *loved* your father. We were already lovers by then."

Cait opened her mouth. Shut it.

An uncomfortable silence filled the hospital room.

"You're not going." Ross exchanged a long look with his wife. "Nobody is going. And that's final."

They didn't know Rhys, Cait reasoned. They didn't care about him. They loved her, and they loved each other, and the fairness of one half-mortal's fate didn't even enter into their decision.

But Rhys had loved her, too.

Or at least, Cait thought, torn between hope and anguish, he had cared for her enough to sacrifice himself for her sake.

The debt he had taken on was her parents'; but the responsibility for his fate was hers.

Even if she hadn't exactly figured out what to do about it yet.

I went to the fair folk on Midsummer's Eve . . .

Cait let her parents bring her home. She gave herself time to heal. She made an appointment to have her stitches removed and endured four more rabies shots spaced over the next month. She called Jill to congratulate her roommate on her engagement and to beg off their rendezvous in Hot Springs. She even applied to the graduate program in Library Science at the University of North Carolina, Chapel Hill, to begin in the spring semester.

And on June twenty-first, Cait packed her bag for a campus visit, said good-bye to her parents, and walked off the trail south of Wayah Bald.

The sun slanted gold and green through the trees. The air was warm and still, with the stickiness of an approaching storm. Cait trampled the rioting wildflowers, trying not to think. She didn't look for the trail blazes. She wanted to get lost.

Under the shadow of a deep rhododendron, a little man waited on a fallen log like a lump of lichen, his clothes the color of fallen leaves and feathers in his hair.

Cait's steps dragged. Her heart rocketed to her throat. She coughed to clear it. "Puck?"

CHAPTER 7

The little man grinned, revealing pointy teeth. "Ay, Puck."

Cait raised her chin. "Or should I call you Goodfellow?"

"Puck or Hob or Robin Goodfellow, it's all the same to me." He hopped off the log. "Took you long enough to get here."

Cait tried very hard not to feel offended. "It's Midsummer's Eve. I thought that was the best time to find you."

"Unless I'm wanting to be found. You're nearly too late."

Her heartbeat quickened. "Too late for what?"

Puck shambled through the woods at surprising speed. "We'll have to move quickly."

Cait fell in beside him, her thoughts and her feet struggling to keep pace with his. "Are you taking me to—" *Hot breath, white fangs, flaming golden eyes.* The healed cuts on her arms and legs burned with remembered fire. The gold chain pulsed in her pocket.

Cait swallowed. "—to Rhys?"

Puck shook his head. "I wish I could. But he's wild now, and wary of the Queen."

Cait was feeling pretty damn wary herself.

"So are we going . . ." Her voice failed. She tried again. "Are you taking me to the Queen?"

"Horns and hooves! No."

She was a little reassured. But only a little. "Then where are we going?"

Puck stopped and shot her a curious look from the corners of his bright black eyes. "You mean, you don't know?"

"I don't know anything," Cait confessed. "I just wanted to find you."

The *sidhe* smiled—not his usual mocking, mischievous smile, but something warmer, almost affectionate. "And so you have. But if you did not know what you were seeking, how did you know where to look?"

"My father said . . ." *The minute she sets one foot off the trail, Puck will take her straight to the Queen.* "He seemed to think you would find me," Cait said carefully.

"Miles from where we met before." His tone made it a question.

"Yeah, well . . ." Cait puffed as she followed him up a rough slope littered with branches and dotted with pink and yellow flowers. "I looked at the map. Wayah Bald . . . Wayah means wolf in Cherokee. I figured that was, like, a good place to start."

"You are more clever than I thought," Puck said.

Cait flushed. She hadn't felt clever. More like "desperate" and "grasping at straws." Simply getting this far had tested her ingenuity and resolution, and the main task, whatever it was, still lay ahead. Approval, even approval from the Queen's stooge dwarf, was ridiculously encouraging.

"Thank you," she said.

"Are you also brave?"

She was scared to death.

"I'm here," she said as steadily as she could. "And I'm willing. Is that good enough?"

"It will have to be. Or your lover is lost."

Cold fingers traced down Cait's spine despite the oppressive heat and the sweat she was working up climbing the mountain. But she felt a spark of anger, too. "She's his mother! Hasn't she done enough? She's already cursed him. Does she have to kill him, too?"

"The Queen does not kill her young," Puck said matter-of-factly, in the tone he might have used to say, *The Queen does not eat her young*. "But she will not save him."

"Save him from what?"

"The Wild Hunt rides tonight. And their quarry is the Queen's son."

The Wild Hunt.

A memory caught Cait of Rhys's voice rising and falling in the firelight while the snow fell outside their shelter and he told her the story of the Wild Hunt, who harried the damned across the sky.

She stumbled. "What do you want me to do?"

"You must ride with them," Puck said. "You will never find young Rhys else, or keep up with the pursuit."

Her heart quailed with the impossibility of what he was asking.

"I'm not much of a horseback rider," she said.

Puck grinned, his teeth very pointy. "It's not a horse I'll be giving you to ride."

Like that made it any better.

"And then what?" she asked.

Puck was silent.

"What do I do then?"

He gave her another sidelong look. "Why, then you must do as your heart bids, for I've no better guidance to give you."

Daylight faded as the sun sank in a bloody welter of clouds. Cait's legs ached, her feet were swollen, and she had a stitch in her side. After six weeks off the trail, she was out of shape.

You're nearly too late.

She dragged herself up by gripping the trunk of a sapling. Puck scuttled ahead. At least concentrating on her sore feet and tired muscles as they climbed took her mind off what would happen when they got to the top.

She had always been stubborn. Like her father, her mother said.

She tried to be compassionate and fair-minded. Like her mother, her father said.

But pity or fairness or pure pigheadedness weren't all that drove her now.

It was the memory of Rhys's rigid shoulders and taut, white face as he confronted his mother for her sake. *Take me in payment. And let her go free.*

It was the way he said her name, standing in the waters of the pool, the silver reflection sliding lovingly over his upper body and his eyes molten gold. *Caitlin.*

Just her name in his dark, fluid voice.

Caitlin.

I'm coming, she told him, tears pricking her eyes, her breath sobbing as she climbed.

No. The answer came forcibly enough to make her slip. *It is too dangerous. You don't know what you're doing.*

Cait took a deep breath to steady herself. *It's okay,* she

thought back tentatively, although it wasn't, really, and if she was hearing voices in her head she probably had lost her mind. *Puck is helping me.*

No answer.

Cait crested the hill, trying not to feel bereft. At least she wasn't crazy.

But as they emerged from the tunnel of dark-leaved rhododendron, Rhys's voice brushed her mind like the wings of a moth in the dark. *He is the Queen's servant. He is not to be trusted . . .*

Puck rubbed his hands together. "Here we go."

Cait felt like a bug, trapped between the lowering bowl of the sky and the mountains stretching in every direction. She shivered in the wind from the western peaks. A storm was building, piling the clouds with a massive hand along the horizon. High, high above, the sky broke through, the moon a flat, pale disk against the deepening blue. But the clouds were gray, and as they rolled forward, darkness covered the hills.

"And here is your ride," Puck said, as if he were announcing her date for the prom.

Stones clattered, and a black, shaggy pony trotted out from among the black, rounded rocks. Its fat sides were as solid as the hills and its mane was long and tangled.

Cait regarded it with misgiving.

The pony rolled its yellow eyes back at her, exposing long, yellow teeth in a grin like Puck's.

"Is it . . . safe?" she asked.

Puck shrugged. "It is the Pooka. It is not safe, but it is fast. The Hunt will ride along the ridge lines and harry the woods until they find the wolf. You must be with the leaders at the end, or they will tear him to pieces before you can stop them."

"Why are you doing this? Why are you helping me?"

Puck hesitated. "The *sidhe* do not take sides. It is not our nature. But I called your father my friend once. And the child Rhys . . . I had the minding of him often enough. He was a solemn baby." His smile flashed, and this time Cait did not recoil. "Mayhap you will make him happier."

The wind blew. The clouds boiled up. The Pooka stamped its hooves, striking sparks from the rocks. Above the mountains, heat lightning played. The rumble chased it across the sky.

"It will be soon now," Puck said. "Mount."

Cait scrambled awkwardly on the Pooka's broad back as a man strode out from the trees, a horn at his side and hounds at his feet.

She blinked and almost lost her balance. Not a man. Seven feet tall, he was antlered like a stag and all gold: gold skin, gold hair, gold horns, gold . . . eyes.

Rhys's eyes, in the gold man's face.

Her breath left her.

"Who is that?" she whispered, trying to keep her teeth from chattering, desperate not to attract the horned man's attention.

Puck looked surprised by her ignorance. "The Hunter King."

Okay. If there was a queen, it made sense there would be a king. But what freak of fairy jealousy or politics would drive him to hunt the Queen's half-human, bastard son?

The hounds milled around the horned king's legs, lifting their heads to the wind. They weren't truly dogs any more than their master was really a man. Their long legs were oddly jointed, and their lolling tongues were the color of flame.

Cait shivered and averted her gaze to the hunter, solitary under the darkening sky. "He looks . . . familiar."

"Ay, he would. He is Rhys's sire."

Her heart, which had been pounding in her chest, lurched into her throat. "But . . . Rhys's father was human."

"He was once. No longer."

The Pooka snickered, tossing its head in the rising wind. Cait gripped a handful of raggedy mane.

The storm was almost upon them, roaring and tearing through the trees. Lightning forked over the hills. The Hunter King raised his horn to his lips and blew one long note that rolled like thunder.

"Be ready for it!" Puck shouted.

Ready for what? Cait thought, but before she could get the words out of her mouth, the clouds stooped, and the Wild Hunt descended like a flock of geese invading a pond, the powerful rush of their passing like the beat of a thousand wings, blinding, deafening. Their clamor filled the sky.

She stared in disbelief as the king strode into the heart of the storm, his hounds surging forward. The wind swept them up and hurtled them into the sky.

The Pooka bunched its great round hindquarters like a cat pouncing on a mouse and bounded into the wind. Cait yelped and tightened her clutch. She had no saddle, stirrups, bridle, or reins. Twisting her fingers in the Pooka's black mane, she clamped her thighs to its barrel sides and hung on for dear life.

The wind howled. Cait was blinded, buffeted by the rain and the hair—hers, the Pooka's—whipping into her eyes. But through the streaking rain and mane, she glimpsed other things riding the storm beside them. Lightning flickered off helms and skulls, glittered in eyes and spear points. She gasped and turned her face into the Pooka's warm neck.

Between earth and sky they swooped and lurched, following the path of the peaks, touching down on the mountain balds where no trees grow. She knew them from her maps:

Wayah Bald to Copper Ridge, Rocky Bald to Grassy Gap. Some crests were overgrown with shrubs, some cleared, but it made no difference to the riders. In and out of the sky, they coursed, sizzling down on grassy flats or churning over the tops of the bushes, scorching the earth with lightning.

If she fell, she would die.

She leaned flat over the Pooka's bunched neck, her fingers tangled in the coarse mane by its ears. Her arms and legs burned. Her hands were numb and throbbing, as if she were back in gym class, twisting above the basketball court, trying desperately not to slide down the climbing rope.

Lightning cracked. The Hunter King, glowing gold, strode like a giant among the peaks. He sounded another long note on his horn, and the hunt brayed and whooped and roared and cackled in response.

She could not see their quarry. She could barely see the ground. But she felt the hunt's fierce satisfaction swirl and swell, like foxhunters in England who claimed to love the joy of the chase, not the thrill of the kill.

Which was fine, Cait thought, from the perspective of the hunters, but it didn't change the fate of the poor fox. Panting. Exhausted. Torn to pieces.

You must be with the leaders at the end, or they will tear him to pieces before you can stop them, Puck had said.

You're nearly too late.

Please, she thought, and *No,* and *Rhys!*

Squeezing her legs on the Pooka's sides, she hunched over its neck, scanning the ground.

There, a darting movement at the edge of the trees . . .

There, a lean shadow against the darker shadow of the rocks . . .

Flattening itself under trees and scrub, zigzagging through weeds and across open spaces, driven from whatever refuge it had sought by the marauding hunt, ran the wolf who had been Rhys.

Cait's heart stopped.

Cornered against a cliff face, ringed by fallen rock, there, at last, the wolf turned at bay as the Hunt tumbled out of the sky.

CHAPTER 8

Too late, too late, too late . . .

Cait braced as the Pooka hit the ground in the midst of the swarming hunt, its flat black hooves sliding and scattering rocks. The shock of their landing jarred Cait's bones and loosened her grip and snapped her teeth together. She fell off, over its shoulder, under its hooves.

The Pooka stepped delicately around her and away with a whicker of horsy laughter. *Bastard.*

Cait lay on the hard ground, struggling to breathe, too stunned to move. And maybe her precipitous arrival had stunned the hunt, too, because they didn't seem to be moving, either.

The wolf howled, a rising minor note that hung on the damp night air and shook her heart.

Rain streaked down. It plastered her hair to her head and her clothes to her body and ran into her eyes. But the cold water in her face revived her.

She pushed to her elbows and then to her knees. She lurched to her feet, using the rocks for support.

The wolf had slipped around her, facing the hunt. Its head lowered. Its hackles raised. The hair stood up all along its back. The white hounds circled just beyond reach, snarling and darting in short, snapping forays. Dwarfed and surrounded, the wolf lowered its head, growling deep in its chest.

Cait clenched her hands, her nails biting into her palms. Why didn't it seek the protection of the cliffs at its back?

And then she realized.

It—he—*Rhys* was defending her.

Protecting *her*.

Still.

The rain abated. Beyond the eager, snarling hounds, the Wild Hunt pressed in silently. The fuzzy moonlight reflected in the gleam of harness, the glitter of eyes. The hunter raised his horn to rally his hounds to attack.

And Cait stepped forward and stood beside the wolf.

The Wild Hunt groaned and swayed like trees in the wind.

She reached down blindly, seeking comfort from the thick fur beneath her fingers. The wolf's lean body vibrated with rage and fear. Or maybe that was her trembling. Her knees felt like rubber bands.

The hunter turned his antlered head to regard her with his golden gaze, and she trembled even more. There were no whites to his eyes, and his pupils were long and narrow like a goat's.

"Step aside, girl." His voice was deep and rusty with disuse. "This is none of yours."

She was stubborn. She had always been stubborn. And maybe stubborn was as good as brave. Cait stuck out her chin. "Yeah? Well, he's not yours, either."

A creaky, hollow sound escaped the hunter's mouth, like

the opening of an empty chest in an abandoned house. With a shock, Cait recognized he was laughing.

"His dam claimed otherwise," he said.

The breeze died. The Hunt stirred and fell still. Cait glanced beyond their glinting spear points and ghostly banners and saw the Queen, stiff in her red dress, shining with her own faint silver light, watching them.

Shit.

"He doesn't belong to either of you." Cait shoved her clenched hands in her pockets, feeling the brush of warm metal across her knuckles, feeling the wolf beside her, tense as a coiled spring. "Not anymore. He's mine."

The hounds whined eagerly as the hunter considered them both with his awful, golden eyes. "He does not bear your mark," he said at last.

Clumsy with hope, Cait fumbled the necklace from her pocket. The links blazed briefly in the moonlight. She knelt and fastened the chain around the wolf's hairy throat, ignoring the leap of her pulse at the hot breath on her cheek, the white fangs so close to her face.

Panting a little with fear and triumph, she dropped her arms from around the wolf and turned to confront the Hunter King. "He does now."

The Wild Hunt sighed. The Queen cried out, in shock or protest.

And warm, hard arms came around Cait from behind and pulled her back against a lean, muscled chest.

"Dear heart," Rhys's shaken voice said in her ear. "What have you done?"

Joy rose in a wave, flooding her heart, choking her throat. "I, um, bound you." She turned in the circle of his embrace, gazing up anxiously into his eyes. "It's a binding chain, right? So they can't have you. You're mine."

"Much good may he do you when he is dead," said the Hunter King.

But Cait wasn't giving up. Not with Rhys transformed and back in her arms. "If you want him, you'll have to go through me," she said fiercely.

Rhys touched her cheek, turning her face to his. "You are not much of a barrier, dear heart," he said, still somewhat unsteadily, but with that undernote of laughter she had heard and loved at their first meeting.

"You make a poor challenge." The Queen's cold, silver voice fell like moonlight in the rocky clearing. "And a worse bargain. Use your head, girl. Why should both of you die?"

Cait stiffened. All her life she had been the good girl who made smart choices, who listened to her head instead of following her heart. Until now. Until Rhys.

Do as your heart bids, Puck had urged.

Well, she'd tried. Hadn't she tried? She'd faced down the Queen and the King and the hounds, she'd ridden the damn Pooka through the storm. She had figured out the riddle of the necklace and turned Rhys back into a man.

And it was all for nothing.

They were going to die anyway.

What could she do against the spears and swords, the tearing claws and trampling hooves of the Wild Hunt? Throw rocks?

She looked at Rhys, despair rising in the back of her throat, and swallowed hard.

The smile in her lover's eyes faded like the last promise of daylight. "She is right," he whispered. He stroked her hair and cupped her face in his hands. "Don't let my sacrifice be for nothing. Save yourself. Go home. Grow old. Remember me."

He kissed her then, so tenderly her heart quivered and her eyes filled with tears.

It *wasn't* right. It wasn't *fair*.

She blinked fiercely. "Screw this. He can't have you."

"You can't stop him," Rhys said, so reasonably she wanted to punch something. "And if you anger him, you'll lose your own chance to go free." He released her. "Go now, dear heart. Go quickly."

"You." Cait turned on the Hunter King, her heart burning in her chest. "You gave up everything for love once. For the Queen."

"Caitlin . . ." Rhys warned.

She shook her elbow free of his grasp. "I'm not *finished*."

The Hunter King's handsome, inhuman face was devoid of mercy or understanding. But he hadn't killed her yet, so she kept talking, praying for him to listen, willing him to hear.

"You let yourself be sacrificed because she didn't love you. Well, Rhys let himself be sacrificed, too. He knew when she turned him into a wolf that he could be killed, that he could die. So, okay, he's not immortal anymore. He's got to die eventually. But he doesn't have to die tonight. He doesn't have to die at your hand. He could still have a long life." Cait caught her breath. "With me."

"Better for him if he died," the Queen said.

She swept forward in her red dress, and the Wild Hunt wavered and drew back from her like shadows from a flame. The King's hounds whined. "Would you condemn our son to long years on this shadow earth, to crawl in pain and sickness to slow death? Better to end it now."

Rhys's face was white in the moonlight.

She was losing him, Cait thought in desperation. She was losing.

"Please," she said to the Hunter King. "You were alive once. You were in love once. Please. Let him go."

The hunter turned his proud, antlered head toward his son. "Is that your will? To live with this mortal woman and then to die?"

"Yes," Rhys said. "If she'll have me."

"So be it."

"No!" The Queen's voice rang like a trumpet. "I will have what is mine."

The horned king's eyes blazed. "He is yours no longer. You gave him to me when you summoned the Hunt. And I release him."

Cait turned and grabbed Rhys. "Are you sure?"

He smiled crookedly. "That I love you? Yes. That you'll have me? Not at all."

She flung her arms around him. "Of course I'll have you."

He held her close, pressing his lips to her hair. Her pulse sang in her ears, but she could still hear the strong beat of his heart. A fresh wind blew through the clearing; and when she opened her eyes, the night was clear and bright, and the clouds were streaking away toward the horizon like horsemen chasing the dawn.

"But I nearly betrayed you," Rhys said.

"When the Queen wanted you to bind me," Cait guessed.

"Even before then." His mouth set in a straight line. "Ursus would not have attacked you except to drive you to me."

"Oh. Well." Cait exhaled. "That was bad. But it wasn't like you knew me then."

His eyebrows raised. "Are you always this forgiving?"

"No," she admitted cheerfully. "But it's only fair to tell you if you plan to seduce me again, I intend to forgive you."

He smiled at her in the moonlight, his eyes hot and the curve of his mouth tender. "I am happy to hear it."

They kissed, and her love for him shook her heart and warmed her down to her toes. The kiss deepened, with tongues and teeth, before Cait remembered their audience and broke away with a gasp. But when she glanced around the clearing, all trace of the fair folk had drifted away with the breeze. They were alone.

In the mountains.

In the dark.

She sighed as the real world impinged on her fairy tale. "I don't suppose you can summon a little *sidhe* magic to get us to a shelter for the night."

"I can do better than that," Rhys said.

"Really," she said skeptically.

He nodded. "Look around. Do you recognize this place?"

She surveyed the circle of trees and rocks, the tall cliff face and the overhang behind them. "Not really."

"It looks different without the snow."

She gaped as the meaning of his words sank in. The cliff? Okay. And the overhang. The firepit and a narrow fissure in the rock and . . . Was that his abandoned camping gear, concealed in the shelter of the rock? "But that was miles from here!"

"There are—you might call them shortcuts—in the *sidhe* world," he said. "You traveled farther than you know that night."

"Wow." She watched as he stooped under the shelf in the rock and dragged his sleeping bag into the moonlight. "So are we going to be able to get home the same way?"

"No, I am fully mortal now."

She had to know. "Do you regret it?"

He looked up from building a fire. "Regret that I can live with you and make a life with you? That I can have children and a family? No. I love you, Caitlin."

She moistened her lips. "Would you say that if you weren't wearing that necklace?"

He grinned and straightened from his position by the fire. Reaching behind his neck, he unfastened the chain.

"I love you, Caitlin," he said, holding her gaze. "And as for this . . ." He spilled the golden links in her hand. "You can make it into rings or save it for our children. I don't care."

He kissed her then and drew her down on the sleeping bag spread by the fire. While the moon climbed in the sky and the forest sang around them, he held her and stroked her and loved her. He took her, took everything she had to give and gave everything of himself in return.

Cait accepted the powerful surge of his body on her and in her and tightened her arms and legs around him, feeling her world alter and align with the two of them at its center.

It was magic.

No, Cait thought afterward, lying with her head on his hard, damp chest. It was love.

She smiled.

Rhys stroked her hair back from her forehead. "What are you thinking?"

"I'm thinking we better not invite your mother to the wedding."

His laughter shook the shadows in the rocks and made the fire dance in delight. The moon sailed full-bellied over the crests of the clouds, and the mountains dreamed.

Author's Note

Dear Reader,

How Caitlin's mother, Janet, won Ross MacLean from the clutches of the Fairy Queen can be found in an earlier novella, "Midsummer Night's Magic," in the anthology Man of My Dreams (Jove, 2004). That story—along with the myth of Eros and Psyche—inspired this one. I hope you enjoy them both!

—Virginia Kantra

DRIFTWOOD

○

MaryJanice Davidson

ↄ

This story is, yawningly,
for Cindy Hwang, again, who asked me,
and Ethan Ellenberg, again, who made it happen,
and my kids, who stayed out of the way, mostly.

ↄ

Acknowledgments

Stories may pop full-blown into a writer's head, but there's a helluva lot more to making a book than that, or me, the author. There's the editor, who calls you up and asks if you want the project. There's the agent, who wades through the eight-point-font paperwork and looks out for you and points out what's good and what's not so good and why you can't write that story for this guy, but you could write the *other* story for this guy. There are the copyeditors (who think I'm not the sharpest knife in the drawer) and proofers (who think same, and are right) and PR staff (I don't know what they think), the sales guys and gals (ditto), the book sellers (they seem fond of me!), and finally, the readers (it's a toss-up). Pull any one of those people out of the equation and . . . no book. Worse, no royalties!

So thanks, thanks, thanks to the unsung heroes of publishing. Since my name is on the front cover, I get most of the attention and the credit, and the blame if something goes wrong, which is only fair, because it's always my mistake in the first place. But, as above, without the whole gang, there's no book, typos and all.

What would I do without all of you?

Author's Note

This story takes place after the events in Derik's Bane *and* Undead and Unpopular. *Also, in the real world, in our world, there are no such things as werewolves, but about vampires, I'm reserving judgment.*

Also, the opinions ("I hate kids.") of the characters in this story do not necessarily reflect the opinions of the author, the editor, Berkley Sensation, or Penguin Putnam.

Finally, you are required to let the air out of your tires before driving out on a Cape Cod beach, and the people who don't do that? Deserve whatever happens to their tires.

Who does the wolf love?
—Shakespeare, *Coriolanus*, Act II, Scene I

C

*He is mad that trusts in the tameness of a wolf, a
horse's health, a boy's love, or a whore's oath.*
—Shakespeare, *King Lear*, Act III, Scene VI

C

A lawful kiss is never worth a stolen one.
—Maupassant

C

Don't mess with the dead, boy, they have eerie powers.
—Homer Simpson

CHAPTER 1

Burke Wolftauer, the Clam Cop, dusted his hands on his cutoffs and observed the black SUV tearing out onto Chapin Beach at low tide. Crammed with half-naked sweaty semi-inebriated humans, the Lexus roared down the beach, narrowly missing a gamboling golden retriever. It roared to a halt in a spume of sand and mud, and all four doors popped open to let a spill of drunken humanity onto the (previously) calm beach.

All of which meant nothing to him, because the full moon was only half an hour away.

Burke dug up one more clam for supper, popped it open with his fingernails, and slurped it down while watching the monkeys. Okay—not nice. Not politically correct. Boss Man wouldn't approve (though Boss Lady probably wouldn't care). But never did they look closer to their evolutionary cousins than when they'd been drinking. *Homo sapiens blotto*. They were practically scratching their armpits and picking nits out of their fur. A six-pack of Bud and a thermos of Cosmos and suddenly they were all miming sex and drink like Koko the monkey.

All of which meant nothing to him, because the full moon was only half an hour away.

Now look: not a one of them of drinking age, and not a one of them sober. Parked too far up the beach for this time of the day, and of course they hadn't let any air out of their tires. They'd been on the beach thirty seconds and Burke counted an arrestable offense, two fines, and a speeding ticket.

He licked the brine from both halves of the clam shell, savoring the salty taste, "the sea made flesh," as Pat Conroy had once written. Clever fellow, that Conroy. Good sense of humor. Probably fun to hang out with. Probably not too ape-like when he knocked a few back. Guy could probably cook like a son of a bitch, too.

Burke popped the now-empty clam in his mouth and crunched up the shell. Calcium: good for his bones. And at his age (a doddering thirty-eight) he needed all the help he could get.

Then he stood, brushed the sand off his shorts, and sauntered over to the now-abandoned Lexus. He could see the teens running ahead, horsing around and tickling and squealing. And none of them looked back, of course.

He dropped to one knee by the left rear wheel, bristling with disapproval at the sight of the plump tires—tires that would tear up the beach in no time at all. He leaned forward and took a chomp. There was a soft *fffwwaaaaaaaahhhh* as the tire instantly deflated and the SUV leaned over on the left side. Burke chewed thoughtfully. *Mmmm . . . Michelins . . .*

He did the same to the other three, unworried about witnesses—this time of year and day, the beach was nearly deserted, and besides, who'd expect him to do what he just did?

He walked back up the beach to retrieve his bucket and rake, using an old razor clamshell to pick the rubber out of his teeth. He belched against the back of his hand and reminded himself he wasn't a kid anymore—he was looking at half a night of indigestion.

Worth it. Yup.

CHAPTER 2

Serena Crull heard someone come close to her hole and went still and silent as . . . well, the grave.

This was an improvement over what she had said twelve hours earlier, upon tumbling ass over forehead into the eighteen-foot-deep pit: "Son of a biiiiiiiiiiiiiiii . . . ooommpph!"

This had been followed by: "Shit!"

And: "Son of a bitch!"

And: "Ow."

Which had been followed by roughly twelve hours of sulking silence. She had tried climbing out: no good. She'd just pulled more slippery sand down onto herself. She hadn't bothered to try jumping: she wasn't a damned frog. She'd once jumped down, but it was only a story or so and, frankly, it had hurt like hell. Not to mention she hadn't stuck the landing. Jumping up? Maybe in another fifty years.

Then the sun had come up, and she'd *really* been

screwed. She scuttled into a corner (or whatever you call the edge of a hole that gives shelter), pulled some sand over herself, and waited for the killing sun to fall into the ocean one more time. What she would do after that, she had no idea.

And she was starving.

She was dying and she was *starving*.

Okay: She was *dead* and she was starving.

From above: "Hey."

She said nothing.

"Hey. Down there." Pause. "In the hole."

She couldn't resist, could not physically prevent her jaw from opening and the nagging voice from bursting forth, it was just so exquisitely *stupid*, that question: "What, down the hole? Where else would I be? Dumb shit."

Longer pause. "I'll, uh, get help."

"Don't do that. I'll be fine."

"Someone'll have some rope in their truck."

"Why don't you have rope in your truck?" she couldn't resist asking.

"Don't need it."

It was amazing: the man (nice voice—deep, calm, almost bored) sounded as indifferent as a . . . a—she couldn't think of what.

"I don't, either."

"Don't either what?"

Nice voice: not too bright. "Don't need a rope. I do not need a rope. No rope!" No, indeed! A rescue right now would be disastrous. She could picture it with awful clarity: heave and heave, and here she is, thank goodness she's safe, and what the hell? She's on—She's on *fire*!

As her hero, Homer Simpson, would have said: "D'oh!"

"How did you even fall in there?" her would-be rescuer was asking. "It's impossible for there to be a deep hole on the beach. The sand would fill it up."

"I'm not a marine biologist, okay?" she snapped.

"Geologist," he suggested. "You're not a geologist."

It was amazing: she'd spent the day alone, in hours of silence, terrified of the sunlight, hoping she wouldn't face an ugly death, and now she wanted her rescuer to get the hell lost.

"Get the hell lost."

Pause. "Did you hit your head on the way down?"

"On *what*?"

"You seem," he added, "kind of unpleasant."

"I'm in a *hole*."

"Well. I can't just leave you there."

"Oh, sure you can," she encouraged. "Just . . . keep going to wherever you were going."

"I didn't really have anywhere to go."

"Oh, boo friggin' hoo. Is this the part where I go all dewy between my legs and talk about how I'm secretly lonely, too, and how it was meant to be, me falling on my ass and you hauling me out? And then we Do It?"

"Did someone push you down there?"

"Shut up and go away. I'll be fine."

"Maybe the fire department?" he mused aloud.

"No. No. No no no no no no."

"Well. You can't exactly stop me."

She gasped. "You wouldn't *dare*."

"Even if you are crazy. I can't just not help you."

"Go away, Boy Scout."

"It's just that I can't hang around too much longer."

"Great. Fine. Have a good time, wherever you're going. See ya."

"I have this thing."

"Okeydokey!" she said brightly, her inner Minnesotan coming out, which was an improvement over her inner cannibal, which wanted to choke and eat this mystery man, claw strips of flesh from his bones and strangle him with them, then poke a hole in his jugular and drink him down like a blue raspberry Slushee Pup. "Bye-bye then!"

"But I could maybe keep you company until it's time to . . . for me to go." Another pause, then, in a lower voice: "Although that might not work either."

"Aw, no," she almost groaned. "You're going to talk down my hole, then go away?"

"Yeah, you're right. That won't work."

"For more reasons than you can figure, Boy Scout."

"I don't have a cell phone, is the thing."

"Me neither. Aw, that's so sweet, look how much we have in common; too bad we're not having sex right this second."

Pause. "You keep bringing up sex."

"Yeah, well. It's been a long fargin' day."

"Fargin'?"

"Shut up, Boy Scout."

"It's just that you don't have to worry."

"That's a humungous load off my mind, Boy Scout."

"Because the thing is, I can't . . . you don't have . . . it's that I'm not attracted to you at all."

She clutched her head. "This. Is. Not. Happening."

"I don't mean to hurt your feelings."

Insanely, he had. "Hey up there! For all you know, I'm an anorexic blonde with huge tits, skin the color of milk, and a case of raging nymphomania."

Another of those maddening pauses. "Anyway, that's not really the problem. The problem—"

"Bud. I so don't need you to tell me what the problem is. Please get lost."

She heard a sudden intake of breath, as if he'd come to a quick, difficult decision, and then there was a *whoosh* and a *thud*, and he was standing next to her.

CHAPTER 3

*F*ive minutes later she was still screaming at him. *Right* at him. The hole was only about three feet in diameter. They were chest to chest. And she was loud. Really loud.

". . . left your *brains* up there, Boy Scout, not that you ever were that *heavy* in the smarts department in the *first* place!"

"It just seemed like a good idea, is all."

"Seemed like a good idea?"

"Wow. You're really loud. While you're yelling, I'll make a step, and throw you out."

"You'll make a what and what me what?"

"Make a step with my hands. Like this." He bent forward to show her, and they promptly bonked skulls.

"Ow!"

He could feel himself get red. "Sorry." And red wasn't the only thing he was getting. What had he been thinking? She was right: he'd left his brains up there with the seagull shit.

"This was your solution?" she scolded, rubbing her forehead. "No cell phone, no rope, and now we're *both* down here?"

"It's really small down here," he said, trying not to sound tense. "It didn't look that small from up top."

"It's a hole, Boy Scout. Not a cavernous underground lair."

He scratched his arm, and when his elbow knocked against the side of the hole, sand showered down, which made him itch more.

"Can you breathe okay?" He tried not to gasp. "Is there enough air down here? I don't think there's enough air down here."

"Oh boy oh boy. I am not believing this. You actually took a terrible situation, made it worse, then made it *more* worse. Are you all right?"

"It's just that there's no air down here." He clutched his head. "None at all."

"You're claustrophobic and you jumped down into a hole?"

He groaned. "Don't talk about it."

"But why, Boy Scout?"

"Couldn't just leave you here. But you're not really here." He sniffed hard. Her hair was a perfect cap of dark curls (he thought; there wasn't much light down here) and under normal circumstances he would find that extremely cute. He sniffed her head again. "I don't think you're here at all."

"Boy Scout, you have lost what little tiny cracker brains you had to begin with." She managed to fold her arms over her chest and (he thought) glare at him. "If this is some elaborate ploy to impress me in order to get laid—"

"I can't have sex with you. You're not here." He gasped again. "I can't breathe. How can you breathe?"

"Well, apparently I'm not here," she said dryly. "And don't get me started on why the whole oxygen thing isn't a problem for me. I— What are you doing?"

He stumbled around and was scrabbling at the sandy walls, digging for purchase and doing nothing but pulling a shower of sand down on them both.

"Boy Scout, get a grip!" She coughed and spat a few grains of sand at his back. "You're just making it worse!"

She was yammering at his back and he didn't hear, couldn't hear, sand was everywhere, in his mouth, in his ears, in his eyes, and it was so close, it wasn't a hole, it was a grave and it was filling up, filling up with him in it.

He clawed at the wall, pulled, yanked, scrabbled, tried to climb, and he could hear the woman yelling, screaming, feel her blows on his shoulders and they were as heavy as flies landing.

Then the moon was there. The moon came for him in the grave and took him out, took him up and out, and he was able to gouge himself out of the grave with two ungainly leaps and then he was screaming, screaming at the moon, howling at the moon, and she wasn't screaming anymore, the grave was full and she was quiet, at last she was quiet and he ran, ran, ran with the moon and his last thought as a man was, "What have I done?"

CHAPTER 4

"It's around here," Burke said, so ashamed he couldn't look up from the sand.

"Around here?" Jeannie Wyndham, his pack's female Alpha, poked at the small dunes with a sneakered toe. "That's pretty vague for a guy with a nose like yours. Is this the spot or isn't it?"

"I . . . think it is. It's hard to tell. I can't smell her at all. I can just smell me. And I'm all over the place. After I got out of the gra—hole, I just ran."

Michael, his pack leader, was crouched and balanced on the balls of his feet as his yellow gaze swept the area. He said nothing, for which Burke was profoundly grateful. He couldn't have borne a scolding, as much as he deserved one.

"Burke, give us a break," Jeannie said, sounding (no surprise at all) exasperated. "You stumbled across a woman who needed help—"

"And I left her to die."

"—and you did what you could. You guys are— Every werewolf I've ever *met* is such a screaming claustrophobe you should all be on tranqs, but you jumped into a hole to try to save her before you Changed. She didn't have a chance in hell anyway."

Burke could think of several chances the poor dead woman might have had, but it wasn't prudent to correct Jeannie, so he stayed silent.

"There, I think," Michael said. There was a deep depression in the sand, a jumble of footprints—and wolf tracks, leading away. "You're right, Burke. I can smell you all over the sand, and a few other people—tourists who just came out for the day, people just passing by—and that's it. Certainly there's no scent of a woman who'd been trapped in the bottom of a hole for over twenty hours."

"Well, if you can't smell her, and Burke can't smell her . . ." Jeannie trailed off, then mumbled, "He needs a girlfriend."

"I'm not making it up."

"Of course not," Michael said with a hard look at his wife. She stuck her tongue out at him, and he continued. "But there have been, ah, concerns. You've lived alone most of your life. No one sees you. The only time any of us see you is if I summon you—God knows I don't do that unless it's a real emergency, or to meet a new baby—"

Burke didn't say anything, but he knew where Michael was going. Werewolves were *not* solitary creatures. They were designed to mate young and drop lots of pups. Rogues—even gentle ones—made everyone nervous. Now they thought that the stress of never having children had driven him over the edge. If he hadn't been so miserably ashamed, he would have laughed.

"At least yesterday was the last night of the full moon," Jeannie said, shading her eyes as she watched the sun dip into the ocean. "Or there'd be no talking to either of you in another five minutes."

"I came back to the mansion as soon as I could," Burke explained. "When I woke up this morning, I was in Vermont." No surprise. He had run and run and run, but had never managed to leave his shame and guilt and horror behind.

"Well, no one's around. Why don't we do a little digging and see what, uh, comes up?" Jeannie asked with *faux* brightness.

Burke knew, as did Michael, that despite the deepening gloom there *were* people around, but no one was close. And in any case, digging holes in the beach wasn't exactly suspicious behavior. Hell, people paid money for clamming licenses *just* to dig at the beach.

He dropped to all fours and began to scoop out great handfuls of sand with his hands, ignoring the shovels Jeannie had brought.

"Cheer up," Jeannie said, shifting her weight uncomfortably from foot to foot. "There probably isn't anybody— I mean, we might not find anything."

"And if we do find anything, it wasn't your fault."

"Excuse me," Burke said politely, "but it was *entirely* my fault. I appreciate you coming out here with me."

"Like we're going to let you dig around in the dark by yourself, thinking you'll stumble across a corpse? Yuck, Burke! Besides, the whole thing's a joke. You're only the nicest, gentlest, quietest werewolf out there. You'd no more kill a woman than I'd break Lara's arm."

"Not that she couldn't use that sort of thing," Michael said shortly; he was saving his breath for digging.

Burke grunted and kept digging. He knew Lara, a charming creature and the future pack leader, and frankly, he wondered how Jeannie had *kept* from breaking the high-spirited girl's arm. The cub wasn't even in her teens yet, and some of her exploits were already legendary, like the time she jumped off the roof of the mansion and used her quilt as a parachute; except it hadn't worked out quite the way she planned and she'd come down like a stone, breaking one ankle and scaring the holy old shit out of her parents.

Heh. That had been a day.

"How long—are we—going to dig—before we decide— Burke isn't a killer?" Jeannie panted.

"Until we find the—" Burke froze, reached deeper, and felt his fingers closing around . . . a forearm. He leaned back and pulled, tears stinging his eyes from the sand. Yeah, the sand and the thought of that poor woman dying alone, dying in the dark, dying as the sand filled her nose and lungs and finally stopped her heart.

Dying alone.

"Oh my God!" Jeannie screamed in a whisper as he stood, pulling the body free from the sand until it was dangling from his strong grip like a puppet whose strings had been cut. "Burke! Oh my God!"

"You— I guess we'd better try to find her family," Michael said, recovering quickly, which was why he was the boss and Burke was the Clam Cop. "If we can't, we'll give her a proper—"

"Oh no you *don't!*" the body snapped, swinging in the air and kicking Burke in the shin. "You didn't dig me up just to plop me into another grave. And *you*," she snarled, as sand showered from her hair, her face, fell from her shoulders and her clothes and fangs—*fangs?*—and hit the beach. "I'm starving and it's all—your—fault!" So saying, she lunged forward, fastened to Burke's shoulders like a lamprey, and sank her teeth into the side of his neck.

CHAPTER 5

It took the combined strength of Jeannie and Michael, plus a lot of tugging and yelling and threatening, before the dead woman was pulled off. Everyone was scratched and bleeding before it was over.

"Don't talk to me," the dead woman said, wiping the blood off her chin and backing away from them. "Don't talk to me, don't look at me, don't bury me."

"But . . . you . . ." Jeannie groped for the words and ended up waving her arms in the air like a cheerleader who'd forgotten her routine. "You can't . . . you . . ."

Michael cleared his throat. "Ma'am, you're dead. You have no scent, you have no pulse. You, uh, should lie down and be dead."

"Aw, shut the hell up." She whirled and pointed a dirty finger at Burke, who had been trying to figure out if he was terrified or relieved. "And you! The number of your gross offenses against me grows by the hour! The *half* hour! Now leave. Me. Alone!"

She whirled and stomped away, her fists clenching as she heard all three of them hurry after her.

She turned back. "Leave. Me. Alone. Any of that unclear? Any of you not speak such good English?"

"I get it!" Jeannie cried with the hysterical good humor of a *Jeopardy!* contestant. "You're a vampire!"

"No, she isn't," Burke and Michael said in unison.

The body stomped her foot, and all three of them took a step back. "Of course I'm a vampire, morons! What else would I be? A Sasquatch? Nessie?"

"There are no such thing as vampires," Michael said gently. "I think you must have gone into shock when you were buried and that protected you until we could rescue you—"

"*Rescue* me?"

"And the whole thing has been too much for your system and now you think—"

"Oh, what crap. I don't need to breathe, *ergo*, I didn't suffocate, and I couldn't get out of the hole during the day. *Ergo*, I wasn't buried alive. Are you honestly telling me that werewolves don't believe in vampires?"

"The existence of one doesn't prove the other," Michael said stiffly. "I believe in witches, but that doesn't mean I believe in leprechauns."

"How'd you know they were werewolves?" Jeannie asked, examining the scratch on her left elbow.

"Because Boy Scout lost all his little tiny marbles, went into a screaming fit worthy of a Beatles fan, turned into a wolf, and jumped out of a twelve-foot hole. Call me crazy."

"Crazy," Jeannie said brightly.

Burke touched the bite mark on his neck, which was already scabbing over. It would explain a lot: her relative calm at being in such a fix, her utter lack of scent, and, of course, her walking and talking after being buried alive for more than twenty-four hours.

All his life, he had been told legends of wolves and fairies and water witches, and a grizzled beta had once claimed to have seen a demon, but never had he heard of a vampire, or even seen one.

Until, obviously, now.

"You're alive," he said, and it was impossible to keep the relief out of his voice, though he tried. Despite his efforts, both Jeannie and Michael turned and gave him odd looks.

"Newsflash, Boy Scout: I've been dead for forty years. Sorry about the . . . you know—" She gestured vaguely in their direction: all three were scratched, bitten, disheveled, sandy. "I was hungry and the thirst got a little away from me. Now, I gotta go. I'd eat a rat just for the chance to have a hot shower."

Without another word, she turned and moved off into the dunes.

Burke looked at his pack leaders. "Good-bye," he said simply.

Michael stuck out his hand and they shook. "I guess we won't be seeing you for a while. If ever."

"What?" Jeannie asked.

"I don't know," he replied honestly. "I guess it's up to . . . to . . . I don't even know her name."

"We'll keep your house for you. Everything that's yours will always be here for you."

"What?" Jeannie asked again.

"Thank you, Michael. I appreciate your help tonight. Do I have your leave to go?"

"You have my leave, O brother, and good hunting and

many cubs," he replied, the formal good-bye of a pack leader releasing a beta male from his care.

"You're going after her? You've decided you're going to be mates and live happily ever after even though she's dead and you don't even know her name?"

"Good-bye, Jeannie."

"Burke!" she yowled, but he ignored her and loped off into the dark, a true rogue, now.

CHAPTER 6

Somehow, Boy Scout had flanked her, because he was waiting for her in the parking lot, the fluorescent lights bouncing off his black hair, making it seem very like the color of blood.

"I have a shower," he said by way of greeting.

"One side, Boy Scout. I've seen all of you I'm gonna."

"And a house. You could stay there and . . . and rest during the day and do your business at night."

Hmm. Tempting. Credit cards could be traced, a decent hotel wouldn't take cash, and she didn't want anyone to see her coming and going. Shacking up with a stranger for a night or two was— Wait. Had she lost her mind? Because she was actually mulling it over. Crazy guy's offer. As if he hadn't left her in the biggest fix of her life just last night.

Well. Second biggest.

Although, her gentler self argued, he had tried to help her. Badly, but the effort counted for something, right?

"Please," he said, and that did it. She was undone; it wasn't the "please," it was how he looked when he said it: miserable and hopeful all at once.

"Oh, all right," she grumbled. "Maybe for the night. I hope one of these cars is yours."

"It's not. But my house is just over the dunes, past the Beachside Motel." He pointed at a row of lights in the distance and she sighed internally. It had been a rough couple of nights, and she wasn't up to a hike, undead strength or not.

She opened her mouth to bitch, only to feel herself be swept off the warm pavement and into his arms. "It's not far," he promised her, and went loping through the lot and into the dunes.

"Boy Scout, you're gonna break your fargin' back!" she hollered, secretly delighted. When was the last time she had been picked up and carried like a bride over the threshold? Her mama had died when she was a toddler; her dad was too busy working two jobs to pick her up; cancer had taken him her first year at the U of M. After that . . . "I weigh a ton!"

"Hardly," he said, and the sly mother wasn't even out of breath. He raced with her across the sand, past the motel, up a small hill covered with stumpy, stubbly bushes, and then he was setting her down on a sandy porch. She turned and looked, and could barely make out the lights of the parking lot. Boy Scout could *move*. But then, she'd seen evidence of that just the night before.

He opened the door and made an odd gesture—half wave, half bow.

She walked into the house. "No locks, huh? Doncha just love the Cape."

"No one would dare," he said simply. "Will the lights hurt your eyes? We can leave them off if you prefer."

"No, the lights are fine."

Click.

They blinked at each other in his living room, both getting their first good look at the other, and both entirely pleased by what they saw.

For her part, she saw a tall, thin, black-haired man with gray eyes—the only gray eyes she'd ever seen, true gray, the color of the sky when it was about to storm. He was dressed in dirty shorts, shirtless and barefoot, and as tanned as an old shoe. Laugh lines—except he never laughed, or smiled—around those amazing, storm-colored eyes. His legs were ropy with muscle and his arms looked like a swimmer's: lean and strong. His hands were large and capable-looking. His mouth was a permanent downturned bow; even when he tried to smile, he looked like he was frowning. She liked it, being in a generally bad mood herself; sometimes it was nice to be away from perpetual smilers, and Minnesota had more than its fair share.

Burke saw a tall woman (she came up to his chin in her bare feet) with a classically beautiful face, strong nose, wide forehead, pointed chin. Black eyes, skin the color of espresso. Long, slim limbs. Wide shoulders that made her breasts almost disappear. Unpainted toes and fingernails; filthy linen pants and a T-shirt so dirty he had no idea what the original color was. And if he closed his eyes he couldn't see her: she gave off no scent of her own, only sand and sea. She was like a chameleon for the nose; she took on the smells around her, the smells he loved. He thought her accent was the same way: she didn't sound like much of anything. She didn't drop her R's like the locals, had no Midwestern twang, no Southern drawl. She didn't sound like anything. Or, rather, she sounded like just herself, and that was exactly right.

And there it was: that sense of rightness about her, the sense that she was for him and he was for her. Even though only one of them knew it.

That was all right. He was a patient man.

She mistook his silence for something else and glanced down at herself, the first time he had seen her self-conscious: "Ugh, look at me. I must stink as bad as I look."

"You're beautiful."

"Ugh, stop it right now."

"But you are," he said, puzzled.

Her brown eyes narrowed as she studied him. "Boy Scout, get those thoughts out of your head right this minute."

"Thoughts that you're beautiful?"

"Uh-huh. I'm not beautiful; it's the vampire mystique. It's like . . . like a hormone I give off. Makes it easier for me to bite you. Any vampire can do it."

"You don't smell like anything; how can you be giving off a hormone?"

"Because, trust me, I'm not beautiful. I've got a big nose and big feet and tiny tits and my hair never grows so I always look like a shorn sheep."

He was dizzy with the wrongness of her self-perception. "Huh?"

"This will never work out. Not in a thousand years."

"Huh?"

"Look at us."

He smiled.

"No, really look."

"I don't care that you're a vampire."

"You don't even know what a vampire is, or does."

"So? You'll show me."

"And the age difference?"

He shrugged.

"Boy Scout, I've got at least fifty years on you! I was thirty when I died!"

"So call a nursing home."

"And . . ."

"And?"

"You're white."

He waited for the rest of the explanation, and she had to resist the urge to put her fist through his television set. "I'm black, you're white. Are you listening?"

"You mean— You're a bigot?"

"*I'm* not! Everybody else is! And don't even tell me how trendy it is to be black or to have a black girlfriend because trends are cyclical, they are, and one day you'll wake up and I won't be trendy and then where will we be?"

"Miss," he said patiently, "do you want that shower or not?"

"Boy Scout, you're not hearing a thing I'm saying, are you?"

"You have eyes like chocolate," he said dreamily.

"You don't even know my name."

"Oh. Well. Mine's Burke Wolftaur."

"Of course it is. Great disguise, by the way, werewolf. Running around on the beach right before a full moon, got the word *wolf* in your damned last name, *real* bright."

He shrugged. "I was on my way back to my house; I would have made it in plenty of time if I hadn't run into you."

"Oh, so it's *my* fault you're a dumbass?"

"Yes. And all the packs' names go back to the same roots. There are hundreds of Wolfs, Wolftons, Wolfbauers, Wolfertons, right here on the Cape."

"I repeat: great disguise, dumbass. I'm Serena Crull, by the way."

"Cruel?" he asked.

"C-R-U-L-L."

"Oh."

"Well, at least my name isn't Serena Vampireton, ya big putz."

"The bathroom is down the hall and on your left. I'll find some clean clothes for you."

"Had lots of lady friends stay over, hum?"

"No, you'll have to make do with my clothes."

"Ah, let the fashion show begin!"

"You'll be lovely," he said flatly, as if stating a fact: It will rain tonight. It was too cloudy to stargaze. You will be lovely.

"Boy Scout, you are one weird white boy, anybody tell you?"

"Never to my face," he replied, and went to find her something to wear.

CHAPTER 7

*B*urke shut the fridge and turned around, then nearly dropped the gallon of milk on his foot. Serena was standing *right there* and he hadn't heard a thing.

"That's disconcerting."

"Thanks, Boy Scout. If that's for me, don't bother. I don't drink . . . milk."

"It's for me, actually. I can still taste the sand from last night." He poured himself a large glass and drank it all off in a single draught, like it was beer. He could use a beer, but there wasn't a drop in the house. He scowled at the gallon container, then poured himself more.

"How are you feeling?" he asked.

"I was about to ask you the same thing." She grabbed a napkin from the small pile on the kitchen table, stepped forward, and wiped his upper lip. "I can't hardly see where I bit you anymore."

"Fast healer. Fast metabolism."

"Honey, tell me." She stepped back—almost too quickly, he thought, as if she was afraid. Not that he could exactly tell—it was maddening not to be able to smell her emotions. And tantalizing. But mostly maddening. "So?" She whirled in a small circle. "How do I look? Ready to call *Vogue*?"

"You look fine," he said, which was a gross underestimation. She was wearing one of his white strappy T-shirts, which only emphasized her small, firm breasts and the sweet dark smoothness of her skin. Frankly, the shirt emphasized that her breasts were all nipple, which made him want to pull it off to see, which made him want to—

"Fine," he repeated, wrenching his mind back on track. Trying, anyway. "You look fine."

"Well, the sweatpants were never gonna work, so I found a pair of your shorts." As it was, they came down to her knees and made her look irresistibly cute; she wiggled her bare toes and he smiled. She was still damp from the shower; water glistened in her tight cap of black curls.

He hurriedly drank more milk. Pity that wasn't what he was thirsty for.

"Well, I appreciate the clothes and the shower and the late-night snack—" She tapped her throat by explanation and he nodded. "But I'd better hit the trail, as they said in the old Westerns right before they killed all the Indians. Excuse me: Native Americans."

"Hold on. I want to help you."

"Help me out of these shorts, maybe," she joked, and he hurriedly looked away so she wouldn't realize how close she was to the truth. "Naw, I think we've bugged each other enough for one night—well, two nights. Don't you?"

"You can't do it by yourself."

"Do what?"

"Whatever it is you came here for. You're not a native,

and you're not a tourist. Something brought you to the Cape. I want to help you with it."

"Why?"

Because you're beautiful. Because I was a coward. Because you know what I am and you're not afraid. Because I know what you are and I'm not afraid. Because. Because.

"I feel bad," he said carefully, "about last night."

She waved his cowardice away with one nail-bitten hand. "That? Forget it."

"Never."

She raised her eyebrows at his tone. "I mean it. I made a fuss, but it was no big. It was sweet—yet dumb—of you to jump in at all. You couldn't help your nature, any more than I can help biting people on the neck. And I quit apologizing for *that* about thirty years ago."

"Still, you're rogue." *Like me.*

"Rogue?"

"Out here by yourself. Alone. You don't have the pack to help you. But I'll help you."

"Boy Scout, I really don't think you will."

"On my word as a former member of the Wyndham Pack, I will."

"Boy Scout, you don't want any of this, trust me."

"I left you once and it almost killed you."

She snorted. "Not even close."

"I can't leave you again. At least—" He groped for a way to lighten the moment, make a joke. What would a real person *say*? "At least not until we get you some decent clothes."

"You're sweet, but you shouldn't offer to jump into something when you don't know what it is."

Patiently, he went over it again. "I don't care what it is. I want to help you. Frankly, I don't see you leaving this house without me right behind you. I'm an excellent tracker." A bluff, with her lack of scent, she could probably lose him in half an hour.

She scowled, then shrugged. "Have it your way, Boy Scout. You rang the cherries: I'm not a tourist. I'm out here for a reason. In fact, I'm out here to find a vampire and kill him. How 'bout that?"

"Oh, murder?" He put the milk back. "That's fine with me."

To his amusement, she was so shocked she sat down.

CHAPTER 8

"See, the thing is—"

"It's fine, Serena."

"But see, it's like—"

"Do you want to leave now? Or do you need to, I don't know, rest?"

"Listen to me. I . . . we . . . have to find the vampire who—"

"Who sired you?"

She made a face, her dark nose crinkling like she smelled something bad. Since he hadn't taken the garbage out for a day or two, it was entirely possible. Perhaps they shouldn't be having this meeting in the kitchen. Perhaps another room. Like the bedroom. Ah, the—

"Boy Scout, you're not listening. Nobody says 'sired'; a vampire makes you or he kills you. In fact, a lot of us say we were killed, even *if* we were made. Are you— Was that a yawn?"

"I haven't been sleeping."

"It *was* a yawn! What, I'm boring you?"

"I'm just not interested in the details."

"The details like who we're going to murder."

"According to you," he said coolly, "our victim is already dead."

That gave her something to think about, he could see; she leaned back in her kitchen chair and stared up at the ceiling for a minute. Finally she brushed her ear—a charming monkey gesture—and said, "Well, okay. Technically, the guy we're going to stake doesn't breathe and doesn't have a pulse, or not much of one, and he's been running around dead for at least sixty years. But still. It's a very serious thing."

Burke managed to conceal another yawn.

"I can't believe," she said, shaking her head, "that you don't at least want the details."

"Oh, sure, I want them. Who, when, and how, I suppose. He's probably going to be a hard kill." He smiled and Serena shrank back in her chair. "You certainly were."

"Okay, first of all, when you grin like that, you've got about a million teeth. Second of all, the *who* is the vampire who made me, yeah. The *when* is as soon as I track the mother down, and the *how*—we have to stake him in the heart or throw him into a tanning bed or something like that."

"Crosses? Holy water?"

"Will hurt him but probably not kill him. And don't be waving any of those things around *me*, Boy Scout."

"Does the stake have to be made of—"

"Any kind of wood. And it has to be through the heart. Anywhere else, he'll just get right back up and keep coming." She added bitterly, "Don't ask me how I know this."

Burke ground his teeth. "Did he hurt you?"

"Huh? No. I mean . . . not physically."

"But you want him dead for making you dead."

"No. For making my friend dead. I want him dead for lying. He *lied*. He didn't tell me the truth. I mean the whole truth. He let me believe that whoever he bit would be a vampire. He didn't tell me . . . didn't—" She covered her face with her hands and went silent.

After a minute, Burke said, "He bit you."

"Yes."

"And you came back."

"Yes."

"You were lonely."

Serena's hands came down; her eyes were big with wonder. "Yes. Once the hunger—the being new, the being crazy of a new vampire—once that wore off, I found my friend. My best and greatest friend, Maggie Dunn."

"She missed you."

"She was so *happy* that I was alive. Sort of alive. You know. And—"

"You talked to your friend. Or Maggie asked you. It doesn't matter."

"That's right," she choked. "It doesn't matter."

"You thought, or she thought, being a vampire would be a fine thing. Friends forever. And your sire—the one who made you—he obliged. He didn't tell you—what? Did he not perform all the rituals? Did he do it wrong out of spite, or to keep his pack's numbers down?"

"He didn't tell me, and I only found out later, that being a vampire . . . it's like the measles. It's something you catch. Or don't catch. You could get bit by the same vampire a hundred times, and ninety-nine of those times, nothing would happen. Or he'd drink too much and you'd die. But that one time, the hundredth time, you'd come back. I thought—I didn't know it was a fargin' *virus*. I didn't know it was a damned head cold. And he didn't tell me. Didn't warn us."

"Your friend didn't come back."

"My friend." She took a shuddering breath and obviously wasn't used to it, because she almost tilted off her chair and onto the floor. "My friend died screaming. And I let it happen."

"And this was . . ."

"Nineteen sixty-five." She smiled. It was a wobbly smile, but it was there. "Free love, you know."

"Why . . . now?"

"I finally found him, that's why now. There's a new regime in place, and the king helped me track him down."

He blinked, processing this. "The king."

"King Sinclair. The king of the vampires. He made the Minneapolis librarian track Peter down for me."

"Peter?"

"Innocuous name for such a scum-sucking son of a bitch, isn't it? Anyway, the old boss didn't give two shits for problems like mine. I knew better than to even ask—we all just kept out of his way. It was a bad time for most of us. But then—"

"Things changed."

"I heard the new king and queen—"

"There was a coup for power? The old leader lost? Was killed?"

"Yeah. So I let things settle down a bit and then I went to St. Paul and— Never mind all that, point is, I got an address, I even got the name of the restaurant he runs."

"Your leaders—they know what you'll do when you find Peter?"

She nibbled on her lower lip. "The king does. He understands this kind of stuff. I got the feeling—I think he keeps the queen out of a lot of the bloodier stuff, you know? She's kind of new to the game."

"Ah." He knew about new mates, having seen (from a distance) Jeannie's struggles to fit in with the pack. He didn't blame this Sinclair fellow at all for keeping his woman out of the boring bloody details.

"That's it? 'Ah'?"

"There is nothing else, right?"

"Yeah, but . . . that's it? You got nothin'?"

"Do you know what my mother told me every night before I went to bed?"

"Uh . . . stop being such a chowderhead?"

"No. She repeated the family motto: Kill or be eaten."

"Swell."

"Isn't that your situation, as a vampire?"

She shifted in her chair. "I—I don't think of myself—I mean, I don't think I've ever killed anyone. It's a myth that vampires have to kill you to feed. Half a pint and we're good for the night. Sure, we're a little bit nuts in the beginning—a brand-new vampire is pretty much out of her mind for a few years. But you get ahold. It's like anything—you deal."

He touched his neck, which had entirely healed, and smiled at her. "Good to know."

"But it sounds like being a werewolf is really, really stressful. No wonder you live away from it all."

"That's not why I live away from it all," he said, and got up to put the milk away, and they both knew the discussion was over.

CHAPTER 9

*B*efore she realized it, the night had disappeared and the killing dawn was lurking around the corner. Serena could hardly believe it. They'd spent the entire night in the kitchen, plotting.

Born and bred on the Cape, Burke knew the local geography and tourist traps, and recognized the name of Pete's restaurant, Eat Me Raw. He told her it was "up Cape" in "P-town," whatever the hell that meant. Not for the first time, she thought it wasn't so crazy, hooking up with the Boy Scout.

"We could drive there now," he said, looking at her doubtfully, "but you'd have to ride in the trunk. And stay in the trunk until the sun goes down."

"Tempting offer, but no thanks. Let's just crash here and we'll hit the road first thing tonight. You've got a whole day," she teased, "to come to your senses."

Without a word, he got up and escorted her to the basement of his small, pleasantly untidy house. It was a finished basement, cool and dark, partly used for storage. Part of the basement had been made into a bedroom, with one small south-facing window, which he efficiently taped a dark beach towel over.

"All rightey then," she said, looking at the neatly made double bed. The room screamed "guest room"; there was no personality to it at all. In fact, Burke's entire house (well, the parts she had seen) had very little personality, as if occupied by a ghost, or someone who didn't care much one way or the other. "Good night."

"Good night." He stood very close to her for a moment and then (she thought—hoped?) reluctantly moved away. "Call me if you need anything."

"Oh yeah. You betcha." She cursed her Minnesotaisms, which surfaced in moments of stress.

The door shut. She was alone in the sterile guest room. Which was too bad, because she hadn't been laid in about twenty years (the thirst tended to take over everything, including the sex drive and the need for manicures) and Burke would obviously be a—

But that was no way to think. That way was trouble, pure and simple. She had a mission to complete and when Pete was dead, when his lying head had been cut off and she'd kicked it into the ocean, when Maggie had at long last been avenged, then . . . then . . .

Well. She didn't know. But that was for later. For now, she climbed between clean sheets and, when the sun came up (she couldn't see it, but she could sure feel it, feel it the way bats felt it, the way blind worms in the dirt felt it), she slept.

And dreamed.

This was delightful, as it hadn't happened often. She

hadn't known vampires could dream at all until it started happening to her about five years ago.

In her dream (wonderful dream, delightful dream) she and Maggie (Maggie!) were walking around in Dinkytown, just a few blocks away from the apartment they'd shared as college students. It was the fifties, and they both wore black capris and white men's shirts tied around their twenty-year-old midriffs. Maggie wore ballet flats on her little delicate feet (oh, how she'd envied Maggie her feet) and Serena wore saddle shoes, which were the slightest bit too tight, but who cared? The sun was shining and oh, it was good to be young and alive and eating ice cream cones and welcoming the admiring glances from the fellows on the sidewalk in June, in Minnesota, in summer, in life.

"Place has twenty flavors of homemade ice cream, glorious hand-cranked ice cream like Grandma makes, and you always pick vanilla." Serena took another bite of coconut chip and tried not to look smug.

"Never mind my choices, let's talk about yours. You've given up happiness for how many decades, and for what? To avenge me? For what? Because you feel guilty?"

The ice cream suddenly tasted like ashes, and Serena had to fight the urge to spit out the bite. "I don't want to talk about that now. This is supposed to be a nice damned dream."

"Tough noogies, chowderhead." Maggie brushed her bangs out of her eyes and Serena noticed the ragged bite marks—chew marks—all around her friend's neck. Something had been at her, and hadn't been nice about it, either. "You managed to literally stumble into some happiness, and what? Did you jump on him and try to make a baby?"

"I can't have—"

"Or did you drag him down into your sick old shit?"

"Maggie, he has to pay!"

They both knew the "he" Serena was talking about. "Sure he does. But do you?"

"I don't know what you—"

"You never did, honey. That's why I'm the scholarship student, and you're running around dead on Cape Cod. No lover, no home, no nothing. Just your bad old self. And for what?"

"Maggie, I can hear you *screaming* in my *sleep*. Vampires don't even dream and most of the time I dream about *that*."

"That's on you, honeygirl." Her friend looked at her with terrible affection, the vanilla melting in her fist, the blood running down her blouse front. "You didn't want to spend eternity alone; who would? So here we are, both dead. But now you've got another chance—and you're wrecking that one, too. The first time was piss-ignorance. Not your fault. But this? Willful."

"It's not—"

"Well, you always were the stubborn one." Her friend grinned, all teeth and gums and blood. "And I was the pretty one."

"Maggie—"

"See you 'round, honeygirl."

Maggie vanished. The stores vanished. The old-fashioned (at least, to her twenty-first-century eyes) cars vanished. The sidewalk patrons vanished. There was only her, and her stupid coconut chip ice cream cone, and her too-tight saddle shoes, and—

—the guest bedroom.

It was night again and the thirst was on her; her mouth felt like dust, her mouth felt dead. Dead. Like Maggie, long dirt and bones in her lonely grave. The grave Serena had helped put her in. Had *led* her to.

She shoved back the blanket and was on her feet, then up the stairs and headed for the door. She had to drink before she could think, and she certainly wasn't going to chomp Burke again, poor boy. She had enough guilt on her shoulders without—

"Where are you going?"

"Don't sneak up on me, Boy Scout," she said without turning around. "Bad habit."

"But where are you going?"

"Breakfast. Well, supper. Can't say when I'll be back."

She hadn't heard him cross the room, but suddenly his arm closed over her elbow. "Rules of the house," he said simply, looking down at her with his storm-colored eyes. "You have to eat what the host serves." He tugged the neck of his T-shirt down, exposing his jugular. "Me."

CHAPTER 10

*I*n a perfect world, she would have logically reasoned out why it wasn't appropriate to bite the boy, the infant—cripes, how old *was* he?

In a perfect world, she would have used her superior vampire strength to shake him off and gone traipsing down his porch and onto the beach, picked some drunken tourist and slaked her thirst, then come back and coolly discussed Pete's upcoming murder.

Neither she nor Burke lived in a perfect world; they yanked toward each other at the same moment (a clam between them would have shattered), mouths searching, tongues exploring, and then she reared back like the beast she was and bit him, pierced the vein with her teeth and sucked.

And nearly reeled; his blood was the richest, most satisfying drink she had ever had in all her years of being undead. In all her years, period. He tasted like salmon fighting upstream, like rabbits fucking under the moon, like wolves bringing down cattle.

They staggered around his living room in a rigid dance, fingers digging into each other's shoulders, and he pulled her (his, really) T-shirt off with one rip down the back. Not to be outdone by a mortal, she did the same. She hoped he had a stash of Clark Gable–type T-shirts somewhere, because he was now short two.

They tripped and hit the couch, Burke on the bottom, and she broke free and groaned at the ceiling. A bad idea with a full mouth; she caught a rill of blood with her thumb, then sucked on it.

"Good?" he asked.

"Burke. Oh man. You just don't know."

"It's my high-fat diet," he said seriously, staring at her tits. "Um. All nipples. Come here."

"Your high-fat diet includes nipples?"

"Shhh." His arm circled around her and he pulled her down, sucking greedily, even biting her gently, and she wriggled against him, pushing at her shorts, pulling at his.

She kissed the top of his head and shoved her breasts harder into his face, delighting in the feel of his mouth on her flesh. "Oh, Burke." She sighed.

"Mmmph."

"Not to put any pressure on you. But Reagan was in the White House the last time I got laid."

Her nipple slid from his mouth with a popping sound and he replied, "That's the opposite of pressure. It's been so long, you probably don't remember what good sex is."

"Come on!" she screeched, delighted. "It's like riding a bike."

"Hardly," he grunted, seizing her by the thighs and levering her over his mouth. She clutched the back of the sofa to keep her balance and promptly went out of her mind as his tongue searched, darted, stabbed. She couldn't imagine the upper-body strength he had, how he could so effortlessly hold her entire weight just above his mouth. The sheer physics of it was—was she thinking about physics?

Get your head in the game or you'll miss it. Good advice. Not to mention, she could feel his tongue all over, not just where . . . where it actually was. *Umm.* She shuddered all over and thrust against his face, no more able to stop her movements than she could have given up blood. And her orgasm was upon her like the finest rush imaginable, surging out of nowhere and shocking the shit out of her—she had never been one to come in less than five minutes, never mind less than five seconds.

She lost her grip but he did not, and the momentum brought them both tumbling to the floor, smashing the coffee table in three pieces on the way. Neither of them especially cared. They had one goal, and that was Serena's penetration: a shattered coffee table could not have been more irrelevant.

Burke crushed her lips beneath his mouth and shoved her legs apart with his knee; she locked her ankles behind his back as he pushed into her with no niceties and no apologies—just what she wanted, needed, silently demanded. Their bellies smacked together faster and faster, and they clawed and bit their way to mutual orgasm.

"Oh man," she said when she could talk.

"Hush."

"I'd fall down, if there was anywhere to fall."

"I knew you'd wreck this by speaking."

"Aw, shut it."

He brushed splinters out of her hair. "You owe me furniture."

"Ha! After that, you owe me a hundred bucks."

"Is that the going rate these days?"

"I have no idea," she admitted. "I just said that to sound tough." She was silent, considering. "I have no idea why I just said that, either."

"Well. You are tough." He gently disengaged from her limbs, picked her up like a doll and put her on the couch. He looked rueful as he examined the various shredded cloth that had been two outfits only five minutes ago, then said, "I'm ready for a burger or a steak or something. Are you—" He touched the bite wound on his neck. "Full?"

"Sure. Like I said before, we only need a little bit. But maybe you shouldn't be jumping around like that," she warned, getting up to put a hand on his arm—too late, he had already darted into the kitchen. "Sometimes vic—people are a little light-headed after I—"

He snorted, his head deep inside the fridge. "Eggs would be good. Eggs with a side of eggs. And a hamburger. Two hamburgers."

"I can hear your cholesterol going up, just listening." She was amazed at how energized he was. Werewolf, she reminded herself. All the time, not just during the full moon.

He brought down a bowl, rapidly cracked a dozen eggs into it, found a fork, and started whisking.

She came over to him and stared at the eggs. "Do you miss solid food?" he asked.

"No. The smell of it makes me ill. I can't believe you're going to eat half the food in the house."

He cocked a dark brow at her. "Half?"

CHAPTER 11

"It's good that we got the sex out of the way," she said as they sped toward Eat Me Raw. "Now we can focus on—you know."

"The murder?"

"Right." She was a little taken aback at how coolly he said it, like it was a fact of life, something unpleasant but unavoidable, like taxes. "The sex thing would have just distracted you."

"That's probably true," he said cheerfully.

"But you know," she felt compelled to add, as she was compelled to ruin all good things in her life/death, "there's nothing in it for us. I mean, no future."

He was silent, concentrating on the road.

"It's not like I can give you a family. My ovaries quit working the same day everything quit working. Not that I ever wanted a family," she added in a mutter. "I hate kids."

"Me, too."

"Liar!"

He blinked at her. "Well. I don't *hate* them. I don't hate anything. But I must admit, they bug the shit out of me."

"Me, too! I mean, I know we all had to go through it, and kids have to learn, blah-blah, but do they have to learn right next to me? You can't go to a restaurant anywhere and have a nice glass of wine without some toddler throwing Saltines in your hair."

"And the parents . . ." he prompted.

"Oh, man, they are the *worst*! Always obsessing about when their kid takes a shit, or doesn't take a shit, or is a slow talker, or talks too much, and showing you meaningless crayon scribbles and going *on* and *on* about what geniuses their little Tommy or Jenny is. Ugh!"

"Try being in a pack, and knowing the baby barfing all over your shoes is destined to be your boss someday."

The sheer horror of the idea consumed her for a moment. "Okay," she said at last, "that's bad."

"Making nice to a toddler who takes a dump in the corner, because she's going to be the pack leader someday."

"Man!"

"And the parents, who are your bosses right now, think it's swell when the kid breaks a window by throwing her baby brother through it. So there's broken glass everywhere, the baby's laughing and shitting, the kid's laughing, and the parents are all 'isn't she a genius?' and 'isn't he a brave little man?' "

"I don't know how you stand it!"

"That's why I live alone. Lived alone," he corrected himself.

She let that pass. "Is it weird for a werewolf to not like kids?"

"Extremely. As in, perversion. We're supposed to be married by the time we can legally drink, and have two or three cubs by the time we're twenty-five."

She snickered at "cubs."

"But, I like my privacy. I like the beach. I like being able to sleep late on Saturdays and watch dirty movies on HBO whenever I want."

"Sing it."

She settled back in her seat and enjoyed the ride. He had an old pickup truck, beat-up blue with new tires and sprung upholstery. He had had it, he told her, for fifteen years.

Then she thought: I am riding in a blue truck with a near-stranger to go kill Pete, and I'm . . . happy?

Postcoital happiness, she decided. Strictly hormonal. She used to get the same high from eating chocolate.

"So, what's the plan?"

He blinked at her again. "You're asking me?"

"Okay. We go to the restaurant. We find Pete. We take him out back and kill him."

"With the handy stake you happen to have in your— pocket?"

She glared at him. She was dressed, once again, in his gym shorts and a T-shirt, one so old it was no longer black, but gray. Barefoot. He was slightly more respectable looking in faded jeans, loafers, and an orange T-shirt the color of a traffic cone. "It's a restaurant," she said, faking a confidence she didn't feel. "We'll find a big sharp knife and cut his lying head off with it."

Burke shrugged.

"You really don't have a problem with this?"

"He killed you and your friend and who knows how many other girls. I'll eat his heart and have room for a big breakfast."

She opened her mouth, and promptly closed it. Other

girls? Horrifying thought! Of course Pete hadn't stopped with Maggie. And it had been years. *Decades*. How many—

"And he doesn't have to kill them," she said out loud, bitterness like acid on her tongue. "You don't have to kill them. People give more blood to the Red Cross."

"Yes, Serena."

"He didn't have to! I would have—I would have forgiven him for what he did to me, but he didn't have to kill Maggie, too." She sobbed dryly into her hands, amazed that after all this time, she could still cry for Maggie. For herself. She felt Burke's hand on her shoulder, firm, as he pulled her across the seat and into his side.

"You're right, Serena. The beast doesn't have to kill to feed. You're not an animal like I am."

That thought shocked her—she had never thought of Burke as an animal. Not once. She was the bad one. He was—he was Burke.

She rested her head on his shoulder and watched as his reliable blue Ford ate up the miles.

CHAPTER 12

"Party town," she commented, staring at the throngs of people, the dozens of cars crammed taillight to headlight all along the streets.

"Yes," Burke said, illegally parking the truck. "It'll be like this until Labor Day."

"Provincetown. P-town?"

"There you go. You sound like a local."

"I'm not moving out here after—after. I can't stand the accent."

"Yah, sure, you betcha," he teased. "Because you don't have an annoying twangy Minnesota accent. You sound like an extra from *Fargo*."

"Shut up. I hate that movie. And can we focus, please?" She opened the door and hopped out of the truck, but he was already out and coming around the front. He took her hand in a firm grip and led her to the front door of Eat Me Raw.

"Wait! Shouldn't we . . . uh . . . be subtle?"

"We're here to kill the beast," he said. "It's best to get it done."

"So we'll just go in there and ask for him?"

"That was the plan, right?"

"What if he's not here?"

"If he's like most restaurant owners, he's here seven days a week, two-thirds of every day. Night, I mean. Good place to troll for victims. And here?" He gestured to the teeming crowds, the bars, the bright lights, the chaos. On a Tuesday night, no less. "Who would notice a vampire here? Or a missing girl right away?"

"Nobody missed me," she admitted. "I didn't have any family, and nobody believed Maggie. The cops assumed I'd hit the road. Maggie wouldn't let it go and they finally listed me as a Missing Person."

He scowled. "That sucks. I would have knocked over houses to find you. Strung men up by their balls."

Touched, she said, "That's so sweet, Burke."

He shoved open the door of the restaurant and walked in. She felt as though they were actually pressing against the noise from the bar. It was a typical New England raw bar— bright lights and dark wood and yakking tourists. Burke shouldered his way past them and walked up to the hostess stand.

"I'm sorry," the hostess practically screamed, "but there's a ninety-minute wait!"

"We'd like to see the owner!" Burke bellowed back. His voice climbed effortlessly over the din and several women (and not a few men) turned to look. "Tell him an old friend from Minnesota is here!"

"Scream a little louder, why don't you?" she muttered, knowing his werewolf hearing would pick it up. "I'm sure the cops will never be able to find a witness or ten."

As the hostess yelled into one of those cell phone/walkie-talkie things, he turned to her and replied, "We're here to kill a dead man. Tough case for the cops to solve. His birth certificate, assuming they can I.D. him when we finish, is probably just a bit out of date. Legally, he probably doesn't exist."

"He *shouldn't* exist," she muttered.

"I'm sorry!" the hostess yelled. "He's not in the bar right now!"

"She's lying," he said. "I can smell it."

"Well, let's—"

"It's all right, Annie," a stranger said, materializing beside the hostess. "No need to cover for me this time. I'll be glad to talk to these people."

Serena felt Burke jump, and knew why: no scent. She looked at Pete and was a little surprised. The boogeyman, the monster, the thing that haunted her dreams and stole her rest was a balding man in his early forties. Well. Who looked like he was in his early forties. What little hair he had left was going gray. His eyes were a light mud brown, and his nose was too small for his face. He was neatly dressed in a dark suit the color of his hair. He looked like a nurse shark: harmless, with teeth.

He smiled at her. She was startled to see he knew her at once. "Sorry about your friend."

She tried to speak. Couldn't. And she knew—*knew*—why he was smiling. He thought he was safe. His turf, his town. All these *people*. He thought they wouldn't touch him. And he was *old*. For vampires, age meant strength. He thought if worse came to terrible, he could take them.

"Let's step outside," Burke said, and seized Pete by the arm.

"I don't think so," the old monster said loudly. "I'm needed here. I—hey!" They tussled for a moment, and then

Burke literally started dragging him toward the rear of the restaurant. Serena could see shock warring with dignity on Pete's face: make a fuss and get help? Or endure and get rid of them outside?

She could see him try to set his feet, and see his amazement when Burke overpowered him again, almost effortlessly. She could also see the way Burke's jaw was set, the throbbing pulse at his temple. It wasn't just werewolf strength; Burke was overpowering the monster with sheer rage.

"Killing girls," Burke was muttering, as the armpit of Pete's suit tore. He got a better grip. "Killing girls. *Killing girls!*"

A few people stared. But this was P-town and nobody interfered. New Englanders were famous for minding their own business.

"What the hell are you?" Pete yelled back. "You're no vampire!"

"I'm worse," Burke said through gritted teeth. They were in the kitchen now, the smell of sizzling chicken wings making Serena want to gag. "I *have* to kill to eat."

Before any of the staff could react—or even notice, as hard as they were all working—Serena hurried ahead. She figured she might as well contribute to the felony kidnapping in some small way, so she held the back door open for them. Burke dragged Pete out, past the reeking garbage rollaways, past the illegally parked cars, past the boardwalk, onto the beach. Serena bent and picked up a piece of driftwood, one about a foot long and shaped, interestingly, like a spear. She could feel the splinters as she held it in her hand; it was about two inches in diameter.

Pete swung and connected; the blow made Burke stagger but he didn't loosen his grip. "Your pack leader didn't authorize this," he said. "You'll start a war."

Ah, the monster knew about werewolves—that was interesting. Of course, it made sense . . . Pete would want to know who he was sharing the killing field with.

"Serena's my pack. And you're all rogues. Don't pretend you're Europe. Nobody will miss you."

"Nobody missed you," Pete leered at her.

"Not then. But now, yes." She hefted the driftwood, then hesitated, hating herself for it but unable to resist. "Why? Why me, and why Maggie?"

"And Cathie and Jenny and Barbie and Kirsten and Connie and Carrie and Yvonne and Renee and Lynn and so many I've lost count. Why? Are you seriously asking me that? Why? Because that's what we do, stupid. You're—what? Fifty-some years old and you don't know that?"

"We don't do that," she retorted, and gave him a roundhouse smack of her own. "We don't *do* that! We don't have to! You did it because you *wanted* to!" Each shout was punctuated with another blow; Burke and Pete were skidding and sliding in the sand. The sea washed over their ankles. She had to scream to be heard over the surf. That was all right. She felt like screaming. She was, literally, in a killing rage. "You wanted to! She never did *anything* bad and you wanted to!"

"It's what we do," Pete said again, black blood trickling from his mouth, his nose. "The king won't stand for this."

"Who do you think *sent* me, bastard? He's getting rid of every one of you tinpot tinshit dictators. He won't stand for your shit and neither will I!"

"Then why," Pete said, and spat out two teeth, "why are you still talking?"

Good question. She kicked him in the balls while she thought of an answer. She had the stake. She had the anger. She even had a henchman. So why was the monster still alive?

"We don't do that," she said at last, and dropped the stake. She was condemning who knew how many more women to torture and death . . . Maggie was counting on her, wherever she was, and—and— "We don't do that and I don't do that."

"Ha," Pete said, and grinned at her through broken teeth. "All the way from Minnesota. Long trip for nothing."

"Not nothing," Burke said. "She came for me. She just didn't know." Then he broke Pete's neck, a dry snap swallowed by the waves. Pete's mouth was opening and closing like a goldfish in a bowl, and then—Serena couldn't believe it—and then Burke literally ripped the monster's head off and tossed it away like a beach ball. The sound it made was like a chicken leg being pulled from a thigh. Times a thousand.

She spun away from their little group of evil and tried to be sick in the sand, but couldn't vomit. The sound—and the look on Pete's face when his neck broke—and the *sound*—

Burke briskly washed his hands in the surf and knelt beside her. She leaned against him and wiped her mouth.

"I knew you wouldn't," he whispered into her ear. "I told you: I'm the beast, not you."

"I just—couldn't. He was smirking at me and he knew I couldn't and he just—I just—" She closed her eyes and heard the snap of Pete's neck breaking again. This time it didn't make her feel sick. This time it made her . . . not exactly happy. More like . . . peaceful? "Oh, Burke. What if you hadn't come? What if I'd never met you?"

"But I did. And you did. And Maggie can rest. No more bad dreams."

"How did you know I—?"

He kissed her on the temple. "How could I not know my own mate?"

She clung to him, ignoring the surf wetting their legs, their knees. "Your mate? You still want to—?"

"Since you were in the hole and told me to go away. I couldn't leave you then. How could I leave you now? You're for me and I'm for you."

"Just like that?"

He shrugged.

"Just like that," she answered herself. The events of the past two days flashed across her mind: all he had done. For her. Had anyone ever . . . ? Who else could have done so much for her, but the man she was destined to be with?

"I'll outlive you," she said tearfully.

"On the upside, I can't knock you up."

"No kids," she said, cheering up.

He kissed her again. "No kids."

They rose as one and walked to the truck, not looking back when the surf covered Pete's body—both pieces—and took it away.

As predicted, nobody missed him, except the liquor rep, and she quickly found a new client.

No one in the bar who saw Burke and Serena ever forgot them, and no one in the bar ever saw them again. Drifters, in and out of P-town, one of several thousand tourists who came through Cape Cod each summer. Nothing special about them.

No, nothing at all.

MONA LISA THREE

o

Sunny

My thanks to my editor, Cindy Hwang,
for including me among her fortunate few.
To Roberta Brown, a truly amazing agent.
And to Publishers Weekly *and Susan White*
of Coffee Time Romance
for giving me such boffo reviews!

CHAPTER 1

*I*t was the beginning of December in Manhattan, smack, dab in the Christmas season, and we were shopping. But not for presents. Oh, no. For something far more practical—clothing. In a couple days' time, we were heading to Louisiana, my new territory.

The men had insisted that I meet my new constituents dressed like the Monère Queen that I was. Well, three-quarters Monère, at least. That last quarter was comprised of human blood, making me the first Mixed Blood Queen ever; I'd just been officially recognized by the Court. But given that most Monère considered Mixed Bloods to be mutts, mongrels, and the like, I could see my men's point that I dress like a Queen. T-shirt, jeans, and sneakers wasn't quite the image of authority they were used to. Oh well.

The Monère, my guys included, were quite backward in their tastes, actually. Long dresses and loose hair for their women. The plan was to break them in slowly, gently. If I had to wear a long black dress, I could do that. For now.

But since they'd insisted on torturing me, I decided it was only fair to torture them right back. I made them get new clothes as well. For Gryphon, well, the torture was more on my part. He was a vision of masculine beauty with ebony-black hair falling to his shoulders. His long, lean, and delicious build. The white alabaster purity of his skin. The red, red brightness of his cupid-bow lips. So beautiful that you wanted to reach out and touch him, prove that he was real.

He was the first Monère I'd ever encountered, the first man I'd ever loved. He'd come to me a few weeks ago, injured, alone, fleeing his Queen. In saving him, I had really saved myself.

He was my heart. And that vital organ that he claimed *pitter-pattered* within me as he stepped out of the fitting room dressed in the black Prada slacks I had chosen for him. The vibrant blue shirt he wore brought out the stunning cerulean richness of his eyes. Devastatingly lovely.

Another fitting room door swung open and Amber emerged, the other man who held my heart, roughly handsome in a mahogany brown dress shirt. His straight chestnut locks looked tousled as if he had run a hand carelessly through them, and his deep sea–blue eyes were narrowed in a fierce frown.

Huge was the word that best described Amber. Big and brawny, bounded with muscles, he was toweringly tall, majestic like a mountain. A mass of bulges and mounds— bulging biceps that strained the cloth, a mounded, muscular chest, a hard flat belly, powerful haunches, and thick-muscled calves. With his harsh features bold and craggy, Amber was beautiful in his own unique way—in his great warrior strength, in his unexpected tender care of me. He'd saved me. Brought me back from the brink of death.

My two Warrior Lords. My two lovers. It was hard to believe that I wouldn't have to give up one or the other. That I could keep them both. That they would share me, as they put it, alternating in my bed and in my body.

Other sighs, not only mine, were heard around the store. Looking at the two of them, one with the grace and beauty of a fallen angel, the other menacingly big and brawny, with the strength of a towering oak . . . who would not sigh, given this vision?

"The pants are too tight," Amber muttered, redness darkening his broad cheeks.

Actually, he filled out the tan-colored slacks quite nicely—impressively. I circled him slowly, front to back, appreciating the snug fit that showed off the leanness of his hips, the powerful heft of his thighs, and the tightness of his lovely muscular butt, among other things.

"I have to disagree. I think they're perfect," I murmured, unable to resist stroking a discreet hand down the enticing curve of his bottom. Beneath my light touch, his buttocks tensed to rock hardness, making my heart skip a beat. Oh, my.

"What do you think, Chami?" I asked, turning to the third man with us. Chami was one of the three other men recently sworn to my service. The deadliest among them. My assassin.

He was tall like Gryphon, almost six feet, but with whipcord leanness, slender like a greyhound. Sprawled on the couch in limber disarray, dressed in the light green cashmere sweater and olive pants I had chosen for him, with his soft curly brown hair waving across his smiling blue eyes, I was sharply reminded of how deceiving appearances could be. He looked nothing like the deadly killer that he was.

"I agree with Mona Lisa," Chami said, a smile tugging the corner of his mouth. "The clothes show off all your . . . masculine attributes to nice advantage."

Amber growled and Chami laughed outright.

"What do you think, Gryphon?" Chami asked, mischievously turning to the other man to share in the blame.

"If it pleases our Queen," Gryphon replied softly, "that is all that matters."

"You're outvoted, Amber." Reaching up, I wrapped my arms around his thick, brawny neck and pulled the big man down for a kiss.

"Does it please you?" Amber whispered when our faces were only a caress away.

"Yes," I breathed against his mouth.

"Then I shall wear them." A soft press of lips, chaste in action but oh so vibrant in emotion, and he released me. From that one light touch between us, I watched as his blue eyes slowly changed to that extraordinary golden clarity for which he was named—Amber. The eyes of his beast. The color of his eyes whenever he was moved with passion or power. They swirled now with love and devotion, feelings he didn't bother to hide, looking so different from his normal stony façade.

"Does *my* clothing meet with your approval?" Gryphon asked, pulling my attention back to him.

I ran my appreciative gaze down his lovely form. "Yes," was my husky reply. "Very, very much so."

Pleased, Gryphon smiled with a quick flash of dimples, here then gone like a tender flickering tease that made one want to entice them out again. "Good," he said, "then it is your turn now."

I groaned. Amber perked up. They changed back into their regular clothes and we made our way to the women's section of Bloomingdale's. The formal wear.

"This one," Gryphon said, holding up a long gown. Black lace overlying black silk.

"This dress," said Amber, holding up another glittering, sweeping black confection.

"And this," said Chami with his choice. Sleek, narrow, long and, of course, black.

I tried on all of them, to the men's vast appreciation. At five foot eight, I was tall for a woman, with a lean athletic build and a modest bosom, far from lush. My eyes were my best feature, dark like my hair, tilted up exotically at the sides. Other than that, I was average. But beneath my men's heated, approving eyes, I felt beautiful, desirable . . . cherished. A novel sensation.

I ended up buying all three gowns. There. Torture, I mean, shopping all done. Now it was back to work, packing and closing down my apartment.

Under a black-velvet star-studded sky, with the first quarter moon lending its slender slice of light to the night, we walked back with our purchases to my Lower West Side residence down in the Village.

The other members of our group were at the Pierre Hotel. And I was suddenly very, very glad we had decided to stay there, notwithstanding the hefty expense, when I opened the door and found a demon in my apartment.

CHAPTER 2

*D*emon dead was perhaps a more accurate description. They were not creatures from hell as we think of them, although they did live there—in Hell, that is. Demon dead are Monère who died, yet retained enough psychic energy to sustain their existence in another realm—a forever twilight where no life, no colors, existed. They were dead but not gone. And not really dead, although not really alive, either, as we knew it. Their hearts did not beat, they did not breathe. But they felt, they yearned, they bled. And they could kill.

They were incredibly strong and dangerous. Something that even the Monère feared.

My encounter with Kadeen, another demon dead, had almost killed me and my men. Of course, he'd ended up being the one killed, but not by my hand. By his prince's—the High Prince of Hell, Halcyon, who was sweet on me and courting me in his own way. Who said he loved me. I'd asked Halcyon to find another to love. Because the attention his interest in me engendered was hard wear-and-tear on my body.

This was the third demon dead I had ever encountered. A lot, if you consider the fact that most Monère went their entire long lives without encountering a single one. So far, they'd been either friend or foe. I wasn't sure which one this was. I didn't know at all how to react.

My men must have sensed something wrong in the utter stillness I'd frozen into, in the sudden speeding of my heart. Strong arms wrapped around me and pulled me back from the doorway—Gryphon, I knew his touch—as Amber and Chami surged into the apartment.

"No, let me go, Gryphon," I said, mouth dry.

Reluctantly, he released me when a few long moments passed by and there were no sounds of fighting within.

I stepped into my small apartment and found Amber and Chami standing near the door as frozen as I had been. They were having as much difficulty deciding how to react as I had because the demon dead facing us was a she.

She sat perched on my tiny love seat, fitting comfortably because she was tiny herself. But she was a small thing in height only. The rest of her was . . . well, lush. No other word for it, with her full generous breasts and hips, and hourglass waist. Even the golden-hued skin and long nails, sharp as knives, distinctive to all demon dead . . . even those merely added to her attraction. She was all shades of brown, from her large dark eyes to her full pouty lips, more mauve than red. Her hair was a color I had never seen before—gold. Bright and glistening, almost metallic in sheen. She was stunning in a soft kittenish way, sensuality oozing from her very pores. Every man's dream. Hopefully not my nightmare. Because to cross the portal from Hell into this realm, you had to be strong. Really, really strong.

No matter how delicate, how lush, how sex-kittenish she appeared, she was powerful. The good news was that she wasn't screaming and chasing after me in her demon beast form, trying to kill me. The bad news was that she was here. What did she want? For that matter, how had she found me? Did the demon dead know enough about the human world to flip through the Yellow Pages?

"So, you are Mona Lisa," she purred. Her voice was as luscious as the rest of her, full-bodied, rich and throaty, satiny smooth. It literally licked across your skin in a tactile caress. The men shivered lightly, almost imperceptibly, but enough for me to know that they felt it, too. My nipples tightened involuntarily. Shit. I'd almost rather that she was trying to kill me. A touch homophobic? You betcha.

I licked my dry lips. "Yes, I'm Mona Lisa. Who are you?" Not quite rude, but not my most polite, either.

"I am Lucinda." She said it like it should mean something to me, but it didn't. Her eyes narrowed slightly. "Halcyon's sister."

His sister? Halcyon had a sister?

Well, crap. Now we really didn't know how to handle her.

"All of Hell is abuzz with your name. A woman important enough to the High Prince that he killed another demon in challenge over you. Halcyon has not executed someone like that for . . . oh, what is it now . . . a hundred years?"

I flinched because I knew who he'd executed a hundred years ago. Kadeen's father. And the son had been trying to challenge Halcyon ever since. The High Prince of Hell had ignored him up till now . . . until Kadeen had snatched me, mauled me, ripped into my throat, and drank down my blood. Then Halcyon had accepted his challenge and had killed him.

Unfortunately, the demon dead do not die—or would that be, die again—easily. Inside, the deepest part of me, I still trembled with the battle, the horror, so fresh in my memory.

"Well, as you can see," I said, my voice dry and raspy, "I am not much."

Lucinda threw back her head and laughed. A light, melodious, tinkling sound that shivered down your spine in a delighted caress, stroking things inside you that she had no business stroking. I shifted uncomfortably and decided that her laughing was a bad, bad thing. I'd try not to make her do it again.

"How modest. Is that your attraction?" She stood up suddenly and all of us tensed.

But even though my heart raced, my feet remained planted because I'd already decided how to handle her. She was curious about me. Hopefully, once she satisfied that curiosity, she would leave. It was a game plan of sorts. So I stood there as she walked closer. Although walk was not quite the word for how she moved. Swayed. Swayed would be a much better word.

Standing, her lush shape was displayed even more obviously. She wore a silk shirt like her brother, only it was the color of deep burgundy, the color of blood, instead of the white that Halcyon usually favored. And it molded to Lucinda's shape in quite a different way than it did to him. Her black leather pants looked as if they had been painted on her. Now here was tight. Amber's pants, in contrast, had merely fit him well.

She brushed against Amber, who was standing protectively before me. And even though she reached only halfway up his massive chest, he almost jumped when she touched him. His fists clenched, unsure of what to do.

"How big and tall you are," Lucinda purred, looking up at

him, a smile curving her full lips. Her gaze trailed down his face until her glance fell like a loving caress upon his neck, on the slow pulse that beat there strongly at the base of his throat. She looked at that bounding pulse like a woman looked at chocolate, as if imagining how it would taste, how it would melt in your mouth. Only it wasn't chocolate she was craving.

"It's okay, Amber," I murmured. "Let her through."

At my soft command, Amber stepped away and let her approach me. She seemed blissfully unconcerned with the fact that Chami and Amber flanked her on either side now. Either she knew they posed no threat to her unless she tried to harm me, and she was not planning on harming me. Or she was arrogantly sure of her own power and ability to protect herself. She stopped directly in front of me, her head reaching only to my chin, and then did something that no human would have done. She smelled me.

"You smell like the night," Lucinda said, her nostrils flaring delicately as she took in my scent.

"We were walking outside," I said a bit breathlessly, my heart pounding at having her this close to me. Close enough to touch. Close enough to rip out my heart or slice off my head with those lethally sharp nails—two of the ways to kill a Monère. Of course, I wasn't a full-blooded Monère, so I was probably even easier to kill.

She examined me from head to toe in a thorough scrutiny, a thorough scenting. "You smell of power. And the smell of two others cling to your skin."

She turned, a dainty demon, and stepped up to Gryphon. He'd frozen into that unnatural stillness that they were all capable of holding themselves in, as if they were carved from stone. Only his eyes moved, following her as she leaned in close, took in his scent.

"You, Warrior Lord," Lucinda said softly, her eyes running appreciatively over his stunning loveliness before moving on to Amber. "And you," she said, looking up once more at the giant. Slowly, she reached out and stroked her hand just above Amber's arm, as if caressing something solid but unseen. "Two powerful Warrior Lords."

She flowed with sinister grace to the last of my men, Chami. Laughter was not in his eyes now, nor was the boyish charm he usually sported evident upon his lean face. That boyishness was as deceiving as the rest of his appearance. It had been a long time since he had been a boy, over a hundred years at least. Monère lived up to three hundred years of age. They were considered mature at a hundred, seasoned at two. There was a coolness to Chami's eyes now, a seriousness much more in keeping with his deadly nature as he let her smell him.

"Ah, but this one . . ." Lucinda turned her unsettling gaze back to me. "This one you have not claimed. His scent is not upon your skin. Nor yours upon his." Her eyes narrowed thoughtfully. "I smell Halcyon's scent upon your neck, but nowhere else on your body."

Gee, all that from one sniff. My hand lifted to my neck, the skin tingling where Halcyon had bit and tasted me. The wound had healed, was no longer there, but the remembered feel of where he had pierced my skin lingered still like a phantom memory. And the memory was not one of fear.

"Halcyon has not even taken you to his bed," Lucinda murmured with surprise, shaking her head. "And yet you hold him as if in thrall. Is that your allure for him? The tease, the chase? The anticipation?"

"I am not teasing Halcyon," I said. "I do not wish to be his lover. As you can already tell by smelling me, my bed is full."

"Ah, yes. Your two lovers." Lucinda smiled, sauntered over to Gryphon, and brushed the back of her fingers down the side of his face in a light caress as he stared impassively down at her.

An unfamiliar feeling swept over me—hot, sharp, like taloned claws. Jealousy.

Slowly, carefully, I pulled Gryphon away from her touch. "Mine," I said, baring my teeth at her. "Don't touch."

She laughed again with wicked delight. "Oh. Now I glimpse your attraction to my brother. A little cat showing her claws." She swayed seductively back to Chami. "What about this one? Can I touch this one?"

I looked at Chami but could read nothing in his carefully blank eyes. "Only if he wishes you to," I finally said.

Lucinda leaned forward and pressed her soft full curves along Chami's long slender length. One hand ran down his chest in an almost touch, brushing again just above his skin. "Such lovely thrumming power," she murmured, looking up into Chami's eyes. "So, my delicious one. Do you want me to touch you?"

"What do you want?" Chami asked bluntly.

"A drink of your blood," Lucinda replied, an eerie echo of Halcyon's words to me when we first met.

Chami's blue eyes glinted like hard diamonds, but his face paled even more than its usual whiteness. "Will you leave us then?"

Her lips curved slowly, lusciously. "Yes, I've seen what I've come to see." And the almost touch became true touch as her hand moved that one last inch of distance and stroked his chest.

"Then take your drink and kindly depart."

"Chami, no," I protested. "You do not know what it is like."

"On the contrary," Chami said. "I know exactly what it is like."

I shook my head. "It will not be like what you experienced with Kadeen."

"That can only be considered good, milady."

Kadeen had ripped into him and almost drained him dry. It was incredibly brave of Chami to willingly allow another demon to touch him after that savage experience. And he was doing so to protect me. To get rid of her. But he didn't know what she could do to him with a simple taste. Nothing like what he was expecting. And I didn't know how to tell him that.

"It is my wish," Chami said to me softly and glanced back at Lucinda. "I only ask that you be gentle when you take the drink you desire. A drink, not a draining."

"Agreed. Gentle . . ." Lucinda laughed huskily and the sound was like the soft tickling brush of fur stroking over your naked skin, chasing a shiver through us all. "Yes, I can do gentle."

With an almost tender gesture, she drew his head down to her. And he came to her, trembling.

"So sweet," she murmured against his lips.

"I am far from sweet," he whispered harshly.

"Sweet and gallant. You fear me and yet you yield to me . . . for your Queen."

My hand clenched Gryphon's hand tightly as Lucinda turned her mouth slowly into Chami's throat. One tiny hand held Chami secure behind the neck, the other lightly gripped his shoulder. Lifting up on her toes, with her small luxuriant body pressed against the slender bend of his, they looked like lovers embracing. Until her lips drew back, and her teeth lengthened and sharpened.

Gently, she ran the tip of her long, sharp fangs once, twice, across the pulse bounding slowly, powerfully along his neck. He shuddered, shook in her arms but did not fight her. Gently, almost tenderly, she sank those fangs down into his flesh until those mauve lips pressed tight against his skin and the strong column of her throat worked, swallowing.

I watched as Chami's eyes glazed over and then widened in surprise. As the tension that sang in him relaxed beneath her thrall. As she took him over, drank him into her body. And gave him back pleasure instead of pain. Pleasure like nothing else in this world.

And I wondered. Did his groin tingle, ache, throb as sensual tendrils raced like invisible caressing hands over him, inside him? Was almost agonizing pleasure swelling up within him, then bursting from him as he cried out, held her tight? As he jerked and shuddered helplessly against her. As light shone free from his body, called forth by his pleasure, liming him in harsh brilliant beauty—a true child of the moon. What he was. What we all were. Monère. Supernatural creatures descended from the moon, faster and stronger than humans. Descendants of another race from another planet long dead.

The blinding brilliance of the moon's rays slowly faded back into Chami. Now it was Lucinda who held him. Who laid him down gently on the ground, the scarlet red of his blood brilliant upon her lips like lipstick. And I wondered . . . did Chami wish even now, sated, almost insensate, for more of that sharp, painful ecstasy?

Lucinda licked his blood from her lips slowly, savoringly, her eyes heavy-lidded and languorous.

"A small taste of me," she whispered. And I shuddered and shivered in remembrance of Halcyon's words to me. *A small taste of me, as I taste you.*

Lucinda straightened and her gaze lifted to regard me once more. "Let Halcyon fuck you. Maybe then his fascination with you will fade. That fascination endangers you both." With those words, she walked out the door, closing it softly behind her.

I rushed over to Chami and knelt beside him. "Chami, Chami. Are you all right?"

His eyes, when he rolled them up toward me, were still dazzled, his pupils darkly dilated. He was still floating in the glowing aftermath. My eyes lowered to the wetness staining the front of his pants. Tears of his pleasure. Evidence of his orgasmic release.

"You knew," Chami said, his voice languid, dreamy.

I met his pleasure-punched eyes and nodded. "Yes."

"Merciful Mother." His voice rolled out slowly, stretched softly. "How can you resist that?"

And though his whisper had been but the barest sound, his question echoed long and loud and haunting in the sudden silence of the apartment.

CHAPTER 3

*I*t was quiet after Chami left. To change, he said, though a part of me wondered if he was hurrying after Lucinda to give them both another taste. Another drink of his blood for another drink of her pleasure. But even as I wondered, I didn't try to stop him. The real danger to us had passed, from her and from our other enemies who we had either killed or banished. We were safe enough for now. And Chami, especially, could look after himself.

We all had special gifts. Chami's unique power could be discerned from his full name, Chameleo. A name given to him for his chameleon ability to blend with his surroundings so that he became invisible.

Guilt kept me silent because Chami had no one in his bed. Nor did Aquila or Tomas, the two other guards sworn to my service. And even though I had made it clear before I had taken them on that I would not be sleeping with them, still I felt guilty. Because Monère men gained power from sleeping with a Queen. Gryphon and Amber had gained enough power from mating with me to become Warrior Lords, able to sustain their own life without a Queen. Able to rule their own territories should they so choose. But they had chosen, instead, to be with me.

The question haunted me—had I been less human in my morality and more willing to take many into my bed as other Queens did, would Chami, Tomas, or Aquila gain enough power to become Warrior Lords as well?

But I could not be less human. My humanity was stretched thinly enough as it were, taking both Amber and Gryphon as lovers, although not at the same time. No, not that. Alternating weeks. Stunned with relief that they were not leaving me, I'd only just promised to try it.

How could you resist that? Chami had asked. And the answer, truthfully, was not easily. Had I met Halcyon first, my elegant Demon Prince, I could have loved him. He was gentle, extraordinary, and so lonely. It was his loneliness that called most strongly to me, because before I met Gryphon and he brought me fully into this new world, I was lonely and alone in a sea of humans. Raised among them, but different, always apart like Halcyon was among the Monère. I resisted Halcyon only because Gryphon feared him. While Gryphon shared me generously with Amber, he was insanely jealous of Halcyon.

Halcyon does not belong to you, Gryphon had told me. *He is not one of us. And being with him does not strengthen but endangers you.*

I resisted Halcyon's lonely sensual allure because I could not bear the thought of losing either Gryphon or Amber. I could not bear to be alone again after just having found their love and knowing what it was like to be loved by them— deeply, passionately, intensely, with body and soul. The same way I loved them.

A finger ran down my neck, startling me from my thoughts, stroking over where Halcyon's neat puncture marks had branded my skin not long ago. And though they were gone from sight, they lingered still: invisible marks. I turned to gaze into Gryphon's eyes, blue and rich like the summer sky.

"Was it like that for you?" Gryphon asked me softly, silkily.

My throat went suddenly dry at his question, at the way he had asked it.

"It was the price for bringing me back, a sip of my blood," I said with only the slightest quaver. "He could have kept me in Hell." Almost had.

"Did you enjoy it like Chami?" Gryphon asked. His voice deepened, lowered, grew more softly menacing. "Or did you enjoy it even more?"

I'd never been afraid of Gryphon before. Never. But looking into those blue swirling eyes, hard and hot and laced with an indefinable emotion . . . something like fear—a thrilling touch of it—chased down my spine and raised goose bumps on my skin.

I backed up as he advanced until I was stopped by something solid, something tall, something unmovable. I rolled my eyes up. "Amber," I whispered. He was a solid blocking wall behind me, Gryphon a silky threat in front.

"It is said that a demon dead can give great pleasure," Amber said quietly, his deep voice rumbling through my back, "so that one would do almost anything to experience it again and again."

Always before, Amber's bigness had been a comfort, never a threat. But now, with Amber behind me, Gryphon before me, jealousy and insecurity singing in their voices both . . . now his bigness was far from comforting.

"I-I chose to return to you," I said, stuttering. "To you both."

"But did you consider, for one brief tempting moment, staying with him?" Amber asked, his voice deep and dangerous as his broad hands came up to grip my shoulders lightly, imprisoningly.

I could not answer Amber, dared not, because for one brief mad heartbeat of time I had. If Amber and Gryphon had not been waiting for me above, I would have stayed in that other realm with Halcyon, surrounded by his love, returning it.

"We can please you as well as he can," Gryphon murmured, bending down to place a kiss upon my neck in the spot where he had touched me before—Halcyon's invisible brand. "Differently. But just as much."

I shivered beneath the light press of Gryphon's lips, scared by the dark promise in his words. Scared even more by my reaction to them, because—God forgive me—the sensual threat dangerously lacing his words chased deliciously through a hidden, murky part of me. The thought of sex not totally safe, not totally sweet, with a hint of danger . . . A part of me—that frighteningly dark, cruel part of me that was slowly emerging—thrilled to the potential violence. Within me, secret parts softened, warmed, heated, and clenched with a deep, pulling throb. The pungent fragrance of my growing arousal perfumed the air, filled my nostrils. Made me close my eyes in shame, in want, in need. I was torn, both wanting to fight that dark side of me and embrace it.

"There is nothing to prove," I said, my voice tremulous. "You . . . you do please me. Both of you."

"Then let us please you again," Amber said. "Let us please you together."

I gasped as he pressed his teeth to the other side of my

neck, as he laved my tender skin with his hot, rough tongue. Amber's teeth and tongue on one side. Gryphon's cool, soft lips kissing me on the other side. I exploded into heat. Moaned my need. Gasped for air. Grasped desperately for thought, for control. But there was none.

The part of me that was Queen, my *Aphidy*—the innate, sexually attractive force between Monère men and their Queen—burst out from me, a wild and uncontrollable force set free. It rippled through the air like an invisible arrow, finding and seeking its targets with unerring ease.

Amber and Gryphon cried out, arching against me as it struck them full force. As it brushed against their own power, flaring it up in response to mine, so that we were suddenly engulfed in a drowning cloud of rising energy, of burning passion.

Amber's teeth bit down into me until he almost, almost broke skin but not quite, making me cry out with painful pleasure. Gryphon nipped me sharply on the other side, stuttering my breath. His hands reached down and with one pull, tore open my shirt. Buttons scattered in a noisy roll on the floor, but the sound was drowned out by our pants, our cries. My bra came undone and Gryphon's long, smooth fingers cupped my aching breasts, pulled low sounds from my throat, while down below, larger, rougher hands shoved my pants and underwear down my legs. I kicked free of them and felt Amber cup me, felt the hard press of his broad hand against my dewy lips.

The feel of smooth gripping hands above and callused fingers below made me buck my hips back against Amber and arch my chest out toward Gryphon. But the frustrating barrier of cloth pressed against my bare skin.

"Your clothes," I gasped. "Take them off."

Unable to wait for them to obey me, I blindly grabbed

Gryphon's shirt and pulled. The sound of ripping cloth rent the air, and the violence of it, the tearing sound of it spurred us to an even greater frenzy. Amber ground his groin against my bottom, heavy, full, and wonderfully hard. His hands left me, and a moment later I felt the brush of his hairy chest against my back.

Belt buckles—one, then another—clanged against floor. Knives thudded to the ground. And then we were all, finally, fully naked.

They sandwiched me between them, Amber's thick length a burning brand low in my back, Gryphon's hardness a nudging prod against my soft belly. I felt empty, so empty. Needing—aching—to be filled. But how could I take more than one man into me? There was only one place I could think of, and it would not accommodate them both. I shook my head, tried to fight clear of the sensual haze, then could only gasp as Amber sank two wide fingers between my legs.

"No, you're too big for her. The other way," Gryphon said, his words making no sense to me. Amber was big, yes, but he was able to fit into me.

Amber's fingers slipped out, and Gryphon spun me around to face Amber. I tried to clear my mind so I could understand what Gryphon meant. But then it was too late to think. I could only feel as Amber lifted me up and sank me down upon his length.

"Oh, God," I choked, as his incredible thickness slowly invaded me. He was so big, so thick, so wide that he had to work himself into me. I was stretched, wonderfully, terribly stretched, as with a grunt, with a series of hard little shifting thrusts with his hips, he pushed himself into me one inch, then another, and another and another . . .

Like a circuit suddenly connected, I began to glow. Amber's skin began to shine, turning us into creatures of light.

Behind me, Gryphon's slender fingers caressed down where Amber entered into me and I stiffened, tightened up, causing Amber to give a deep, reverberating groan. One of those slender fingers, wet with my own liquid desire, crept up to circle my anal pucker.

"Gryphon, what are you doing?" I asked in a high unsteady voice.

His chest brushed my back in a silky caress as he rubbed himself against me.

"Let me be in you as Amber is in you," he whispered against my neck, making me shudder.

Oh God, I thought, as I realized what he was asking. As I realized that that was what I wanted, too.

I shivered. Said, "Yes."

One more circling, wetting caress, and then he pushed that finger into me. And that slender digit was as tight an invasion in me back there in my virgin anal hole, as Amber's wide thick length filling me in front, sinking into my vaginal sheath.

"Oh God, oh God," I whimpered as he pushed into me, as they both pushed into me. My body clenched involuntarily, spasming around finger and rod, drawing out Amber's deep groan and Gryphon's soft moan. But instead of keeping them out, my inner clenching seemed to suck them both in, until Amber hilted within me and Gryphon's finger was pushed fully in to the webbing. And somehow, he felt as big as Amber did in me. I trembled and panted between them, pinned and stretched by them both.

"Oh, how sweet and tight you are," Gryphon crooned and the room radiated with our light, was brilliant with our glowing pleasure.

As if given some signal, Amber bent his head and took a tightly beaded nipple into his hot mouth. He sucked and tugged on the incredibly sensitive, elongated tip at the same time that Gryphon pulled his finger halfway out and then pushed back into me with slow determined force. I cried out and exploded. Shafting brilliance burst from me like a physical expression of the undoing within me. Waves of convulsions overtook me and ecstasy blinded me to all but the rhythm of my own body spasming and clenching around the two thick things that stretched me, filled me, were within me. And I held them tightly, as if they were my only anchors in a world gone trembling wild.

The ground tilted and careened as my devastating release passed, and I realized, when my senses were able once more to sense normally, that we were on the floor. Amber was lying on his back with me braced on top of him, and he was still hard and thick within me, still glowing as my light absorbed back into me. His golden amber eyes glittered wild and feral with his leashed passion.

"You didn't come," I said.

"No," he rumbled, and the sensation of that vibration passing up through me—felt most acutely where he still throbbed within me—forced my eyes to close and my breath to stop.

Before I could ask why he had held back his release, the feel of a hard velvet shaft sliding down from behind to touch me in that intimate space where Amber stretched me, shocked me silent. Gryphon's length dipped and glided between my legs, rolling in the honeyed wetness that overflowed from me.

"Gryphon?" I asked questioningly.

"Let me in," he whispered, his warm breath a silky caress shivering my ear as his body blanketed me from above. "Let me come into you fully."

I didn't know what Gryphon meant until his finger slid out of my sphincter. The pull of his leaving tugged sound from my throat, and then I felt another hard presence there, wet from my own fluids, bigger, wider than his finger had been.

"Let me in," he murmured and slowly pushed in.

"Oh!" The melting laxness left my body and I tensed unbearably tight again. "Oh, God . . . Gryphon."

The stretching was almost painful. Pleasure and pain mixed and became sublime. Beneath me Amber arched up, his huge body straining with restraint not to move more as Gryphon slowly sank his shaft into my back entrance. Amber's eyes locked with mine as he lifted his hips, rising up as if to meet Gryphon within me.

"Amber," I whispered as my body began to glow with the moon's lunar brightness once more. Behind me, above me, Gryphon's radiance danced with ours, casting shadows on the ceiling and walls, making us creatures of light, creatures of darkness.

Within me, I felt them touch, separated only by one thin wall. They touched and held still. I writhed, moaned, whimpered, crammed so achingly full I almost couldn't stand it.

"Move," I commanded with a shaky breath. "Dear Lord, move!"

They did. And if I thought that what had come before was torture, feeling them both moving within me, pulling out in opposite directions, then plunging back in to meet within me, in and out, in and out, meeting, converging, bulbous tips rubbing one over the over, sliding my thin membranous wall between them, surrounding me both inside and out, pulling apart and then surging together once again in perfectly synchronized counterpoint movement . . . feeling them moving within me like that was pure devastating pleasure.

Sensation flashed like wildfire, engulfing me in a hot conflagration so that I was burning, burning, crying. Then Amber was swallowing up my cries, his mouth covering mine, his tongue surging into me in the same beating rhythm as how they moved within me, in front and behind. I was burning, stretching, and crying, so that I didn't know where pleasure left off and pain began. The two were intertwined, one. Then even more sensation was added into the stormy, potent mix as Gryphon's hands cupped my breasts, squeezed. As his teeth sank sharply, sweetly, into my neck, piercing me that way as well, tasting my blood.

The pressure—the incredible pleasure—built within me until it was one huge gigantic ache. Waves of intense pleasure climaxed in a cresting crescendo. And the orgasm burst over me, out from me, as if it could no longer be contained. My body heaved helplessly, caught up totally in the bucking throes of climax, lost to control but not to sensation. I felt Amber stiffen beneath me, gripped by his own shooting convulsions. I felt the powerful jet of his pleasure splash against the mouth of my womb. I felt Gryphon shudder behind me, his body seize. Felt the heat and wetness of his own release fill me in another passage.

Slowly, the terrible tension left us. Light dimmed, faded, was absorbed back into us. And we melted one atop the other like fallen combatants after a fierce battle.

CHAPTER 4

So much for alternating weeks. I didn't know how to feel—appalled or delighted that I'd made love to Amber and Gryphon both at the same time. So I shoved the thought away from me. Put it away for another time to ponder. Maybe to savor.

I showered and dressed in a comfortable cotton shirt and cable-knit sweater I hadn't yet packed, sore in places usual and unusual. Gryphon had to wear his new shirt. His old one was completely ruined. First time I'd literally ripped the clothes off a man. Probably wouldn't be the last. I found myself grinning at that happy thought. With the pleasant task of keeping my men clothed, shopping might even become enjoyable.

Amber's old attire was safe and whole, though, and he donned them once more, insisting on saving his new clothes for when we arrived in my new territory.

Packing . . . well, we'd have to finish that another time. I couldn't stay in the apartment after our recent ménage; too discomforting, the thought of it. So we left, and I made the executive decision to take everybody out and have some fun that night. We were in the Big Apple, about to go to Louisiana. I wanted to play . . . on ice. Something I'd never done before. Something I doubted New Orleans would have. And even if they did have skating rinks, none of them would be as splendid as the famous Rockefeller Center rink.

The first time I'd come to Manhattan and walked by the world-renowned center the Rockefeller name had made famous, I'd glanced at the happy, laughing people twirling beneath the giant Christmas tree, the country's largest, skating with their boyfriends, girlfriends, family members, and loved ones, and I had daydreamed one day of it being me down there. An orphan's dream. But tonight it wasn't a dream; it was reality.

My skates suddenly went one way while my body decided to go another, and the slippery blades flew out from beneath me. My arms windmilled—yes, people really do that when they're about to fall—and with a shriek, I landed on my derrière, pulling Gryphon down with me.

The startled look of surprise and mild affront in Gryphon's eyes as he crashed onto the ice set me off laughing so hard that it brought tears to my eyes.

"I'm sorry," I gasped, dabbing my eyes, "but if you could only see the look on your face. Like"—I mimicked his Old World manner of speech—"'How dare this graceless thing happen to me.'" I lay back on the ice and howled.

"I fell," Gryphon said with slow dignity, "because you made me fall."

"Yeah," I grinned as other skaters veered around us, "I know."

Carefully, he tried to pick himself up. The skates slid out

from under him, and with that shocked look of surprise again on his face that I found so hilarious, Gryphon fell splat once more onto his butt—setting me off in another rollicking-rolling, laugh-till-you-split-your-sides fit.

He cut me off mid-chortle with a kiss. "Are you having fun?" Gryphon asked, his tender blue eyes smiling down at me with a soft light.

I kissed him back, face flushed, a happy smile plastered on my face. "Yes."

"Surprisingly, so am I. Though I would much rather be standing with Amber."

Amber was the only one I had not coaxed onto the ice.

"I would crack the ice if I fell," he'd said with inarguable truth. "I shall keep watch while the rest of you frolic on the frozen water." He shook his head as if to say: *The odd follies of humans.*

A pair of black skates swooshed expertly to a stop before us, and I looked up into a pair of dark slanting eyes so poignantly like mine. Dark hair fell in sharp straightness around a face that looked even younger than his sixteen years. It was Thaddeus, my brother whom I'd just recently found. A Mixed Blood like me, he had been abandoned at birth to an orphanage, the same as I. But he had fared better. His adoptive parents had loved him and raised him to maturity until they had been killed by a truck that had drifted into their lane and hit their car head-on. Only Thaddeus had survived the accident and the white fiberglass cast on his arm was a stark, grim reminder of that recent tragedy. We were not immortal, but we sure as hell were harder to kill.

"Show-off," I said to Thaddeus.

He held out a hand and helped me to my wobbling feet. "Hey," he said, grinning as he pulled Gryphon upright next, "it's one of the few things I can do better than you guys." He looked over my shoulder. "Uh, oh. Looks like the others need my help again."

I watched as he skated nimbly off, back to the others in our little group. Rosemary, the only Full Blood Monère woman among us, was gingerly step-walking with her skates, faring pretty well with that method, her plump face flushed pleasantly by her exertions. Tomas and Aquila, my two other guards, chivalrously supported her on either side. They were powerful warriors in their own right. But standing next to Rosemary, shorter than her by a couple of inches and far more slender, they didn't look it. Rosemary stood six feet tall and was built like an Amazon. She had left her coveted position as High Court cook to follow me to my new territory. The reasons for her doing so were several meters behind her—her children, Tersa and Jamie, rare Mixed Bloods like Thaddeus and I. Only they were only half Monère. That quarter difference in blood made a crucial difference. They were essentially human, without a Full Blood's greater strength or gifts.

I watched as Thaddeus slid to a smooth stop before Tersa. She'd fallen. Beside her, her brother, Jamie, was climbing clumsily to his feet. Their flaming russet hair gleamed like Christmas ornaments and their laughter was even brighter with the joy of youthful enjoyment. They were closest in age to Thaddeus and I—Jamie, nineteen, and Tersa, twenty-four. Tersa was actually older than I was by three years but I tended to view her as my junior. She was tiny, petite, only five feet tall, with delicate bones like a bird. But it wasn't just her size that made me protective of her. Weaker, more vulnerable, without my strength, she'd been raped to draw me out to my enemies. To show their disdain for our mongrel blood. Their mother, Rosemary, had left her sought-after post, taking up a position with me, because she knew I would do my best to protect her children. And she was right.

My brother, Thaddeus, was the only one who did not know of Tersa's brutal taking. All the other men were cautious and gentle around her, careful not to touch her or make her feel uncomfortable with their male presence. But Thaddeus didn't know. He held out a hand to her. My breath caught, wanting to stop him, yet too late to do so.

With but the barest hesitation, Tersa reached out and took Thaddeus's hand. Let him pull her up and help brush the ice from her clothes. Then, laughing, they helped clean up Jamie.

"They are good together," Gryphon said quietly, echoing my thoughts.

"Yeah, they are." My family. Thaddeus, the brother of my blood. Tersa and Jamie, the brother and sister of my heart. And the others . . . all of them mine, under my care.

"Mona Lisa." Amber's soft utterance of my name, spoken more than a hundred feet away, came to me clearly through the cacophony of sound. With so much noise bombarding our acute senses, it was a natural habit to tune it down until it became a low background hum. But some things, like the speaking of one's name, cut sharply out and apart from the rest of the din, reaching your ears easily.

I turned my face and looked to where Amber stood at the edge of the rink, his massive size standing him apart from others. But even were my eyes blindfolded, I would have known precisely where he stood from his powerful presence alone. We sensed each other in ways humans could not. That innate draw of a Monère male to his Queen was a strong pull that went both ways. It was always there, sometimes muted. But never forgotten, always felt.

I looked into Amber's stony face, blank with cool control. But I knew every nuance of those solid features so well now. I gazed into his eyes, dark blue like the color of the sea, saw the alert tension filling them, and knew that something was wrong.

I loosened that power that was within me, called it up from deep inside and flung it wide and searching, a tangible force trembling in the air in a full spreading radius outward. Searching, searching until it found one and then another's presence like ours. Two Monère males, Full Bloods, above and behind me. And a short distance beyond them, two other males and a Queen. Her distinctive power brushed abrasively against mine in an irritative, stinging fashion, feeling a bit like fire ants biting your skin—an innate reaction when two queens came in contact with one another. Whereas we were drawn to males and they to us, we were repelled by other queens—nature's way of ensuring that we disperse wide to propagate.

I turned around and looked up to the short encircling wall overlooking the rink, crowded with eager tourists who had come to the city and were enjoying the festive sight of the elaborately decorated giant tree and the circling skaters swishing small and tiny below it. The surrounding wall above us was packed three feet deep with gazing people, but the ones I sought were easily picked out among them. One man tall and dark-haired. The other with light brown hair, shorter, more beefy. Nothing usual about them but for the power they emanated in a low, steady thrum. I recognized their faces. Mona Sera's men.

Chami came to a sliding halt beside Gryphon and I. Aquila and Tomas, aware now of our nonhuman observers, skated back with Rosemary to stand protectively in front of Tersa, Jamie, and Thaddeus.

Technically, I was a Queen—an uninvited Queen—in another Queen's territory, Mona Sera's. Reason enough to hunt me down and try to kill me and my people. Although that wasn't what I really feared.

Why? Because I was Mona Sera's daughter.

Before you get any other wrong ideas here, let me set you straight. Our recently renewed acquaintance was not what you would call a cozy mother-daughter relationship. She'd tossed me out like garbage when I was born because of my mixed blood. I'd only discovered she was my mother when I broke into her home seeking a cure for Gryphon. He'd once belonged to her and she'd poisoned him with silver because he no longer wished to serve her. Mona Sera was like the wicked Queen of the West—okay, I know we were technically in the east, but you get what I mean. She was vicious and cruel. Even among the Monère, who weren't exactly known as the most gentle of creatures . . . even among them, Mona Sera was considered one of their worst Queens.

Before she'd found out I was her daughter, she'd ordered Amber to rape me. Being her daughter hadn't saved me. It was the fact that I was a Queen *and* her daughter that had spared me that fate. I was of use to her. Nothing more. She'd taken me to High Court, and had me acknowledged as a Queen. Though a Mixed Blood, I was a precious Queen nonetheless. And she did so only to have her own fertility and Queen-bearing status recognized; it gained her brownie points with the Council, increased her own value.

She'd given me two gowns, two of her men, Amber and Gryphon, and then washed her hands of me once more.

Whether you live or die now is of no concern to me, she'd said.

Now some might think that giving me two of her men was a generous gesture on her part. Trust me, that wasn't the case. They had become too powerful for her, and she did what Queens typically did when that happened: She tried to kill them. They were dying when she'd given them to me— Gryphon from the liquid silver she had poisoned him with,

Amber from sun poisoning. She'd roasted Amber under the sun's hot rays, under the guise of punishing him for disobeying her, until he was one gigantic, weeping mass of boils and pus.

Mona Sera had only given Gryphon and Amber to me because I had asked for them and because they were dying. She hadn't expected them to live; no one had. But I'd saved them and now they were mine.

We left the ice and changed back into our shoes. I didn't really think Mona Sera was here to try and kill us. But with my mother, you never really knew. Safest, always, to treat her with caution. We made our way to the upper level.

"Stay here, please," I said to Aquila and Tomas. Nodding, they remained at a far corner guarding Rosemary and the kids, as Chami, Gryphon, Amber, and I strode forward to see what my dear mother wanted.

Gryphon nodded first to the shorter, stocky warrior. "Kyle." Then nodded to the taller, dark-haired one. "Francois."

They nodded back.

"Warrior Lord Gryphon. Warrior Lord Amber," Kyle said, politely addressing them by their proper titles.

These two men had once hunted Gryphon at their Queen's order, and had considered Amber as good as dead. I wonder what they felt at their brethren's elevated status, Warrior Lords now instead of roadkill. Were they jealous of them or happy for them? Nothing showed. Their eyes and faces were blank, wiped clean of all emotion and expression, as Amber and Gryphon's had once been. Impassive, as all of Mona Sera's men had to be.

"My Queen seeks a word with Queen Mona Lisa," Kyle said, glancing over at two black cars parked at the curb. Both were Lincoln Town Cars, ubiquitous to Manhattan, looking innocuously like the thousands of others used for private car service here in the city. But the occupants within these two cars were not human businessmen or women returning home after a long day's work.

"Queen Mona Lisa will be happy to meet with your Queen," Gryphon said, "out here in the open."

"Will the park bench meet with your approval?" Kyle inquired.

The bench he spoke of was situated midway between us and the Town Cars. It was occupied at the present moment by a young couple, wrapped up in kisses and each other's arms.

"Yes," Gryphon said, nodding. "That will be fine."

Francois walked back to the waiting cars while we followed Kyle to the agreed meeting spot.

Kyle cleared it by the simple matter of planting himself in front of the kissing couple. He was a small tank of a man. With his thick arms crossed in front of his barreled chest and a scowl darkening his face, he looked frankly intimidating.

"Go . . . somewhere . . . else," he growled when the young lovers finally became aware of his presence and looked up.

They departed without a word of protest, smart couple. I arched a brow and took a seat on the left side, still warm from where they had sat. Amber, Gryphon, and Chami were silent presences beside me.

"Does that work in getting a taxi?" I wondered out loud.

Humor wasn't something Mona Sera apparently encouraged in her men. Kyle didn't bother answering me. Forget smiling. With a slight bow, he departed to wait by the second car.

Francois opened the rear door of the first car. Head bowed, eyes cast down, he assisted his Queen out of the car. Mona Sera stepped out.

The first time I'd seen her, she had been filled with

power and naked. Well, half-naked. The lower part of her had been a serpentine flow of smooth rippling muscles covered by glistening scales. She'd had no legs, just the body of a snake. Mona Sera was a lamia in her other form. As first impressions went, it had been . . . let's say, impressive.

Even now, fully clothed, she packed the same punch. Not so much because she was beautiful—more striking. Her hair fell long and unbound in a silky wash down to her hips, a true, pure black, so dark that blue highlights reflected from it beneath the crescent moon's silvery light. Her lips were thinner than mine, but the cheekbones, the strong line of jaw . . . I could see her stamp in my own face, and in that of Thaddeus's. What made me want to keep the two of them far, far apart was the coldness radiating from that icy, handsome face. She had eyes like a doll. No, that wasn't right. She had eyes like a snake. Like the reptile that she was—cold and calculating. No warmth, no compassion. Nothing human in those eyes.

Mona Sera stepped out of the car without a glance at the man whose hand she'd taken, treating it—him—like he didn't exist. Only there for her convenience, to serve her. Francois remained subserviently bowing until she swept past him. I sensed another male, but he remained unseen in the front seat of the first car. The driver.

Mona Sera took a seat beside me on the bench, as far away as the wooden planks allowed. "You are still here in my territory," she said by way of greeting.

"We are leaving in few days," I said.

"The sooner you depart, the better." She cast me a very unfriendly look, her black eyes glittering coldly. "Trouble follows you like a dark cloud."

See. Real warm, my mother.

Her comment made me wonder if she knew about Lucinda's recent visit.

"Not just one demon dead, but two now have sought you out here in my city."

Yup. She knew. And she wasn't happy about it. Didn't blame her. Neither was I.

At a snap of her fingers, Kyle opened the second car's door. The odor hit me—hit us all—strongly. A pungent, rotting stench that reached our sensitive nostrils and made us instinctively cringe. The smell of death and disease. Foreign to a Monère. Our bodies were able to heal just about anything almost miraculously fast. The only time before I had smelled something like this was when Gryphon had been dying of silver poisoning.

My heart gave a little extra beat when I saw whom Kyle helped out of the car. Beldar, one of Mona Sera's stronger remaining warriors. His hair was white, though that wasn't completely accurate. He was actually blond, but it was a shade so light, so pale, that it appeared white. Beldar looked up and his eyes met mine.

He had green eyes. Not the mixed brown-green of hazel, but pure emerald green like what you would see in a tropical rainforest. Vibrant, stunning. Even ill and weak he was still beautiful, perhaps more so because his fragility allowed me to really see the pure beauty of his features for the first time—the full line of his lips, the lovely flaring arch of his brows, the straight aquiline nose. Features you normally didn't notice when his face was laughing and mobile beneath the shine of his forceful personality. His charm, then, sparkled at you, blinding you to all else. But now he wasn't smiling, he wasn't being charming. He was barely walking.

Supported by Kyle, he shuffled forward until he fell heavily onto his knees before us. Gently Kyle released him and stepped back to join Francois, standing to Mona Sera's right. Our two groups were split neatly down the middle of the bench, with Beldar between us like a sacrificial victim.

People glanced curiously at our little group but kept on walking. It was Manhattan. People were allowed to be odd here. A man kneeling on the cold cement before two women was nothing.

"Still cleaning house, Mona Sera?" I asked. "Another strong warrior you decided to poison with silver?"

Mona Sera smiled. It was not a pleasant expression. "Oh, no. This I did not do. The blame for this rests on you."

I arched a brow. "Me?"

"You brought a demon dead here among us. It is not running silver that sickens his body. He was bitten."

"Bitten?" My heart suddenly racing, I turned my head to look up at Chami. He stood beside me, strong and healthy, his power and presence untainted by sickness. The tiny marks on his neck were clean, healing, not rotting. I turned my gaze back to Beldar, swaying weakly before us on his knees, but could see nothing obvious. His wound was not visible to our eyes, only discernible by our acute sense of smell.

"Lucinda's bite did this to Beldar?" I asked.

"Not Lucinda." Mona Sera's lips curled. "Her hellhound."

Chills feathered down my spine like an icy hand. "A hellhound? Here? What is one doing here?"

"That is what I wished to ask *you*," Mona Sera said coldly. I saw something in her eyes then that I'd never seen before. Fear. A trembling dark shimmer of it.

She leaned toward me, and the abrasiveness of her nearness scraped rawly against my nerves like tiny claws. "Your presence brought it here. This"—she swept a hand toward Beldar—"is your fault. You are costing me yet another warrior, daughter mine. And I do not like it," she spat, her eyes glinting like black onyx stone. "Fix him. And return him."

I had a bad feeling where she was going with this. I was the only healer of sorts within the area. No healer, apparently, had wished to swear into Mona's Sera's service. "You want me to heal him?" I said, just to be sure.

"Yes. If Beldar dies, I will take one of your men in his stead." Mona Sera's eyes flicked past me to the other half of our group, watching and waiting in the distance. "Or perhaps your woman."

She meant Rosemary, a Full Blood Monère female. Tersa, a Mixed Blood, didn't even exist in her eyes. I watched as Mona Sera's eyes flicked dismissingly over Jamie and Thaddeus. Had she seen the likeness? Guessed that Thaddeus was her son? Would she even care?

"No," I said, shaking my head, feeling panic welling within me. "You cannot blame this on me."

"Oh, but I do." She turned those black moribund eyes back to me. "Heal him or forfeit one of your own for what you will have cost me."

"I-I don't know if I can heal him. What about the healers at High Court? Would they be able to help him?"

"You may try that if you wish, if he lasts that long. He was bitten but two hours ago and already the decay spreads across him like a living eating thing. If you wish to bring him to High Court, do not tarry long. But as to whether the healers there can cure him, even they will not be able to tell you. No Monère has even been bitten by a hellhound."

I was feeling more and more faint. "Never?"

"No, because no hellhound has ever been seen in this realm before." Her hard eyes drilled into mine. "Do what you wish. I shall return tomorrow. For Beldar or another. It matters not to me."

She stood and with a swirl of her long black coat, disappeared into the backseat of the first car. Kyle and Francois stepped into the second car and they drove away.

Gently, Amber went to Beldar's side. Kneeling, he wrapped an arm about the smaller man's waist.

Beldar gasped with pain. "No! Let me . . . let me hold on to you instead, old friend." Braced against Amber, he pulled himself to his feet and allowed Amber to guide him onto the bench.

Aquila, Tomas, and the others joined us.

"Who was that?" Thaddeus asked.

I looked into my brother's eyes. "That was our mother, Mona Sera." I'd never told him about her before and he'd never asked. He'd been smart enough to realize that had there been anything good to say about her, I would have told him.

"No," Thaddeus said, his voice soft but firm. "The woman I just buried was my real mother. The one who loved me and raised me. Not the one who gave me away."

I caught his hand in mine and squeezed. "She did us a favor by giving us away."

Thaddeus squeezed back, smiled slightly. "Yes, it would seem that she did." Worry came into his eyes as he looked at Beldar. Worry mixed with pity. "Can you heal him?"

"You heard?" I asked.

Thaddeus nodded.

"I don't know," I whispered. God help me, I did not know if I could heal him.

God help us all if I couldn't.

CHAPTER 5

*B*efore I became a Monère Queen, I was a nurse. But my nursing skills, good though they were, was not why Mona Sera had brought Beldar to me.

As we rode in a taxi back to my apartment, I turned my hands over to gaze at my palms. Embedded in them was the reason why she had sought me out—my Goddess's Tears. They were moles the size and color of pearls. Two moles buried deep in the heart of my palms, one in each hand. I'd had them all my life. And all my life, I'd been able to sense injury and sickness with them and ease pain. But not heal, though I had sensed the power within me to do so. That had remained dormant until I had come into contact with others of my kind and had entered the Monère's secret society, a violent and dangerous world. There, I had used these moles— marks the Monère had only heard about in their lore and legends but had not seen since the time of their great exodus from the Moon, their dying planet that they had abandoned four million years ago. I'd used the Goddess's Tears to heal and to hurt. And the injury I was capable of inflicting had been enough to have the rogue bandits who'd kidnapped me consider cutting off my hands. My mother had spoken true . . . trouble did seem to follow me like a dark cloud. But if there had been peril, there had also been grace. I rubbed those pearly moles now, felt the tiny bumps, and wondered if they could save Beldar. If they could save us.

The taxi came to a halt in front of my Greenwich Village apartment, and we got out. Braced between Amber and Gryphon, Beldar managed to hobble to the elevator. Chami and I followed behind. I'd sent the others back to the Pierre. If I was going to have sex, I wanted to have it in relative privacy, away from the acute senses of the others.

Why was I thinking about sex? Because that was the way I healed.

Yeah, I know. Not the most convenient gift, mine.

The elevator doors pinged open and we stepped onto the seventh floor. Though Beldar's harsh panting and choked groans sounded loud in our ears, a human would have barely heard them. Nor would they have smelled anything. Had anyone seen him, he would have appeared drunk, listing and unsteady, having to be supported by others. But there were no eyes to watch him in the empty corridor other than our own.

I opened the door and he staggered in, leaning heavily against Amber. He sank down—collapsed, really—onto my small love seat. My apartment, like most apartments in Manhattan, was small. It was essentially only two main rooms; the tiny kitchen and even tinier bathroom did not count. The main space had a small dining area near the front door. The rest of the oblong space was the living room, a sitting area comprised of a rust-colored love seat and a green-patterned armchair.

The remaining room was my bedroom, which was even smaller than the living room space. Basically just my queen-sized bed—which I'd gotten, incidentally, before I'd known I was a Queen, in case you're wondering—and a crammed-in dresser. Hip-wide walking space only in there.

I really didn't know where to put Beldar, wouldn't know until I'd seen how badly injured he was. And something in me shied away from doing that because I knew it was going to be something horrible, something I'd want to run screaming from instead of embrace.

I shut the door behind me, and the locks snicked loudly into place. Bracing myself, I turned back to look at him. Beldar's eyes were closed, his head tilted back, resting against the love seat. His skin was pale and clammy, and his heart was beating fast for a Monère, sixty beats per minute instead of the usual thirty, pounding like a fierce drum in my ears.

The smell was even worse in the enclosed room, and the putrid stench of rotting flesh rolled my stomach. Fighting not to gag, I walked over to the windows and opened them, gasping in a few breaths of fresh air. But that didn't really help because my own fear was bitter and metallic in my mouth. I didn't know if I could do this. Even if I could find pleasure, make myself shine, make him shine, I didn't know if I could heal him.

Gryphon came up silently behind me. "What's wrong, Mona Lisa?"

"I don't know if I can do this," I said softly.

His arms came around me and I leaned back into the comfort of his embrace, gazing blindly out the window into the blackness of night.

"You sound fearful," he said with surprise. "You have never been afraid before."

I laughed, but it was not a happy sound. "I have always been afraid, Gryphon. Always."

"Then I had not seen it before. I have only seen your fearlessness, your great heart." He turned me in his arms, peered deep into me with his sharp falcon's eyes. He was a gyrfalcon in his other form, and keenness of sight all the way down into another's soul was one of his gifts.

"You doubt yourself," he said with soft amazement, "when you never have before."

"I'd never failed before. But I failed with you. I couldn't heal you when you were dying. And Beldar smells much worse than you did even near the end, weeks later, when you were rotting away from the silver poisoning you from within. What happens if I fail with him, too?"

"You did not fail with me," Gryphon said softly. "You simply found another way to save me. If you cannot heal him with your power, we will find another way with him as well."

His trust humbled me. But his words made me think, gave me an idea. One I didn't like but had no choice but to pursue. Looking into Gryphon's beautiful eyes, this man, this miracle whom I loved so much . . . it was the hardest thing to be the Queen that they called me, and ask what I asked next of him.

I took a deep choking breath and made myself do it. "Gryphon, you've interacted the most with the demon dead. Are the most knowledgeable about them among us. I . . . I must ask you to search for Lucinda. Perhaps the demon dead princess will know how to heal Beldar. I'll do my best to heal him, but in case I can't . . . Take Chami with you and try to find her, please. For me. For all of us."

Gryphon brought my hand up, and pressed a gentle kiss to the back of my fingers. "Of course. I shall go do as you ask." He strode to the door, Chami beside him, and I watched them, feeling a terrible knot of worry and fear twist my stomach as I sent them out into danger.

"Be careful," I called out to them because I could not stop myself. "If you cannot . . . if the hellhound is with her . . . Don't let yourselves be hurt. Come back to me safe and whole, and as you said, we will find another way."

Gryphon smiled, a tender curve of his lips. "As my Queen commands." And then he and Chami were gone. Only Amber remained. Amber, me, and a dying Monère warrior bitten by a beast from Hell.

I took one last deep breath of cool night air and walked over to Beldar, eased him out of his long coat. Then, kneeling before him, I began unbuttoning his shirt. It was stained on the right side by a dark wet substance—the source of the foul stench.

"I've dreamed of this," Beldar said, his mouth quirked up in a weak smile. "You kneeling in front of me, your hands touching me. Of course, I hadn't imagined myself in quite this much pain."

"I, no doubt, was the one in pain," I said tartly, a hard glint entering my eyes.

"Ouch." He gave me a rueful smile. "Still don't forgive me for when we first met."

"When we first met, Beldar, you were going to rape me. No, I do not forgive you. You would have taken me without a qualm, wearing that pleasant smile that even now graces your lips."

"Ah, but I would have thanked you afterward," he said like the charming bastard he was, grinning with a shadow of his old charisma.

While it was true I hadn't forgotten, would never forget, I also wasn't as mad as I pretended to be. We'd been intruders, Gryphon and I, stealing into Mona Sera's dwelling. And when Beldar had pounced on me, it had actually been in an attempt to save Amber from their Queen's wrath. Amber had refused to rape me, so Beldar was going to do so in his stead. Twisted, and yet still gallant in a perverse way.

And so, even though my fear of that time was still a sharp memory within me, my hands were gentle as I pushed open his shirt . . . and gasped. Not a smart thing to do because it drew more of that terrible smell into my lungs.

He'd been bitten on the right side, just below the ribs. Terrible ripping tears that had turned his flesh into jagged raw meat with deep gouging grooves. And yet that wasn't what made me gasp. It was the color of his skin surrounding that awful bite that filled me with such revulsion.

Blackness had seeped malevolently beneath the surface of his white skin, swirling, spreading slowly in a sluggish creeping advance even as I watched, like a dark hand of corruption moving insidiously within him. Like an evil hand of death, despoiling the clean flesh it touched, changing it into putrid mush.

It had spread across his entire abdomen and was moving up his chest. The blackish discharge oozed from the hole in his side like fecal drainage, making the nurse in me wonder if his bowels had been perforated. But only for a moment. The Monère part of me that could smell him knew that it wasn't stool that leaked out his side but rotten, decaying flesh.

"Merciful Light. It looks even worse than it feels," Beldar said faintly. "And it feels really, really bad." A painful shudder rippled through him.

A sharply indrawn breath turned me to Amber, to find him kneeling beside us. Wetness glistened his eyes as he gazed upon the horror that was Beldar. Any doubts about whether Amber cared for this man ceased to be as I looked into those deep sorrowful eyes. Yes, Amber cared. He cared deeply.

"Do not fear, Beldar," Amber murmured. "Mona Lisa shall aid you."

The total faith I heard in Amber's words shook me. How could he believe in me like that? Completely, with such absolute trust?

Beldar's face suddenly twisted. "Oh, Goddess!" he cried, as another agonizing wave of pain wracked his body, and the corrupting darkness crept further up him. "Hurry, please," he gasped, fear wild in his eyes. "If you are going to try and save me, do so quickly while there is yet something to salvage."

I gazed at him helplessly for a moment. With his fear echoing within me, desire was the farthest thing I felt. Then a wonderful calm stole over me, that stillness that sometimes came upon me before a battle, when I knew there was nothing else to do but go forward. The doubt, the unusual hesitance in me faded away, disappeared as I realized there was no one else to help him. Only me. We no longer had time to doubt and worry. Only act. And I knew what I wished to do.

My right hand came up to cover the ravaged side of him, to barely touch the ruined surface gently. Putrid slime wet my hand, coated it. But it was the pain deeper within that decay that called forth my own power to the fore, pulling it from the center of me. It flowed up my body, and washed down my arms and out through my hand in a powerful rush. The Goddess's Tears embedded in my palm tingled and warmed, reverberating my hand as that energy spilled down into his wounds, taking away his pain, balming it like a cool wind as it searched and assessed and found that the damage within him was deep and malignant, frighteningly so.

"Oh, my," Beldar breathed, turning wondrous eyes to me. "You took away the pain."

"Only temporarily. And only the pain. I cannot heal you that way."

"I know," he whispered. "You heal with sex." And with the pain gone, the look in his eyes became more heated, more male.

I shook my head. "No intercourse, Beldar. Amber will be the one in my body, bringing me as I bring you."

"No sex?" he said, pained. "I'm dying, Mona Lisa, truly dying. But you are killing me even more."

I touched his sweat-dampened face. "You are not mine, Beldar. I must return you. I would not be doing you a favor returning you more powerful than you came to me. You walk the line already with Mona Sera. I do not wish to be the one to tip you over so that she feels threatened, so that she feels she has to destroy you."

He froze under my hand in that unnatural stillness the Monère were capable of. And I did not know if it was in fear, or because he was not used to a woman's gentle touch, making me wonder how long it had been since anyone had touched him in kindness, in tenderness?

"You think optimistically," Beldar said quietly. "In terms of a future when I do not know if I truly have one. When I saw you that first time with Amber, there on the dungeon floor as you tried to save him, both of your bodies aglow, filled with our moon's marvelous light, I thought then that if Amber were to die, being with you, being in you like that, would be a wonderful way to go."

Slowly, carefully, he brought up a hand to lay it over mine, to press my fingers even more into him so that my palm cradled his cheek and jaw. Turning his head ever so lightly back and forth, he rubbed himself against my hand. "I still feel that way. That it would almost be worth dying for if you touched me as you touched him. With care and compassion and kindness." With those words, Beldar laid himself bare, let me see him naked without his cheerful, blithe mask. As I gazed into his serious, beautiful green eyes, I did not know how to respond.

"If it does not work," Beldar said quietly. "If you cannot save me, then will you take me into yourself?"

I'd been reared among humans and had enough of their blood in me so that intimacy with a man was not something I shared lightly. A bond was forged between people who joined their bodies one with another. And I was possessive enough that I wanted to keep those that I claimed. But if Beldar was going to perish, then for that short period of time before he went, he would be mine in truth. Only mine. My touch would be the last he knew. My kiss, the last to touch his lips.

"Yes," I said, in a husky rasp. "If it does not work . . . then yes."

Mixed emotions flurried across Beldar's face. "I do not know now what I wish for. For you to heal me . . . or not heal me."

I laughed softly and let heat seep slowly into my own eyes. "No intercourse does not mean no pleasure, Beldar."

He turned dazzled eyes to his old friend. "I envy you your Queen, Amber. It must be joyous to belong to her."

"Yes," Amber said. "She is more. Better. We are fortunate."

"I am the one who is fortunate," I said, rising to my feet, my thoughts centered on what needed to be done. "Help me remove his clothes, Amber, and your own while I wash my hand and retrieve the bedding from the other room."

"And then I shall remove yours when you return," Amber rumbled, his eyes bleeding from deep blue to that pure startling golden amber. His cougar eyes.

Pulling myself away from the hot sensual promise in those eyes, I went into the bathroom. Cold water ran over my hands as I washed them in the sink. Drying them, I went into my bedroom, tore the comforter from the bed, and brought it out into the living room. Spreading it over the carpet, I tossed the pillows I had also carried with me down on top of it.

"This will jostle him less," I said softly to Amber, "and give us more room to maneuver."

With that striking gentleness that I always found so surprising in one so big, Amber lowered Beldar down onto our makeshift bed, Beldar's bare legs and naked pale arms looking so white against the blackness eating the center of his body.

In the short moment of time I had been gone, Amber had managed to rid himself of his clothing. Big and brawny, he was a shocking contrast against Beldar's injured frailness, his skin gleaming white and pure and whole like the healthy animal that he was. Muscles bulged in Amber's arms, shoulders and chest as he laid Beldar down on top of the comforter. The sinewy columns of his legs flexed and swelled, his powerful thighs bulging as he knelt, moving in that natural, graceful, unselfconscious ease that I envied. I would never be as comfortable as he was, unclothed.

My eyes moved down him as Amber stood up. And the sight of him dangling long and thick, stirring, coming alive, becoming wider and fuller, made me flush with heat. I stood unmoving, a pliant doll, as he came to me and with gentle care, lifted the T-shirt over my head. Those large fingers, surprisingly nimble, undid the clasp of my bra and I watched as those twin cups dropped to the floor, a splash of whiteness. Instinctively, my cheeks burning, my hands came up to cover the small, delicately rounded curves of my breasts.

A sound of protest came from the ground. "No, please. Don't cover yourself." Beldar's eyes locked with mine, vivid, pleading, flashing with a deepening green fire. "Let me see you," he whispered.

Trembling, I dropped my hands back down to my side. Closing my eyes, I felt the cool night air whisper across my skin, felt my nipples peak and bud beneath that breezy touch.

"You're beautiful," Beldar said softly. "Beautiful."

I shook my head, knowing I was not. But didn't tell Beldar to look away. Dying cut him a lot of slack. I kept my eyes closed and let his remain open.

I felt the waistband of my jeans tighten and then loosen. Heard the rasp of the zipper sliding down. Felt the worn denim and then my underwear being pushed down my legs, leaving me horribly, vulnerably naked. My hands fisted, my jaws clenched. I shook with the control I exerted to remain still under Amber's gentle disrobing.

Beneath his urging hand, I stepped out of my pants, shaking like a leaf blown by a strong wind. A hand tilted up my chin. "Open your eyes," Amber said softly.

My lashes lifted and I stared into his brilliant amber eyes.

"Drop your shields," he murmured, stroking his fingertips along the softness of my cheeks.

"What do you mean?" I asked.

"You keep leashed your natural attraction to us, your *Aphidy*, barricaded behind a high strong wall of your will. Allow it to come out and it will be easier for you." He bent down and pressed his lips against mine in a soft sweet caress. "Lower your shields," he said, and capturing my lower lip with his teeth, bit down hard enough for it to both hurt and please.

With a gasp, a jerky sob, I loosened my control. Like a wild animal suddenly set free, the inner power within me that was always near the surface, roared out with breathtaking force, spilling from me and hitting the others.

They cried out and suddenly Amber was crushing his mouth down on mine, forcing my lips open, plunging a wide, thick tongue inside, hunting, seeking, finding, capturing my tongue with his, kissing me with almost punishing force, as if he would eat me alive. I opened my lips wider, slid my tongue against his, and pushed and parried, teased and tantalized, hungry mewling sounds spilling from my mouth as I ate from him in turn.

Amber's strong arms wrapped around me and the world tilted and cloth brushed against my heated skin. I found myself on the ground, my face only inches away from Beldar. His luminous eyes, sparkling like precious emerald gemstone, were opened wide, dazzled and dazzling. His lips were parted; full, flushed, cherry-red . . . alluring. I leaned over and tasted him, too.

Beldar groaned as my lips met his, and his mouth moved against mine with a terrible hunger.

"Let me in, let me in," he pleaded, and the echo of his words, so like Gryphon's, sent a flush of tingling heat through me. I parted my mouth and he swept in and took control of the kiss, his agile tongue hungrily learning the contours of my soft inner flesh, the smooth surface of my teeth, the feel of the wet slide of my tongue against his, rubbing, sliding, gliding against mine, entwining them and then sucking my tongue into the cavern of his own mouth.

The taste of him was tart and tangy, like sweetness edged with something sharper. He murmured, groaned, breathed into my mouth, one hand sliding to the back of my neck to hold me to him, the other hand smoothing down my shoulder. Then like a lure he could not resist, he cupped my breast, rubbed a thumb over a taut nipple, peaking it even more. I made a soft sound and he ate it down.

"Blessed Lady, you are so sweet, so sweet," he cried and swallowed me up in another kiss.

Behind me, Amber pressed his heated lips down my back, and nibbled my shoulder, making me push back and writhe against him as one big hand flattened across my belly and pulled me back against him so that he pressed, thick and long, against my bottom, a hard shaft riding between my cheeks.

Before me, I slid a hand up Beldar's hair-prickled thigh until I held him full, thick, and aroused in my hand. He nipped my lower lip as Amber had done earlier, a sharp sweet stinging bite. I rewarded him by wrapping my fingers hard around him, pulling a low agonized sound from deep in his chest. But like the nip he'd given me, I knew it wasn't pain he felt but pleasure.

Amber's splayed hand smoothed even lower down my belly, sliding into my triangle of hair. A thick, callused finger pushed slowly inside me with testing roughness and I bucked back against him, squeezing that coarse finger with delicate, clinging inner muscles. At the same time, unconsciously, I squeezed what I held in my hand. Beldar groaned long and hard into my mouth, and he bucked forward, pushing himself within my tight grasp.

He tore his mouth from mine, pressed his heated face against me, and panted in my ear. "Oh, Goddess. Oh, Goddess. Yes, yes, more."

And then I couldn't hear anything. Could only feel as Amber pulled his finger out and began pushing his much bigger, much wider penis into me.

I wasn't stretched enough, wasn't wet enough. I was moist but not soaking wet. I was dry enough, tight enough, to feel every pushing, stabbing, stretching inch of his pulsating hardness moving into me, invading me. And it was wonderful, wonderful with that touch of discomfort. I could feel him even more, even sharper, with that edge of pain mixing with the incredible pleasure.

Light began to shimmer my skin, turning me into a luminous glowing thing, leaving Amber with no doubt as to what I felt. We only glowed in pleasure. And it was pleasure that inundated me, a painful pleasure.

I turned my face into Beldar's. "Shine," I whispered against his full, tender lips, "Shine for me," and lapped across the parted seam of his mouth. With my hands, both of them now, I pumped Beldar's hard velvety shaft in my closed fists in time to Amber's stretching, insistent push-and-slide entry into me.

I pulled—up and up. One long slow squeezing pull, almost terribly tight—and Beldar rewarded me with another groan, with the shimmer of his own pleasure lighting him from within.

As Amber pulled out of me, his fat mushroom head bumping and gliding along my responsive inner tissues, making me catch my breath, I started with my other hand at Beldar's base, pulling slowly, tightly, up his root as my other thumb swirled over his weeping crown, rubbing over his sensitive tip, anointing him with his own essence.

I lifted my thumb and brought it to my mouth, my tongue flicking out to taste him as Beldar watched with harsh breath and glittering eyes. I savored his essence, swirled it along my tongue and opened my mouth to his, sharing his own taste with him. Grating a rough oath against my lips, he plunged his tongue into me. Pushing, retreating. Sliding in, sliding out. Again and again in a heavy surging rhythm, fucking my mouth as I tightened my lips around him and sucked his tongue, my cheeks hollowed out, my mouth a receptive oral sheath for his thrusting aggression. He murmured, muttered, made wild sounds against my lips. And then he was tearing sounds from me as his fingers clasped my nipples, tugging and squeezing them, rolling them between tight thumb and forefinger in rhythm to his thrusting tongue and his sliding, hot-frictioned movement in the sheath of my hands.

The sensation of Beldar's hands, lips, tongue, and fingers, his pulsating hardness in my hands, and Amber's thickness pushing, pulling in me . . . It all built and built in a powerful spiraling tension within me, winding me tighter and tighter. The room glowed brilliantly with our incandescence, with our bright light as I twisted and climbed and stumbled to the very top of the cliff, teetering there for a long precarious moment, heat filling me up, swelling, brimming. And then spilling over.

I reached blindly down with one hand as I felt my contractions begin and found Beldar's tightly scrunched balls. One squeeze and I spilled him over, too. He pulsed and jerked in my hands, and wet fluid splashed onto my stomach and chest, so hot. And then I was taken over by my own release. But even then . . . even then I did not forget. My hand released his pulsing length and found his wet oozing side. And the reason for all this, the purpose, was foremost in my mind amidst our tumultuous release.

Heal—I thought, I willed, even as I shuddered and trembled. *Please heal!* And crying, convulsing, I spilled the hot energy of my climax and of Amber's jetting release into that wounded, blemished spot, channeling everything pouring out from us there, with strength and with prayer.

Please, Mother Moon. Please help me help him. Save us. Save my people. I can't—won't!—give any of them up.

My light peaked and began fading back into me, and I felt Amber's incandescence mute and dim. But the room still glowed. Beldar still glowed.

I removed my hand, pulled back from Beldar so I could see. And wanted to cry in anguish. To say *no!*

The torn flesh had healed. But his skin still had that dark

stain, that malevolent blackness against the pure white of the rest of him. But the darkness was different somehow. He gleamed from within like a shiny unearthly thing. Radiance burst from him with almost harsh brilliance, lighting even that dark rotted core of him so that it gleamed and sparkled like black diamonds caught beneath the sun. But it wasn't the sun that shone. It was the moon—our life source, our energy. The essence of who we were.

Amber shifted, pulled out of me, and lifted up on an elbow to gaze uncertainly down at Beldar. "What's happening?" he asked.

"I don't know," I whispered, as befuddled and caught up in the wonder of what I was seeing as much as he.

Beldar looked down at himself. But as the light started to change, to grow even brighter, fiercer, his expression of awe gave way to one of frightened panic. His eyes rounded and he threw back his head, screaming in hoarse pain. His body thrashed and rolled in agony.

"What's wrong?" I asked and grabbed his hands, pinning him down so he wouldn't hurt himself as he tossed and turned.

"Hurts," he cried. "Dear Goddess, it hurts. Worse than before. *Ahhh!*" He bucked suddenly, his body arching up off the ground, almost lifting me with him, as a violent spasm gripped him. His feet pedaled frantically against the floor, moving him clockwise around me, as if he could desperately outrun the pain that way.

"What's the matter?" Amber asked, grabbing Beldar's ankles, anchoring him still. But the moment Amber touched him, he knew. As I had known with that first contact.

"He's warm. Almost hot," Amber said softly, and his eyes, when he lifted them to me, were frightened.

By nature, Monère were cold-blooded creatures, their skins cool, their heartbeats slow. Night was their domain and they slept during the day when the hot sun ruled the sky. As a Mixed Blood, I was different. I could walk the days as well as the nights. I could withstand the sun, the heat, as well as the cool darkness. But Full Bloods could not.

I didn't know if what was happening was because of me. I didn't heal this way. My curative process was quick and clean. They were usually miraculously whole right after I channeled energy into them. It had never been like this before, a prolonged, protracted, intensifying process. Nor had anyone continued to glow for so long after I had stopped. Was the human part of my energy flow somehow making him warm? Or was it part of the corruption itself? Most importantly, how long could Beldar's body tolerate the increased temperature?

He writhed and tossed on the ground in pitiful distress and we could only anchor him by wrists and ankles while he burned. And burned was the word for it. The black light glowing through his chest and abdomen became almost unbearably brilliant and warm. Black shards of light glittered and gleamed through the front of him like the sun pulsing through a dark prism. But as he tossed and moaned, begged and cried in tearful writhing agony, the blackness seemed to grow lighter. He sparkled brilliantly, a harsh black-and-white thing.

Slowly, so slowly that I wasn't sure if I was seeing the truth of what was, or of what I wished it to be . . . slowly that emitting light gained ascendance over the darkness, overpowering it, shining through it . . . burning it away. The dark edges shrunk, slowly eaten away by the pure cleansing white light.

Beldar simply lay there now, moaning softly and panting, slicked with perspiration as he continued to glow, as light slowly overcame darkness. But it was a cool dampness, not a warm one that drenched his skin.

"It's burning the corruption away, Beldar," I said, caressing his wrists in comfort now rather than in restraint. "Soon," I crooned. "It's almost done."

His chest heaved, filling and emptying like a bellow. "I pray that it finishes soon, either way. As long as I never experience that pain again. Dying would be better than going through that again."

"Hush," I admonished gently. "You're not going to die. You're going to live." I was certain of it now as the warmth in his skin faded even as the darkness within him disappeared. When the last speck of that rotten blackness vanished in a stunning blaze of glorious white light, the radiance was gone. Like a switch suddenly flipped off, he suddenly stopped glowing, and the light vanished back into Beldar in one quick flash.

I ran my hands gently over the new skin on Beldar's chest. His flesh was smooth, whole, healed. I felt only solid muscle and untorn skin beneath my palms as I slid my hands lower, over his abdomen. Sensed only wellness through my tingling moles.

"You're well," I said, smiling brilliantly.

He lay there on his back, looking completely wrung out. "I feel as if I've been to Hell and back."

"I did that once," I said quietly. "I felt as if I were being torn apart."

"That pretty much describes it." Beldar's lips curved into a tired smile. "You healed me."

I shook my head. "I'm not sure that I did. My powers don't work like that. Maybe it was simply your own lunar light within you. Maybe that healed you once it was brought out."

"No," Beldar said with soft surety, "you healed me."

CHAPTER 6

We ended up taking turns showering. I went first at the men's insistence, even though I thought Beldar should go before me—the putrid smell still clung to him.

Amber efficiently bagged the comforter and Beldar's shirt, both stained with slimy blackness, and threw them out. The room smelled much better with them gone. Beldar ended up wearing one of my size large T-shirts, one of the ones I usually wore to bed.

"It smells of you," he said, his emerald green eyes somehow looking even larger and more brilliant with his damp hair slicked back away from his face.

I didn't know how to treat him now. Not with the combative banter we usually thrust and parried our words with. We might not have had intercourse, but we'd been intimate, and I discovered that that in and of itself created a bond. Less strong but still there. And somehow, I could read him better now. I saw the sadness that filled those eyes for one brief moment before he slid his usual carefree mask back on, a charming roguish smile once more gracing his lips.

I felt an answering sadness in me that I had to give him back into Mona Sera's cruel rule. That he couldn't belong to me.

I didn't know what to say, so I said nothing.

The doorbell rang and I went to the door and opened it without looking because I knew by their slow heartbeats who were on the other side of it—Gryphon and Chami. But they weren't alone. Another, whose heart did not beat, stood beside them. Lucinda. And in front of her was what looked like an amazingly big dog.

I backed up slowly and instinctively away from that big dog because I knew that wasn't what it really was.

I'd never seen a hellhound before, had only heard their hellish baying, but as I looked into those yellow eyes—not amber but almost a true yellow, like the burning fires of hell, feral and frighteningly intelligent—I knew that that was what stood before me. A hellhound almost as big as me, its head reaching nearly to my shoulders, brindle black and brown in coloration.

It padded silently into my apartment and for one wild moment, I seriously considered giving in to my body's screaming urges and throwing myself out the window to escape it, even knowing that it was seven stories down to the bottom, a distance I could not survive. It was a gut primal reaction to danger, the desire to flee. These creatures ate big bad demons, gobbled them down. Even the demon dead fled before them. It took a huge straining effort on my part not to run screaming away from it.

I moved slowly backward until I bumped up against Amber. His hands lifted to my shoulders and began to shift me behind him, but I resisted, shaking my head slightly. Beldar was a still, unmoving presence beside Amber, though that wasn't completely true. He was still in the sense he wasn't running, but he was moving—trembling. Almost violent tremors shook his entire body.

We were all deathly still, fearful that any sudden moves might trigger violence. Only Lucinda strolled casually into the apartment with swaying lithe ease. Gryphon and Chami entered and closed the door behind them, and the latching sound it made seemed loud and portentous in the harrowing silence.

"You lied to me," Lucinda said, her eyes cool, wide, and alert. "No one here has been bitten."

"They didn't lie," I said hoarsely. "Beldar was bitten but he's healed now."

Lucinda gave an almost evil laugh. Melodious, tinkling even, but with a malice that made your skin creep. "Now I know you surely lie. No one heals a hellhound's bite."

Well, hell. How do you argue with a demon dead princess? "It's the truth. Can't you smell it, the decaying scent? It lingers still on Beldar."

Both mistress and beast padded over to Beldar, and he looked as if he didn't know which to be more frightened of, Lucinda or the hellhound. Beldar's eyes grew enormous but he didn't run. More than I could have done, I think, faced with the two of them so close they could touch you, kill you, rip you apart. Or simply bite you again and leave you to die in rotting corruption.

"You must be Beldar," Lucinda crooned. One long, sharp fingernail scraped down his cheek. He shuddered and I wondered it if was in fear, or in reaction to Lucinda's sensual voice slithering over him in a tactile caress.

"Yes," he rasped, a faint sound barely audible. He looked as if he were trying not to breathe too hard. Be still and maybe the beasts before him would not tear him apart.

A long pointy fingernail stroked down Beldar's chest, slipped under his T-shirt and lifted it up, baring his tense, ridged abdomen.

Lucinda's head lowered and her cheek brushed against Beldar's nipple. "I do smell something . . ." She turned her head slowly back and forth, rubbing against him almost like a cat, and drew in a deep breath ". . . here."

There was a dazed expression in Beldar's eyes, helpless and bewildered. Fear was there, yes. But also arousal. Shocking, unexpected, sexual excitement was growing against his will. He hadn't known what a demon dead could do to him.

Beside Lucinda, the beast's great jaws yawned wide and open, revealing something no earthly canine possessed—a double row of razor-sharp fangs. As if one row wasn't already enough. A long pink tongue rolled out and lapped against Beldar's healed fleshed in the exact spot where he had been bitten, leaving behind a flushing redness, as if sandpaper had scraped across that skin. Beldar looked as if he were about to keel over or throw up.

Lucinda straightened up and captured Beldar's eyes. "Did Brindell bite you?"

Brindell, apparently, was the hellhound's name.

"Yes," Beldar said faintly, his voice dry and crackly. "And Mona Lisa healed me."

All eyes, including those frightening yellow ones, swung to me.

I never did well being the object of everyone's scrutiny. Made me want to distract them. "If you can't heal a hell-hound's bite, Lucinda, as you say, then why did you come?" Even without serving as a distraction, it was something I wanted to know.

Something flickered in Lucinda's eyes. "I was going to kill him. Free him from his pain. Give him a chance to make the transition to Hell before all his energy was completely consumed."

A mercy kill. That was unexpectedly—kind. More like what Halcyon would have done. Not, I would have thought, something Lucinda would do or even think to do. Perhaps she was more her brother's sister than she looked. More than her stunning, lushly cruel appearance suggested. Or maybe she simply wanted to clean up her mess, get rid of the evidence, as they say. But then again, when Beldar died—and he would have done that fairly soon—all evidence would have disappeared with him. I didn't know what to think.

"How did you heal him?" Lucinda demanded, her eyes fixed on me with cool, sharp appraisal.

"I brought forth his light. I think his own light ate away the corruption."

"Ah, you made him glow, did you, you naughty girl." She gave a shiver-inducing low chuckle. "His light or your power? Which was it, I wonder."

Hopefully she wasn't thinking of conducting an experiment. Like having Brindell bite Beldar again or someone else, then Lucinda making them glow to see if they healed. It was a nasty, nasty thought. I didn't like having it in my head.

The hellhound glided over to me. I tensed, unable to help myself, as the great brindled beast sniffed my face, lingering around my mouth, and moved downward. I flinched as it sniffed my crotch. Gee, maybe it had more in common with its canine brothers—or would that be sisters?—than just the "hound" at the end of its name.

Satisfied with me, the creature snuffled curiously at Amber, standing behind me, then rolled out its long pink tongue in a knowing doggy grin as if to say: *Ah, so that's who I smell on you.*

It seemed uncannily intelligent, those yellow eyes, as if it understood all that had been said. Closing its mouth and those frightening teeth, it swung back to sniff at me once more. How fun.

"Brindell seems to be as fascinated by you as my brother is," Lucinda murmured, and I didn't know whether to be outraged or not on Halcyon's behalf at having his sister compare him to a dog. A hellhound, demon beast, or not, was still essentially a dog. Hell's version of one, at least.

"Perhaps it is the human blood mixed within your veins," Lucinda pondered thoughtfully, her hand resting casually on Beldar's chest, still bared, as if she had forgotten where it lay. "It makes you different. Stronger instead of weakening you as it does to others, so that you have both sides' strength without the weaknesses."

Lucinda turned her contemplative eyes back to Beldar, and her gaze fell to the slow bounding pulse in his neck. It sped up beneath her dangerous attention. "I wonder if your blood would taste of her magic. Or would it carry a hint of the corrupting darkness that almost consumed you? What do you say, Beldar? Hmmm? A little sip of your blood, and then Brindell and I shall leave you."

It was almost funny. With Beldar a head taller than Lucinda, she looked tiny beside him, like something he had to protect instead of something threatening him. But the trapped look in Beldar's eyes, the frozen stillness he held himself in beneath her hand, said he knew the real situation. The diminutive demon princess was something to be feared.

"The process by which he healed was strange, erratic," I said, speaking up. "I do not know how his blood would react in you. And I would ask that you not risk it, Lucinda."

She turned her dangerous, slumberous eyes my way. "You say that in an effort to spare your man."

"Yes, but it is also out of concern for you, Lucinda. You

are Halcyon's sister," I said with truthful sincerity. "I would not wish any harm to come to you even inadvertently by my hand."

Her dark eyes, so like her brother's, narrowed in inscrutable thought. "How odd you are. No wonder he finds himself so drawn to you." Then she blinked, as if clearing away her thoughts. "Brindell," she called softly.

The hellhound swung away from me and padded obediently to her mistress' side. Without another word, Lucinda and her hellhound departed.

Beldar sagged against Amber as the door closed. I think we all sagged a little. Feeling as if gelatin were holding me up instead of solid bones, I sank shakily down onto the love seat.

"Not one of my best ideas, asking you to bring Lucinda back," I murmured weakly. "She wouldn't have been able to save Beldar anyway."

"No, but you were able to," Gryphon said. He gazed at Beldar, strode to the other man, and gave him a tight embracing hug. And I realized that Beldar had been Gryphon's friend, too.

"It is good to have you back, brother," Gryphon said, stepping back.

"It is good to be whole once more. And to garner a taste of the bounty you and Amber both enjoy." Beldar's tone was light, but the emotion shadowing his eyes was not. "You lucky bastards."

"Yes," Gryphon said softly, as the three of them turned to look at me—Amber, Gryphon, and Beldar. "Yes, we are. Very, very lucky."

CHAPTER 7

When night fell again, we sat on that same bench in Rockefeller Plaza where all this had begun, waiting for Mona Sera. I sat in my usual left corner, with Beldar seated on my right. Amber, Gryphon, and Chami stood to my left, slightly behind me. And though Beldar sat on "their" side, versus "ours," he still felt a part of our group. There was no animosity, no wariness toward him on the men's part, nor him toward them. Only a touch of sadness.

Beldar was unusually quiet and serious, as if his glib and charming surface skin had burned away with his rotted flesh, leaving him naked and tender. And I . . . I seemed to be as quiet and serious and as solemn as he. We sat in silence until Beldar broke it.

"I will continue to hope, you know," he said, his brilliant green eyes fixed on the road in front of us.

"For what, Beldar?" I asked, making myself turn and look at him, something I had been avoiding doing up till now. His long white hair and shocking green eyes were as startling and beautiful as always. But the sight hurt me somehow rather than pleased me. Made my heart ache.

"That one day I, too, will become lucky."

Simple words, with not so simple meaning. They stabbed me sweetly because I wished it, too, in my heart of hearts—that he belonged to me. But wishing was just that, wishing. It did not make things come true.

"I do not think Mona Sera will ever give you up, Beldar," I said in a low voice.

His eyes continued to restlessly sweep the cars that passed. An almost-silent sigh lifted his chest. "You are correct. Mona Sera would sooner see me dust and ashes than have you acquire another of her men. She threw Gryphon and Amber away like broken toys, and now pouts like a spoiled child that you troubled to fix them and keep them. And not only that, but make them even better than what they once were. She envies you."

"Me?" I said. It would have surprised me less had he turned and smacked me across the face. "She envies me, her Mixed Blood bastard child?"

"Yes, she is jealous of Amber's and Gryphon's devotion to you. Devotion that she could never inspire. Will never be able to inspire. They served her, a pure Full Blood Queen, out of fear. As do I. As do all of her men. But they serve you, a Mixed Blood Queen, out of love. And they serve you better because of that love. That she will never be able to forgive you for—for making her jealous of you when she considers you less."

It was an oddly perceptive observation, something I would never have conceived of. And yet that wasn't what I had meant. "I meant to say that she will not give you up because she values you."

His lips twisted into a wry smile devoid of humor. "You are correct. She does value me, as you say, or she would have simply let me rot away. Just bringing me to you is unusual care on her part. Yes, she . . . values me, and shall do so up until the time my threat to her outweighs my usefulness to her. Then she shall kill me without a blink, without a tear from those lovely cold eyes. Shall you mourn me then, Mona Lisa? Will you think of me as I will think of you with my last dying breath? Or will you have forgotten me long before?"

His words and the calm acceptance of his fate shook me. "She may give you to another Queen," I whispered.

"And risk having another benefit from something she gave up, as what happened with you?" He shook his head. "No, that is not Mona Sera's way."

"You must not wish to . . . become lucky, Beldar. It is both dangerous and unfair to you because it is unlikely ever to happen. You must be content that Mona Sera does care for you." In her own twisted, selfish way.

"But I am not content," he admonished me gently. "And you must not ask me *not* to hope. It is my sole reason for living now."

There were no words with which to answer him. I could do nothing but sit beside him and quietly bleed from his calm words.

"Do not forget me, Mona Lisa," he whispered softly, in the barest of sound, as two black Town Cars pulled up to the curb. Two cars looking like all the others that had passed by. But these thrummed with the unmistakable power of Monère males, and of the presence of another Queen.

I gazed blindly at those cars. "I . . . No, I won't forget you, Beldar."

My nails bit into my palms as I fiercely willed myself not to cry. I would not send him off with tears in my eyes.

Kyle and Francois emerged from the second car and opened the rear door of the first. Smooth white hands extended from within and grasped each of theirs. Mona Sera stepped out, covered in a flowing black cape covering her from head to toe. The lustrous brown mink collar was her only color.

She walked toward us and Kyle and Francois fell subserviently behind her, ignored like good servants.

Beldar went forward to meet her and bowed deeply, kissing her hand in a smooth courtly gesture. "My Queen, I thank you for saving me." His voice was low with a husky warmth that brought a cool smile to Mona Sera. But his eyes . . . bent over low, bowing at his waist, his eyes glanced back at me. They found and met mine, and his words, I knew, were meant for me, not her.

"You have healed him," Mona Sera observed with not one word of thanks.

"Yes," I said and didn't bother to explain how I had managed to do so. I owed this cold creature nothing.

"When do you leave," Mona Sera asked abruptly, her tone clipped and sharp. Displeased.

"Tomorrow."

"To Louisiana," she said. "Mona Louisa's former territory, once quite prosperous, but no longer so after Hurricane Katrina's wrath." And I saw it clearly, then, what Beldar had seen when I had not. She *was* jealous of me. Of my men and of the territory that I had been awarded.

"Do not think," she continued with cool malice, "that the people there will embrace you as eagerly as they did Mona Louisa. You are far less a Queen than she was."

Louisiana had been Mona Louisa's former domain until she tried to kill me. Okay, not really kill me. Just deliver me into the hand of outlaw rogues who weren't exactly known for their gentle treatment of women. Oh yeah, and for trying to kill Gryphon when she could no longer have him. Bitch. She had a lot in common with my mother, come to think of it.

Now I had to take over what Mona Louisa had once ruled. I had to win over the local Monère there. And as my mother said, I doubted they would welcome me with opened arms. Too bad. They were stuck with me.

"Do not concern yourself on my behalf, Mother," I said mockingly. "I am up to the task before me. And if my territory is less than what it was, rest assured that I shall bring it back to its former glory."

"What unbecoming arrogance you have for a mongrel bastard."

"*Your* mongrel bastard," I returned evenly.

"The only reason I tolerate your presence now. But do not push me, child. And do not mistake our relationship for more than what it is. When you leave tomorrow, do not come back ever again or I shall hunt you down and kill you like the unwanted intruder you are. Is that clear, daughter mine?"

"Oh, yes, Mother dear. Like crystal."

She swept one last hateful glance as us—me sitting there, with my men tall and strong behind me—then she turned and walked away.

We watched as Kyle and Francois returned to the second car, as Beldar gracefully handed Mona Sera into the back seat of the first car and shut the door.

Beldar looked up. Gave me one last searing look, his eyes running over my face as if he were engraving it into his memory. One last lingering glance from those haunting emerald eyes, so strikingly green set against the white spill of his hair, and then Beldar slid into the front passenger seat.

After they drove away, we sat there for a long time in the cool evening darkness, in an almost funereal silence; I mourned not the loss of my mother, but something truly heartbreaking, the loss of one of her men.

Beldar had always been hers, never mine. My mind knew that, but my heart did not. In my heart, I felt as if I had given him up.

"You cannot save everyone," Gryphon said softly beside me.

"I know." I truly did know that. But, oh, how I wished I could.

•

CHAPTER 8

1 watched as Gryphon and Amber carried the headboard and bed frame out of the apartment. Chami and Aquila hefted the mattress easily out after them. It was handy having five strong Monère men helping me move. Made things quick and easy.

In the tiny kitchen, Rosemary and Tersa were busy wrapping the glassware in newspaper and packing them in boxes. Thaddeus and Jamie carted each box downstairs as they became full, loading them onto the waiting truck parked in front of the apartment. They were being donated, along with the furniture, to a nearby homeless shelter.

Do not bring anything other than yourself and your clothes, I had been told. My new home in Louisiana was already fully furnished, and not just with ordinary furniture like the ones I was giving away, but with valuable antiques.

I gazed around the barren apartment that looked larger but more forlorn with its bare walls and naked flooring, and felt no sadness at leaving everything behind. I was taking the

most important things with me, things that really mattered—
the people in my household. My family.

"Is there anything else, milady?" Tomas asked me in his
soft southern twang.

"I think that's it, Tomas, other than the kitchen stuff."
With his light brown eyes and hair, Tomas reminded me of
summer wheat fields swaying beneath the sun. He gazed at
me with his usual quiet somberness. What wasn't usual was
the closed, guarded expression on his face.

"Is something wrong, Tomas?"

His eyes fell, and he shook his wheat-colored hair.

I walked over to him and gently lifted his chin. "Tell me,
Tomas, tell me what bothers you, please."

He lifted his eyes and looked at me like a child lost. "I
thought that I would be the one to go," he said in a low voice.

"Go?"

"The one that you would give to Mona Sera."

My eyes widened. "Why would you think that, Tomas?"

"You love Amber and Gryphon. And Rosemary, as one of
our few women, is too valuable. Aquila is good at business
and can drive. And with his uncommon ability, Chami is
uniquely useful. I have no special skills."

"Oh, Tomas," I said softly. His loyalty was as straight and
true as the sword he had sworn into my service. I knew that
had I chosen to give him up, he would have left me with bewildered eyes and a broken heart, but he would have gone
had I ordered him to, because he had given his word to protect and to obey me.

He was only two inches taller than I was, so that I had only
to lift my eyes a short distance to meet his, giving me an intimacy with him that I did not have with the other taller men.

"You are one of my guards," I told him. "When you gave

me your oath, when I accepted you into my service, I also promised to protect you. I would never give you up, any of you. I would have bargained, negotiated with Mona Sera, had I not been able to save Beldar. But if she had left me with no other choice, I would have fought before I gave any of you to her."

"Mona Sera's men number more than twenty," Tomas said simply.

"Then between the six of us—Amber, Gryphon, Chami, Aquila, you, and I—we would have been equally matched against them. And we would have been fighting for something that meant more to us than simply obeying the orders of a Queen we feared. We would have won. At cost, but we would have won. Never doubt your worth to me again, Tomas. I hold every single one of you dear in my heart."

He expelled a shaky breath, bent low and kissed my hand. "No, my Queen. I shall not doubt you again."

When he straightened back up, I leaned over and kissed him gently on the cheek like a mother did with a beloved child. He rewarded me with one of his brilliant smiles that lit up his plain face, transforming his features into something almost handsome.

I'd found Tomas looking to serve at High Court. Grown too powerful for his Queen, she had simply released him from her service. More merciful, it would seem, than executing him on some flimsy pretense of punishment. Or perhaps he had grown too powerful for her to try that. He had been waiting there, unwanted, ignored by the other Queens, until I had approached him.

I wondered what happened to other warriors who had grown too powerful to be considered safe. Where did they go? Did they, too, become bandit rogues like Aquila had, even though no one overtly threatened their life? Did guards cast from their Queens' courts become outlaws simply because they had nowhere else to go?

No, I could not save everyone. But as I looked into Tomas's sweetly plain face, I was glad, fiercely glad, that there were a few that I could.

EPILOGUE

After I turned over my apartment key and had my deposit refunded to me without question—another nice perk that came with being Queen; having big, intimidating men looming behind me—I took them shopping.

Nice dresses for Tersa and Rosemary—they had politely but completely ignored my suggestion of getting some pants. Not only Monère men, it seemed, were old-fashioned—and more casual clothes for the boys. Young Jamie, who loved American pop culture, which he'd picked up from watching TV, was the most adventuresome among them. He fingered his new blue jeans as if they were more precious than diamonds, and eyed the cowboy boots adorning his feet with something close to awe. He had gazed so longingly at the boots, I hadn't been able to resist buying them for him.

Thaddeus picked out some pants and shirts with casual efficiency, while I had fun dressing Tomas and Aquila. Hmmm, what did you choose for a wild rogue gone respectable? Not so hard a choice, as a matter of fact. Aquila looked nothing like the bandit he'd once been, one of the group that had kidnapped me, in fact. With his Vandyke beard neatly trimmed and a face serious and proper, he looked more like a scholarly professor or the successful man of business he once was. Sharply creased charcoal slacks, a gray-and-black patterned vest, and a simple cream shirt fit him quite nicely.

"Yummy in a quiet, distinguished sort of way," I said, smiling.

Aquila fingered the neatly pressed pleats—only a tasteful few—with obvious pleasure. "Yes, milady, they are. It is very nice to have clothes that actually fit once more, and are not patched."

He'd been wearing donated clothes since helping us escape from the forest. And ill-fitting though the clothes had been, they were far better than the rags he'd worn. A bandit's life, it appeared, hadn't been too profitable.

I let him wander off to select a couple more sets of casual attire, and turned to study Tomas, who stepped out from the fitting room.

A smile broke across my face. The straight-cut black denim—he didn't know they were jeans and I didn't enlighten him—and the rich bronze hue of the shirt contrasted nicely with his wheat-colored hair and light brown eyes. The snug fit of his clothing made him look taller and emphasized his broad shoulders, narrow hips, and muscular arms and chest, all of which had been hidden beneath the looseness of his usual attire.

"Perhaps a size larger," Tomas said dubiously.

"Oh, no. This fits you perfectly," I murmured, twirling my finger at him. "Turn around."

He did so with endearing awkwardness, his cheeks staining a dull red under our interested perusal.

Yup, the rear view was just as perfect, the jeans molding to his backside with loving attention. One thing for certain, all of my guys had great butts.

"Mona Lisa enjoys a snug fit," Amber rumbled softly beside me.

I colored beneath his bland expression and the words that could be taken another, more intimate, way. With Gryphon I'd have had no doubts about a sexual innuendo, but with Amber I wasn't as certain if he had intended it or not. Bits of Amber's true personality were slowly emerging beneath my love and his new freedom, like his tendency toward dominance. I wasn't sure if this was another new aspect of him coming out.

Ignoring his comment, I turned to the others. "What do you think, Rosemary?"

The large cook ran an inspecting eye up and down Tomas. "He looks like a prime cut of meat," she said with a tiny smile.

Simple, dear Tomas flushed even more. My poor men, I don't think they were used to being ogled so blatantly by a bunch of women.

"Get used to it," I said, looking at both him and Aquila.

"To what?" Tomas asked.

"Women looking at you. And you guys can look right back. You, too, Chami," I said, turning to where my chameleon lounged in a chair.

"Can we?" Chami said, arching a brow.

"Yes, indeed. I don't know how many women there will be in our new territory, but any present, unattached and willing, you are welcome to date."

"Date?" Tomas said. "What does that mean?"

"Date means to court, kiss, hold hands. You know." I fluttered my fingers. "To do that kind of stuff with women you are attracted to."

The expression on Tomas's face could only be described as astounded. "You would allow us to do this 'date' thing?"

"Well, yeah. And not just allow it, but actively encourage you to. If there are single unattached women there, and they have a pulse, they are going to notice you guys. Feel free to notice them right back," I said with a grin.

"Does that pertain to us as well?" Gryphon asked, his face smoothed in that remote blankness that let you read nothing.

Is he asking because he wishes to see other women? Because he no longer wants me? a little voice whispered in my ear. Or was he asking because he feared me no longer wanting him?

A bit insecure, me? Yup. And it seemed to go both ways. We were both—or should I say, all three of us—insecure. If I let it, it could drive me crazy. I chose instead to go with my gut feeling.

I walked over to Gryphon, ran a light finger along the hollow of his throat, and smiled like the dangerous feline cat I was in my other form. "If you and Amber so much as look at another woman, I will scratch your eyes out, and then hers."

The blankness left Gryphon's face, and his eyes filled once again with expressive warmth. "When we have such rich bounty at hand, why would we wish to look elsewhere?"

I rewarded him with a light searing kiss. "Aw, you guys always talk so pretty."

• • •

White flakes of snow fell from the sky as we drove to the airport later that same night, like crystallized confetti dropping from the sky. Celebration, not sadness, at leaving this lonely island I had called home. An island packed to its bursting seams with people, but with none that I had been able to call my own. That had changed with the advent of Gryphon into my life, only a short time ago in matters of days and weeks. In terms of emotional commitment, a lifetime ago. New York was my old life. Louisiana was my future. A new home for us all.

We were a ragged lot of outcasts and misfits, composed of those unwanted and those thrown away. But we'd found a belonging with each other. Though we were small in number, we were strong. Together we would keep us all safe. But I wanted more than safety for us. I wanted us to be happy in all our varied needs.

A private jet was waiting for us, another perk of being a Queen. There would, no doubt, be other benefits, along with other problems, that came with the title. That was the trouble with having things. You had to be strong enough to keep them.

Soon we would know exactly what Mona Louisa had left for us. May it be trouble or blessing, peace or strife, there was no other choice but to go forward. Yet even as we moved ahead, I could not help looking back and remembering a pair of vivid green eyes staring at me with such yearning, such soulful need.

Be safe. Be well.

And maybe someday we'd be able to do more than just survive. Maybe someday we'd both get lucky.

Author's Note

Dear Reader,

Enjoy meeting Mona Lisa and her beautiful men? For more, please pick up my first single title, Mona Lisa Awakening, and the sequel, Mona Lisa Blossoming, coming out from Berkley in February 2007. And be ready to pleasure all your senses as she awakens to powers hidden and bliss unexpected. As she ventures into the dangerous Monèrian society and discovers that wicked delight and perilous plight are often mixed as one . . . or two . . . or maybe even three . . .

Till then—

Sunny

www.sunnyauthor.com